DEATH WITH DOSTOEVSKY

DEATH WITH DOSTOEVSKY

Katherine Bolger Hyde

This first world edition published 2019
in Great Britain and the USA by
SEVERN HOUSE PUBLISHERS LTD of
Eardley House, 4 Uxbridge Street, London W8 7SY.
Trade paperback edition first published
in Great Britain and the USA 2020 by
SEVERN HOUSE PUBLISHERS LTD.

British Library Cataloguing in Publication Data
A CIP catalogue record for this title is available from the British Library.

ISBN-13: 978-0-7278-8899-0 (cased)
ISBN-13: 978-1-78029-639-5 (trade paper)
ISBN-13: 978-1-4483-0338-0 (e-book)

All Severn House titles are printed on acid-free paper.

Severn House Publishers support the Forest Stewardship Council™ [FSC™],
the leading international forest certification organisation.
All our titles that are printed on FSC certified paper carry the FSC logo.

Typeset by Palimpsest Book Production Ltd.,
Falkirk, Stirlingshire, Scotland.
Printed and bound in Great Britain by
TJ International, Padstow, Cornwall.

ONE

Emily stood in the middle of the Bede College front lawn and took a long, slow breath of Bede-scented air. The college had its own particular smell composed of the sap of its ancient trees, the brick and stone and polished wood of its century-old main buildings, the crumbling parchment and vegetable inks of the oldest books in the library's rare book room, the sweat and toil of its dedicated students, and of course the ever-present Portland mist, which occasionally thickened into rain.

Today, though, the sky was clear, the air crisp and biting in the city's typical January cold snap. It burned her lungs and invigorated her blood. Here she was a scholar again. No groups of ill-assorted retreat guests to coax into harmony, no beachfront-community issues to wrestle with, and please God no murders to solve. Only herself, a library full of resources on the life and work of Fyodor Dostoevsky, and a tall stack of empty index cards.

At last she was going to embark seriously on the work she'd been toying with for most of her academic career: the definitive English-language work on Dostoevsky's tormented relationship with his Orthodox faith as it played out in his fiction. She felt equal parts exhilaration and terror, for who could ever do justice to such a topic? Yet she was compelled to try.

She hoped to have the library largely to herself, as Bede held no regular classes in January. Instead the campus was home to a uniquely Bede event called Paideia – a month of no-credit, do-it-yourself, often student-led classes in everything from poetry writing to bicycle mechanics. Some students spent the month at home or off on adventures; some came back to campus to participate in the Paideia classes, some merely to party. The atmosphere was lighter and freer than at any other time of year except the post-finals Renn Fayre in the spring.

Except in the library, the bastion of those few harried students who could not bring themselves to take a whole month away from their regular studies. These were mostly seniors taking the opportunity to work intensively on their theses without the distraction of classes. Unless any of them happened to be working on Dostoevsky, Emily should have no competition for the resources she needed or for table space to spread out her old-school index cards, notebooks, and books. Since she no longer had an office on campus, the library would have to be her home base.

With a wistful glance at the third-floor window of her erstwhile office in Eliot Hall and a last bracing breath, she headed across the lawn to the massive library. The stone Tudor Gothic building with its square central tower had been impressive enough in her student days, but since then its size had been more than doubled by a modern addition that did not copy but harmonized with the old style.

Emily planned to greet the librarian, stake out a table, and start collecting the books she'd need. She'd spent most of this day traveling here from Stony Beach and getting resettled in her old house half a block from the edge of campus, so today would not be a real work day. She'd just get everything set up so she could plunge in first thing tomorrow.

At the main desk, she flashed her Bede ID and asked the student worker if she could speak to Miranda Brooks, the head librarian. As she waited, she thought about where she'd like to stake her claim. The best place would be one of the desks set aside for seniors to work on their theses. These had shelves above the tables, which sat next to a full wall of windows and were flooded with natural light. Perhaps during Paideia one of the desks would be unoccupied.

'Emily!' Miranda greeted her, infusing maximum enthusiasm into her habitual hushed library voice. 'Are you back for real? Or is this just a flying visit?'

Emily took the two hands Miranda proffered and smiled at her friend. Miranda had a talent for picking up thrift-store finds and combining them into stunning outfits. Today she wore a pair of high-waisted, wide-legged mustard-colored trousers topped by a peacock blue peasant blouse and a knee-length red crocheted vest. Her tall, slim figure and shingled black hair helped her pull off any look she chose.

'I'm here for Paideia. Finally going to finish researching that book on Dostoevsky. And I'm hoping I can grab a quiet spot here for the duration, since they've given my office away.'

'Of course! We have a number of thesis desks standing empty for the month.'

Following Miranda, Emily rolled her heavy briefcase into the main-floor room of stacks where thesis desks lined the west wall. Each large table had space for four students, two on each side. Miranda stopped at one about halfway down the row. 'Here's a good one,' she said in a whisper, since a student already occupied the far side of the table. 'I know for sure neither of the students who use this side will be back before term time.'

The students had taken all their goods and chattels with them, probably intending to work through vacation, so the half-table stood empty, as if it had been awaiting her. 'Perfect.' Emily unloaded her books on to the shelf above and piled her note-books and index cards on the desk itself. 'Now I just need to grab some books from you, and I'll be all set.' She pulled a list out of her purse.

Miranda cast an eye down the list. 'Oh, dear,' she said. 'I'm afraid a lot of these are in here already. Right on the other side of your shelf.'

Emily stepped around the table and scanned the shelf Miranda indicated. Indeed, several of the titles she needed were ranged there. And the shaggy dark head bent over a laptop beneath them looked familiar.

The young man turned at their voices, a frown of irritation distorting his distinctive features. Daniel Razumov. He'd been in her nineteenth-century European novel class the previous year. In her former life, before she inherited a fortune, redis-covered her lost true love, moved to Stony Beach, and became perforce an amateur detective. Daniel would be a senior now, and he must be doing his thesis on Dostoevsky.

The face that confronted her was long and improbably lean, with pale skin stretched taut over prominent cheekbones, a hawklike nose, and square, stubbled jaw. The dark eyes in their deep sockets burned now with annoyance, but she remembered them smoldering with a perpetual agitation, a restlessness that could not be quelled. His long, thin fingers brushed an unruly black lock off his brow. In class he had habitually pulled at his hair as if trying to extract thoughts from his brain, or perhaps only the words to express them with.

She had two options with Daniel now: try to come to some arrangement for sharing the books and resources they both needed, or pull rank and simply take them. She wasn't officially retired from Bede yet, so she still had staff privileges. But pulling rank wasn't Emily's style, and although Daniel might not be the easiest person to negotiate with, she had always felt obscurely drawn to him. She was sure that underneath all that *Sturm und Drang* he was fundamentally decent.

She smiled at him, and before she could speak, she saw recognition dawn in his face. 'Professor Cavanaugh!' he said, rising to greet her. 'You're back!'

'Hello, Daniel. I'm not back for good, but I'm here for Paideia to do some research.' She gave an apologetic grimace. 'And I'm afraid most of the books I'm going to need are right there.'

His eyes followed her pointing finger, then snapped back to her face, retreating under lowering brows. 'I suppose you're going to make me turn them all in. There goes a wasted month.'

Emily put out a hand but didn't go so far as to touch him. The energy he radiated was such that she feared an electric shock. 'I wouldn't dream of it. I have all the time in the world to do my research, whereas you have a deadline. But I was hoping perhaps we could share? Neither of us can use all the books at once.'

His face opened up as if the Santa Claus he didn't believe in had given him the gift he'd always dreamed of. 'Oh! Of course! Whatever you need, just let me know.' A flicker of trepidation crept back in. 'I'm in the middle of Berdyaev right now.'

'I have my own copy of Berdyaev. No worries there.' In fact, Emily realized, she could now afford to buy all the books she needed; but some of them, especially the Russian-language ones, would be quite difficult to find.

She cast an eye over Daniel's shelf and saw a few titles that were not on her list. Some of them looked like books on psychology. 'What's the focus of your thesis?'

'Dostoevsky's concept of personal identity.'

That would explain the psychology books. 'I'm working on his Orthodox faith, so we shouldn't get in each other's way too much. And I promise I won't disturb you more than I can help.' She wasn't concerned about Daniel disturbing her; he seemed to avoid human companionship as much as anyone she knew.

Next to Daniel's collection of books, acting as an improvised bookend, stood a small statuette that looked familiar. Emily leaned in for a closer look. 'Oh, it's the Bronze Horseman! May I?' She reached out to touch it.

'I'd rather you didn't. It's . . . special.'

She pulled her hand back, a little startled at the refusal. The statuette was bronze and did not look particularly fragile. 'Was it a gift?'

'No. It just – I just – I can't explain it. It's kind of my lucky charm.'

'I see.' Though in fact she had a hard time seeing how that particular statue could be lucky for anyone. The Bronze Horseman was the name given by Russia's national poet, Alexander Pushkin, to the huge equestrian statue of Peter the Great that stood in Senate Square in St Petersburg. In Pushkin's poem of that name, the statue came to life and hounded a man to his death. It was treated as a figure of nightmare in Andrei Bely's novel *Petersburg* as well. What kind of tortured mind did Daniel have to see such a thing as his lucky talisman?

Perhaps she'd come to understand over the course of the next few weeks. For now, she was tired and wanted to get home.

'I'm just dropping stuff off tonight – I expect I'll see you in the morning.'

He answered her bright smile with a curt nod, as if he'd given her too many words already and was regretting it. Emily exchanged a glance with Miranda and left the room.

Her step considerably lighter now that she'd unloaded her case, Emily climbed the short but steep half-block up Woodstock Boulevard to the little Tudor-style brick cottage she'd shared with her late husband, Philip Cavanaugh, for twenty-five years. She'd rented it to the visiting professor who took her place for this sabbatical year, along with her husband, and had bribed the couple with a free month's rent to let her move back in for these few weeks while they were traveling. But the house hardly seemed like her own anymore. She'd rented it to them furnished, but Peter and Lillian had rearranged the furniture and packed away Emily's remaining pictures, books, and ornaments, replacing them with their own.

At least the cats were familiar. She'd left Bustopher Jones at Windy Corner with Katie, her young housekeeper, but brought Kitty and Levin, her matched pair of grays, back to their old home to keep her company. They trotted up to meet her at the door, yowling for their supper. She could tell by their tentative movements and the way they startled at every sound that they were ill at ease here too. Oh well, she and the cats would all get used to the place again before long – probably just in time to move back to Stony Beach.

She hung up her coat and hat, fed the cats, and was leafing through the mail that lay on the mat – none of which was addressed to her personally – when the doorbell sounded loud in her ear, making her jump. A glance through the peephole revealed that her visitor was her dear friend from the French department, Marguerite Grenier, who had provided almost her only link to Bede during the months she'd been away. Emily opened the door to her eagerly.

'Margot! I'm so glad you came. I'm feeling like a dodo that somehow survived into the twenty-first century.'

'I come bearing gifts, *chérie*,' Marguerite replied, holding up a bulging shopping bag in one hand and a bottle of red wine in the other. 'I knew you would have no food in the house and would be too *fatiguée* to go out, so I brought dinner to you.'

Emily kissed her friend on both cheeks. 'Bless you. I hadn't even thought about dinner yet. Come into the kitchen.'

Marguerite set the wine on the table and unloaded a warm baguette, a bowl of salad, and a steaming quiche, plus a smaller bag that she immediately transferred to the fridge. 'A surprise for later. You do have dishes, do you not?'

'Of course. Lillian and Peter only took their personal stuff on their trip.' Emily opened what had been her dish cabinet to find it full of glassware instead. The dishes were on the opposite side. Really, couldn't they have left *something* alone?

She found the necessaries and laid the table for two while Marguerite unearthed and lit a couple of candles in tall bronze candlesticks. 'There. Now we will be civilized, despite the meal being only such a one as I could easily carry.'

'It looks – and smells – heavenly to me.' Emily sat, spread her napkin on her lap, and crossed herself as she said a silent grace, knowing her friend would not appreciate having it said aloud.

Although Marguerite had been a guest at Windy Corner, Emily's new home in Stony Beach, for Christmas, they'd had little time alone together amid the tumultuous events of that week, which included a murder, Emily's engagement to her old flame Lieutenant Sheriff Luke Richards, and her discovery of a half-brother she'd never known she had. So Emily had had no opportunity of catching up on the latest Bede gossip.

'What's been going on in the division? Who's here for Paideia?'

Marguerite rolled her eyes. 'Richard, of course.' Richard McClintock was the division chair, an abrasive, bitter, sarcastic man whom neither of them much liked. 'Konstantin, I think, and Teresa. And Oscar, as you know.' Oscar Lansing was Emily's newly discovered half-brother. He was an adjunct professor in English, the lowest man on the academic totem pole, but Emily hoped she'd be able to do something to help him up a step or two.

'Oh, and Taylor Curzon. She was going to go to Moscow but decided at the last minute to wait until summer. I think she was afraid *ses tétons* would freeze off in the Russian winter.'

Emily groaned. 'Not Taylor. Of all people. Lord, give me strength.'

Unlike Richard, who went out of his way to antagonize people, Taylor Curzon managed to do so with no effort at all. A single woman in her forties, she flaunted her potent sexuality, disdaining all females and sinking her teeth into a different piece of fresh young male meat each semester. More than once Emily had been the one trying to put the pieces of her victims back together after Taylor had sucked the life out of them and cast them aside.

'I hope that doesn't mean her latest prey – or intended prey

– is here as well. I really don't want to have to witness that again.'

'I am afraid you may not be able to avoid it. She has cast her eye on one of your Russian students, I think, and I understand he will be here, slaving away on his thesis.'

Emily set down her fork in sudden horror. 'Not Daniel Razumov?'

'If he is the one who resembles Raskolnikov, *oui*. It is he.'

Emily dropped her head into her hands. She'd come here looking for peace, quiet, and undistracted study. With Taylor Curzon's new target sitting right across from her, she would have been better off staying in Stony Beach.

TWO

The next morning, somewhat dazed due to a poor night's sleep punctuated by the feet of restless cats on sensitive points of her body, Emily arrived at her desk to find Daniel's side of the table empty. With a small and guilty rush of relief – for, although Daniel was quiet, she found interaction with him draining – she organized her piles of cards, books, and notebooks on the table. She frowned at the resultant clutter. If so little wood was visible now, before she had even begun, what would the space look like when she got going properly?

Her mind flashed her an image of the Windy Corner library at Christmastime, when a group of writers – including two scholars – had gathered there to work. Each writer had a laptop, and that appeared to be sufficient to keep all their notes and research in order. Emily waved the treacherous thought away. She was determined to stick with her old-fashioned ways. How could she enter into Dostoevsky's world of quills and quartos if her own work existed only in the intangible miasma of a computer screen?

She steeled herself and set to her task. After an hour or so of good solid note-taking, she stretched and yawned, feeling the need for more coffee. One could bring coffee into the library but not obtain it there, and she hadn't thought to bring a thermos.

As she was debating whether it was worth interrupting her flow to go in search of caffeine, she heard footsteps, and Daniel came into view. Behind him followed a young woman who looked familiar as well. Indeed, that pale, ethereal face, its pure bones revealed by blond hair sleeked back into a flawless chignon, was too striking to forget – though her name escaped Emily for the moment. She watched as the couple approached – Daniel shuffling, head down, backpack on one shoulder and a cup of coffee in the opposite hand, and the girl gliding over the floor with the erect grace of a dancer, a cup in each hand. She must be thirsty.

They paused by Emily's desk. Daniel nodded a wordless greeting. The girl's face opened in a shy smile. 'Professor Cavanaugh? I don't know if you remember me – Svetlana Goldstein. I was in your Intro to Comp Lit class last year.'

'Of course. Nice to see you, Svetlana.' She stood and moved to shake Svetlana's hand, then stopped because both the girl's hands were full.

Svetlana held out one of the cups. 'Daniel told me you were working here. We thought you might like some coffee.'

The flush on Daniel's downturned cheek told Emily that the 'we' was a polite fiction – the coffee had been solely Svetlana's idea. She took the cup gratefully. 'Thank you. That was very thoughtful.'

'Cream and sugar?' Svetlana produced a packet of each from a pocket.

'Just cream, thanks. You think of everything.'

Emily was about to ask the girl about her Paideia activities, but Daniel was leaning toward his own side of the table, his eyes hungry. Clearly he was eager to get to work.

Svetlana noticed this as well. 'We won't keep you.' She smiled again and moved to the chair next to Daniel's while he settled himself. Emily returned to her work.

At midday, her concentration wobbled when Daniel and Svetlana rose from the table and headed out. She glanced at her watch and realized she was hungry, as well as stiff from sitting for so long. She stood and reached for her purse and a book to read over lunch, then put on her coat and followed the students out of the room.

She stopped by the restroom on her way out, so the others were well ahead of her by the time she emerged from the library. Just as well; she would avoid the awkwardness of seeming to want to force herself on their company. The way they walked together – Daniel trudging head down, Svetlana leaning slightly toward him as she matched her naturally buoyant pace to his – spoke volumes about their relationship. It would probably not be one in which a third party was welcome.

At the Commons, Emily got her food from the cafeteria line – a spartan salad, to compensate for overindulgence in Katie's rich food over Christmas, and a cup of hot soup to warm her bones – and scanned the dining hall for a quiet corner, not difficult to find at this time of year. But before she could reach her chosen retreat, Svetlana called to her from the middle of the room.

'Professor Cavanaugh? Would you like to sit with us?'

The true answer would have been no. Among the things Emily did not miss about her old job was getting involved in the drama of students' lives, and Daniel carried drama about with him like an incubus. But Svetlana's musical contralto held a hint of something more than mere friendliness – of entreaty, perhaps. And Emily could never resist an innocent, vulnerable creature who needed her help.

She put on a smile and changed course for the table where the two students sat. Daniel looked up from shoveling food into his mouth and managed a nod. Svetlana positively beamed.

'How is your work going?' she asked Emily.

'Reasonably well. It's a bit odd getting back in the saddle after all this time away. But I did a little work over Christmas, so it isn't entirely foreign.' The girl's conversational gambit seemed to have exhausted itself already, so Emily forged ahead. 'What brings you to campus for Paideia?'

Svetlana shot a sidelong glance at Daniel – a glance full of both love and anguish. He put down his fork to squeeze her hand. Not the anguish of unrequited love, apparently, but requited love could bring plenty of anguish of its own.

'Partly Daniel. He works better when I'm around. But also, I need to do some prep work for Russian Three Hundred. Professor Curzon gave me a D last semester, and I've got to bring it up.'

'A D?' Emily remembered Svetlana as both intelligent and conscientious, and her Russian first name suggested she had some background in the language, at least by blood. How she could have earned a D was baffling. As was the fact that she knew about it – Bede's policy was that students were not automatically notified of their grades, though they could find out if they were persistent enough. 'How do you know?'

Svetlana's fair, translucent skin reddened. 'My father insists I check my grades every semester. He's determined I get into law school.'

Emily could not hide her surprise. Law seemed like the last profession to suit a gentle soul like Svetlana. 'And you? Is that what you want?'

Svetlana stared at her plate, her eyes glistening. Daniel spoke for her. 'Law is what her father wants. Sveta wants to dance.'

'My mother was a prima ballerina,' she said, meeting Emily's eyes. 'Back in Russia, before she met my father. Now she teaches – she taught me. I've always loved ballet. It's what I was born for.'

'Why don't you go for it, then? This is the twenty-first century. You can't let your father control your whole life.'

The sleek blond head shook mournfully. 'You don't know my father.'

Emily tactfully let the subject drop. It was clearly a painful one with no easy resolution in sight. And since, in fact, she did not know Svetlana's father, there was nothing she could do to help. Except, perhaps, find out why Curzon had given the girl a D.

And, speak of the devil, there was Taylor Curzon now, emerging from the cafeteria line and scanning the room like a hawk searching for prey. Her eye fell on their table and sharpened as a triumphant smile spread across her face. Red spike heels clicked over the tiled floor toward them even as Emily willed the heels to turn aside. But Taylor Curzon was not so easily deflected.

She didn't sit, though, but merely stood in the space between Emily and Svetlana, her gaze trained on Daniel as if the two women were not there. 'Daniel,' she said, her sultry voice making his name sound almost obscene. 'You missed our meeting.'

Eyes fixed on his plate, Daniel mumbled, 'I was busy. Had to meet with Professor Uspensky about my thesis.'

'Another time, then. We really must discuss your overdue paper for my class.'

Daniel nodded, still not meeting her eyes. Hoping to deflect her attention, Emily said, 'Hello, Taylor.'

Tossing her long, highlighted curls over her shoulder, Curzon turned as if astonished to discover someone else at the table. 'Well, well, if it isn't our resident heiress. Or not so resident. What brings you back to our humble campus? Not bored with the high life so soon?'

Emily gave a tight smile, determined not to rise to Curzon's bait. 'I'm working on my book on Dostoevsky. I need the Bede library for that.'

'Oh, yes, that quaint little project you always go on about. Do you really think anyone wants to read about an author's *faith* in this day and age? Isn't it all rather passé?'

'Not to me. And honestly, I don't much care how many people read it. I'm doing it for my own satisfaction as much as anything.'

Curzon raised one well-trained eyebrow. 'I suppose you can afford not to care. You don't need the money or the career boost, do you? I understand you're retiring completely after this year?'

'Where did you hear that?' Emily had more or less decided to retire since her engagement to Luke, but she hadn't communicated that decision to anyone at Bede except Marguerite – who was not the type to gossip about her best friend's private affairs.

Curzon shrugged one shoulder, managing to infuse the simple gesture with a languid sensuality. 'Oh, I don't know. Around.' She gave a false smile. 'Is it true?'

'I haven't decided yet,' Emily prevaricated. *And when I do decide absolutely, you'll be the last to know.*

With a smirk, Curzon turned back to Daniel. 'I'll expect you this afternoon, Daniel. You know my hours.' She fixed her gaze on him until he was compelled to look up, if only long enough to nod. 'Ta-ta for now.' She twiddled her fingers at him and turned away.

Not once had she so much as glanced at Svetlana, whose face was now rosy red. The look she shot at Curzon's retreating back would have felled a woman of less unassailable self-confidence, but Curzon's hip-swinging gait did not falter.

The three of them stared at their plates for a moment, their internal waters churned up in her wake. Emily recovered first and was about to make some innocuous remark when they were interrupted again, this time by a young man who looked the age of a student but was dressed more like a professor – and by Bede standards an exceptionally formal professor at that – in the stereotypical round wire-rimmed glasses, tweed jacket with leather elbow patches, loose corduroy slacks, and nondescript bow tie. His brown hair was slicked back with some sort of product that gave it a greasy shine.

'Svetlana, Daniel, how lovely to see you,' he said in a nasal, singsongy voice that grated on Emily's nerves. He set his tray on the table and sat down, as nonchalantly as if he had been invited, then turned to her with an outstretched hand. 'Sidney Sharpe. I don't believe I've had the pleasure.'

'Emily Cavanaugh.' She took his hand and had to repress a shudder – it lay in hers as damp and limp as a slug. She dropped the hand and wiped her own surreptitiously on her skirt.

'Are you a professor here? I don't recall seeing you before.'

She nodded. 'Comp lit. I'm on sabbatical this year but came back to work on a research project over Paideia.'

'That explains it. I just transferred in last semester. I'm studying Russian lit along with my friends here. With a minor in computer science to pacify the hungry career gods.' He smiled at Svetlana and Daniel. Svetlana's mouth twitched in response, though her eyes darted like a cornered animal's; Daniel did not even look up.

Sidney took a large bite of sandwich and spoke again before he had quite finished chewing. 'What are you researching?'

'Dostoevsky. The way his faith plays out in his fiction.'

'Ah, the immortal Fy-oh-dore Mee-hey-lovich.' His atrocious accent hit Emily like a slap in the face. She was glad she would never have him in a language class. Her ears would be scarred for life.

'Daniel's working on the great F.M. too, aren't you, Dan?'

Emily cringed again. She'd never heard anyone call Daniel Razumov 'Dan'. The diminutive sat so ill on him, Sidney might as well have called him Frank or Bill. The look of loathing Daniel directed at Sidney confirmed he shared Emily's opinion. But still he did not speak.

Sidney was unfazed. 'I'm rather fond of the old gent myself. I may do my thesis on him as well. That is, if you two geniuses leave anything unsaid.' He gave an unmusical guffaw that belied the exaggerated compliment.

'I don't believe anyone could exhaust all there is to say about Dostoevsky. Certainly not myself,' Emily said repressively. She took a last spoonful of soup and realized she'd lost her appetite. She gathered her dishes back onto her tray and stood. 'If you all will excuse me, I think I'll get back to work.'

Svetlana shot her a glance of horrified entreaty and hastily gathered her things as well. 'I'll walk with you, if you don't mind.' Daniel followed suit, and the three of them left the table together. Sidney smiled them on their way as if he'd had nothing to do with their hasty departure and was not in the least offended by it.

Once they were outside, Daniel said to Svetlana, 'Have to get something from my room. See you over there.' He squeezed her hand and headed across the quad to the Old Dorm Block.

Svetlana watched him go, her eyes troubled, then turned to walk with Emily toward the library. Once they had left the Commons well behind, she said as if she'd steeled herself for the effort, 'I was hoping to have a minute alone with you.'

Emily gave the girl an encouraging smile. In her years of teaching she'd grown accustomed to students confiding in her. She had the rare ability to listen attentively and to empathize.

'I'm so worried about Daniel,' Svetlana burst out. 'He needs peace in order to work. I was hoping Paideia would provide that, but between Professor Curzon and Sidney . . .'

There was no need for Svetlana to finish her sentence. 'I take it Professor Curzon has . . . taken a special interest in Daniel?'

Emily couldn't bring herself to speak the plain truth – Curzon was trying to seduce him. Marguerite had warned her, and she had now seen the clear signs for herself.

'You know what she's like. Don't you? Once she . . . targets a guy – it's over. Either she gets him into her clutches and then discards him, or if he resists, she ruins him academically. There's no way out.'

Emily nodded. She'd seen it happen too many times. 'And Daniel is resisting?'

'She disgusts him. He'd rather kiss Baba Yaga.' Baba Yaga was the repulsive hag villainess of many a Russian fairy tale. 'Besides, he's . . .' She paused, her translucent cheek flushing.

'He's in love with you.' Emily put a hand on Svetlana's shoulder. 'That's perfectly obvious, even though he's not the demonstrative type.'

'Well, yes.' Svetlana gave a shy smile. 'We'd be engaged by now if—' She faltered.

Emily took a stab in the dark. 'If not for your father?'

The girl nodded, now blushing deeply. 'He wants me to wait until after law school and then find someone . . . "suitable". Which means another lawyer or a doctor, from a wealthy family, and preferably Jewish. Even though I'm not.'

'You follow your mother's faith?'

She nodded. 'We're both Orthodox.'

'As am I.'

Svetlana looked up at her. 'Are you Russian by blood? I never thought – I mean, you don't look . . . and your name . . .'

Emily smiled. 'No, I'm not Russian. I visited a Russian church years ago to get the feeling of it, so I could understand the literature, and I fell in love with the Orthodox faith. I go to St Sergius, across the river. When I'm in town.' Regular access to her home parish was one of the perks of living in Portland that Emily was looking forward to during her stay here.

'Oh, of course. I go to Annunciation.' Emily knew that name as that of a more recently established parish in the southeastern suburb of Milwaukee. 'That is, when I can get there. The bus service on Sundays is pretty bad.'

'You're welcome to catch a ride to St Sergius with me while I'm here. Or perhaps we could take turns between the two.'

'That would be such a comfort.' Svetlana impulsively squeezed Emily's arm. 'I wish I could get Daniel to go. I'm sure it would help him find peace.'

'Daniel strikes me as an intrinsically spiritual person. Surely one day he'll come around.'

Svetlana nodded. 'He is baptized. I'm sure he'll be drawn back eventually. I just hope it doesn't take a complete disaster to make it happen.' Her look of entreaty returned. 'Is there anything you can do, Professor Cavanaugh? About Curzon?'

'Please, call me Emily. I don't know if it's appropriate for me to get involved. Daniel could just report her.'

'But she'd only deny it. It would be her word against his, and as a professor, she'd be sure to win.'

'That may be true if it's only his word. It would help if other victims of hers came forward as well.'

'I think they're all too intimidated. They need an advocate. Someone in authority who's sympathetic. Someone like you.' Svetlana accompanied these leading statements with a winning smile.

'I don't know what I can do, Svetlana. The administration tends to look the other way unless provable harassment is involved. But this is certainly a case of harassment, provable or not. I'll do what I can. That woman is a menace. It's time she was stopped.'

THREE

Fueled by Svetlana's desperation, Emily left her companion at the library entrance and turned north toward Vollum College Center, one of the modern buildings on campus, where Curzon had her office on the third floor. As she approached, she noticed that the door was ajar, so she assumed Taylor was in, but she got no response to her knock.

Calling, 'Taylor?' she cautiously pushed open the door. She'd watched enough detective shows to expect a door left ajar to lead to a body, or at least to the aftermath of a burglary. But the office was empty of humans, dead or alive, and appeared to be in perfect order – books on shelves, papers on desk, pillows on couch.

And on the wall above the desk, a large icon painted on wood. Emily paused, thunderstruck by this apparent indication that Taylor might be a woman of faith. But then she rounded the desk and looked more closely. The icon was clearly ancient: the surface was cracked and discolored, and the Virgin and Child depicted were painted in an old Russian style that dated back to the great medieval iconographer Andrei Rublev. One of the Virgin's fluid, elongated hands supported the Child while the other gestured as if to invite the viewer to focus on him, not on her. The Child's tiny face, deliberately painted to look ageless rather than infantile, was turned upward, while the Virgin's turned down to meet it cheek to cheek in a fond embrace. Both their expressions held infinite affection and love.

Emily was spellbound. To her the icon was an object of ineffable beauty and holiness, but in the right circles it could be worth thousands of dollars. And the chances of its having left Russia legally were slim. How could Taylor have come by it, and why? Because the idea that she venerated it for its true spiritual significance was clearly out of the question.

But someone ought to. Wary of kissing the icon directly because of its age, Emily crossed herself, kissed her fingertips, and barely touched them to the crackling surface. She could almost feel the icon respond, as if it were a living thing.

'I'd prefer you didn't touch that,' came Taylor's voice from the doorway. 'It's quite valuable. In fact, I'd prefer you didn't come into my office without my permission.'

Emily whipped around, red-faced. 'I'm sorry. The door was ajar, and when you didn't answer I was afraid something might be wrong, so I came in to make sure you were all right. Then I saw the icon.' She turned to face it again, drawn by the centuries of candle smoke, incense, and prayers embedded in the darkened varnish. 'It's so beautiful. I had to venerate it.' She paused, but could not help adding, 'Since I don't imagine that happens every day.'

Taylor rolled her eyes. 'It's a work of art. An investment,

nothing more. You do realize that's not the actual Virgin Mary – so-called – and Christ Child, right?' Her voice dripped sarcasm. 'It's just a picture.'

Emily's temper flared, but she knew Taylor was deliberately goading her, hoping for an emotional response. She would not give her the satisfaction.

'Of course I know that, but an icon is not in fact "just" a picture. It's an image that carries some of the grace of the persons depicted. An interface, if you will, between heaven and earth. Countless miracles have resulted from people praying before icons like this one. It really should be in a church where it could benefit the faithful, not hidden away in the office of someone who doesn't appreciate it for what it truly is.'

She paused. 'Not to put too fine a point on it, it should be in a church in Russia.' She wouldn't go so far as to level accusations, but she wanted Taylor to know she had her suspicions.

Taylor shrugged, unfazed. 'You're entitled to your opinion. I don't happen to share that opinion. Now, do you have some actual business with me, or did you merely come to slaver over my prize possession?'

Emily pulled herself together. The icon had driven everything else from her mind, but she did need to say what she had come to say. 'I came to plead with you on Daniel's behalf. He didn't send me – he doesn't know I'm here – but I'm concerned about him. He's a sensitive young man with a lot of potential, and your pursuit of him is interfering with his work.'

Taylor smirked. 'Pursuit? My interest in him is the same as yours – he has a lot of potential, as you say, and I want to help him realize it. Anything more is merely a product of your fevered imagination.' She ran a pointed eye over Emily's figure, from her schoolmarmish bun with its threads of gray to her long full skirt and sensible low-heeled boots. 'My guess is you're having menopausal hallucinations. Hot flashes, am I right? Hormones going wild? Poor Emily. Better go back to your mansion and put your feet up until you get over it. We certainly don't need you here.'

Emily could feel her face reddening and her breath coming short and fast. But it wasn't a hot flash – it was pure fury. Responding to Taylor's taunts would only dig her in deeper, and driving her own point home was clearly hopeless without something or someone to back her up. The best thing she could do right now was to get out before she lost control.

'You haven't heard the last of this, Taylor,' she said through gritted teeth as she pushed past her into the hall.

Wonderful. She'd been reduced to B-movie clichés. But somehow or other she must find a way to bring Taylor down.

Emily worked for a couple of hours, then took a mid-afternoon break. She needed a stretch, some fresh air, and a snack, so she headed to the Paradox, the student-run coffee shop in the Student Union. Its opposite number, Paradox Lost, was closer to the library, in the science building, but Emily always felt like an interloper when she ventured into that realm.

She was standing in line to order when she heard a familiar voice behind her.

'Emily?'

She turned to see a smallish man in his late thirties with light brown hair and a reddish goatee, wearing a threadbare wool overcoat and a hand-knitted hat. Her half-brother, Oscar Lansing. 'Oscar! I was wondering when I'd run into you.' She gave him a quick hug. 'How are you?'

'Not bad. Missing the great food at Windy Corner, though. This is a tough month, money-wise. No classes to teach equals no income.' She knew his income, when he had any, was barely enough to keep body and soul together.

'Let me buy your coffee, then.' They placed their orders and waited for the barista to prepare them.

'I have a plan to do something about your financial situation,' Emily said.

Oscar frowned. 'I told you, Em – I won't take money from you.'

'I know. I mean a plan to get you a better job. At least the beginnings of a plan. Marguerite's going to help.'

He looked askance at her. 'Pulling strings for me isn't any better than handing me cash. I don't want any favors I don't deserve.'

'And you won't get them. All we're trying to do is make sure you get the full consideration you do deserve.'

They collected their coffee and moved to one of the ratty couches that filled the space. 'I guess I can't object too much to that.' He grinned. 'And I suppose I couldn't stop you if I did.' Oscar had already experienced Emily's determination to share her inherited wealth with him in spite of his objections – she had bought him a car as a surprise Christmas gift.

'No. You couldn't.'

He sipped his coffee and stared out the window. Then his hand jerked, sloshing coffee out the spout of the plastic lid. 'There's Lauren!' he said. 'You know, the woman I told you about.' He pointed out a petite Asian woman crossing the quad toward them from the Campus Center building.

'The one you've been dating?'

'That's a bit of an exaggeration. We've gone out, like, twice, and it's been a while. But yes, she's the one.'

Emily watched Lauren, who had not seen them, as she approached. She was tiny and fragile-looking, her smooth skin pinched by the cold, but she was lovely. Perhaps a few years younger than Oscar, though as an assistant professor in psychology she was a rung above him on the career ladder. Even from this distance Emily could see a sparkle in her eye and a quirk in her mouth that suggested a lively disposition. She liked Lauren on sight.

'Bring her to dinner tomorrow night,' she said impulsively. There was still no food in the house to speak of, but she'd have time to remedy that and come up with something simple to cook. It wouldn't be up to Katie's standard, but then the meal itself wouldn't be the main point.

Oscar started. 'Really? Just like that? Out of the blue?'

'Why not?'

'Well, she'd be meeting my family. The only family I have left. That seems like a pretty big step for a relationship that isn't even really a relationship yet. I mean, it would be different if it were a regular dinner party, with other people.'

'Fine, I'll invite Marguerite. Maybe she can scare up a date as well. Will that do?'

He scrunched up his eyes doubtfully. 'I guess.' The door opened and Lauren walked in. 'Will you ask her yourself? I'll introduce you.'

He stood and waved. Lauren waved back and came up to them. 'Hey, Oscar, you're back!' The two exchanged an awkward peck on the cheek. 'How was your break?'

'Absolutely amazing. I'll tell you all about it sometime, but the big thing is – I met Emily. She's my half-sister, and we never knew each other existed until last week.'

He gestured toward Emily, and she stood to shake Lauren's hand – though they'd been closer to the same level while Emily was seated. 'Pleased to meet you, Lauren. Oscar's told me so much about you.'

Her delicate eyebrows shot up. 'He has?'

Emily nodded. 'And I'd love to get to know you. I'm having a few people over for dinner tomorrow, including Oscar. Would you like to come? Please say yes.'

Lauren looked bemusedly from Emily to Oscar. 'Sure, I guess. I mean, thank you. I never turn down free food.'

'Wonderful! I live just up the road. Oscar will show you.' Then she remembered Oscar had never been to her Portland house. 'It's three-eight-five-two Woodstock. The little Tudor. With two gray cats in the window, probably.'

'Oh, lovely, I adore cats! What time?'

'Shall we say seven?'

'Perfect.'

'I look forward to it.' Emily pressed Lauren's hand and kissed Oscar on the cheek. 'I need to get back to work. See you tomorrow.' She grabbed her things and walked out, hoping Lauren would take her place. Oscar did indeed have a great deal to tell her, though whether they were yet close enough for him to reveal everything that had happened at Windy Corner at Christmas, Emily had no idea. She'd have to tread carefully tomorrow night and take her lead from him.

From home that evening, Emily called Katie at Windy Corner, both to check in and to get some advice about her upcoming dinner party. She already partly regretted her impulsive decision, but she did want to get to know Lauren and encourage Oscar in pursuing the relationship, and this looked like her best opportunity.

'Mrs C!' Katie answered. 'How are you? How's Portland?'

'Not bad. I seem to have gotten myself mixed up in some student drama, but I should have expected that. The work's going OK so far. What's up at home?'

'Rolling right along. I've finally gotten the place all cleaned up from our retreat guests, and now I'm concentrating on wedding plans.' Katie was engaged to Emily's young lawyer, Jamie MacDougal, and they planned to marry in the spring.

'Excellent! Anything you want to share, or run by me?'

'We'll have the ceremony at St Bede's, of course. And I'd like to have the reception here, if you don't mind. On the lawn would be perfect, but we can't trust the weather in April.'

'Of course you're welcome to use the house, no problem. But if you really prefer outdoors, how about renting a marquee, like the Brits do? Seems like almost every wedding reception I've ever seen in a British TV show happens in a marquee.'

'That's a thought. But it can get so windy here – a marquee might just blow down.'

'True. House it is, then. I suppose you've got the menu planned out already?'

'Working on it. So many choices. I may be changing my mind right up until it's time to shop.'

'You're not going to do all the cooking yourself, surely? You can't be the bride and the caterer, Katie. That's beyond even you.'

She laughed. 'I'll get help from my sisters on the actual day. I just want to do some of the prep.'

Emily decided to pull rank for once and put her foot down. 'Katie, I'm sure you're doing this partly to save money, and I won't have it. I want you to hire a caterer at my expense. I won't have you setting off on your honeymoon too exhausted to enjoy it. And your sisters deserve to concentrate on being bridesmaids instead of getting stuck in the kitchen.'

'But—'

'No buts. I insist, and that's an end of it. I don't care if you design the menu, assuming the caterers are OK with that, but I will not have you lifting one finger toward shopping, cooking, or cleaning up the food. Is that understood?'

Katie sighed. 'Yes, ma'am.' She might be disappointed on the surface, but Emily could hear the relief underneath.

Another thought struck her. 'And I also forbid you to take Lizzie along on your honeymoon. I will take care of her. Erin and Abby can come over to help when they're free.'

This time the relief was obvious. 'Oh, Mrs C, you are the specific dream-rabbit!' Emily chuckled at the quotation from *Jeeves and Wooster*. 'I was kind of dreading taking her along, but I didn't know what else to do. Erin and Abby will be on spring break from school, but they both work part-time and their schedules overlap, so they wouldn't have been able to cover her twenty-four seven. How can I ever repay you?'

'You've been giving a hundred and fifty percent to this job since I hired you. I'm just repaying you. But since you mention it, I do have a favor to ask.'

'Anything.'

'Not a big one. I sort of landed myself in the proverbial soup. I invited Oscar and his lady-love to dinner tomorrow, but I have no food in the house and absolutely no idea what to cook. I've been relying on your wonderful meals for so long, I can't even remember what I used to scrounge up when I was on my own.'

'That doesn't even count as a favor. Let's see. You need something that's kind of festive but easy to cook, right? Three people?'

'Actually five. Oscar didn't want it to be too intimate, so I asked Marguerite to come and bring a friend.'

'OK.' She paused, and Emily could almost hear her thinking. 'How about this: you know that casserole I make sometimes with the ground beef and noodles and all the cheesy stuff in the middle?'

'Cholesterol casserole. That would be perfect. But isn't it hard to make?'

'Not at all. Practically foolproof. Not that—'

'Foolproof is good.'

'And all you need with it is a salad and some nice fresh French bread. I bet Marguerite knows the best bakery.'

'I'm sure she does. What about dessert?'

'You don't want to stress yourself. I'd have Marguerite pick something up from the bakery along with the bread.'

'Right. What about the recipe for the casserole?'

'I'll email it to you. Oh wait – you don't have email, do you?'

'Nope.' Though it was starting to sound awfully convenient.

'OK, I'll just read it out to you, then. Ready?'

Emily took down the recipe and noted the other items Katie had suggested, along with a few tips for setting a pretty table. 'Thanks, Katie, you're a lifesaver.'

'No problem. Hope it goes well. What's she like, Oscar's girl? Have you met her?'

'Just briefly this afternoon. She's a tiny Asian woman with what seems like a giant-size personality. I like her so far. I'll fill you in after I get to know her more. I'd better go now. Kiss Lizzie for me.'

Emily heard baby babbling and deduced that Katie was holding the phone next to Lizzie's ear. 'Love you, Lizzie-girl! Be good for your mommy, now.'

Lizzie gurgled affirmatively, and Emily hung up. She missed her little family already. This was going to be a long month.

FOUR

Marguerite had gone all French and mysterious when Emily invited her to dinner, so she had no idea who her fifth guest might be. Knowing Marguerite, he could be anything from a twenty-year-old exotic dancer to a silver-haired investment banker or a foreign film star. The only sure thing was that he would be, in Marguerite's personal estimation, *un bel homme*.

By five minutes to seven Emily had the table set, salad made, Merlot uncorked, and casserole simmering in the oven. All that remained was to slice the bread once Marguerite arrived with it. When the doorbell rang, she put the flame to the last candle, whipped off her apron, and ran to answer the door.

Marguerite stood in the doorway, baguette in one hand and a promising white bakery box in the other. She gave Emily the customary kiss on each cheek, then stepped inside to reveal her guest.

Richard McClintock.

Emily had thought that after more than twenty years of friendship, she was beyond being surprised by anything Marguerite might do. But she'd been wrong.

She quickly rearranged her face, which must have registered shock, to approximate welcome. But Richard's sneer told her she had not been quite quick enough.

'Richard! How nice to see you. Please come in.' She stood back to admit him.

The chair of the Division of Literature and Languages ambled across the threshold, pushing his mended wire-rimmed glasses up on his nose. 'Emily,' he said curtly. 'I take it Marguerite decided to surprise both of us this evening.'

She shot a glance at her friend. Marguerite returned a bland smile.

'What would life be without a few surprises? You're very welcome, expected or no. But surely you recognized the house? Have you actually never been here in all these years?'

'Not that I recall.'

Emily recalled having invited him, along with other colleagues, to various get-togethers over the years, but he had never deigned to attend.

'Let me take your coat.' Richard shrugged off his battered parka, and Emily hung it on one of the hooks that lined the foyer. 'Come in and make yourself comfortable. The others should be here soon.'

She showed Richard to the living room, then pulled Marguerite into the kitchen and took the baguette from her. 'What on earth were you thinking?' she hissed. 'You know Richard hates me. And it isn't too far from being mutual.'

'But it is all part of the plan, *chérie*. We want him to like Oscar, no? So we give him a chance to get to know him socially. Oscar is so *charmant*, so genuine, he cannot fail to make a good impression.'

'But don't you see? If Richard knows I'm rooting for Oscar, that will work against him. For God's sake, don't let on about him being my brother. That would drive in the final nail.'

Marguerite shrugged. 'If you say so. *Moi*, I think you worry too much. All will be well. You will see.'

The doorbell rang again. Emily handed Marguerite the bread knife. 'Here, you finish this.'

She opened the door to Oscar and Lauren but kept them in the foyer long enough to whisper, 'Marguerite brought Richard McClintock. Surprise to both of us. Don't say anything about being my brother – he doesn't like me much. We'll just say we met when you came to Windy Corner.'

Oscar looked baffled but nodded agreement. Lauren's eyes lit with excitement. 'How intriguing! What's the deal? Why does it matter if he likes Oscar?'

Emily darted a glance at her brother, hoping he wouldn't take umbrage. 'We're trying to get Oscar promoted. I asked Marguerite to soften Richard up, but this dinner was not part of the plan. Well, not my plan, at least. Marguerite obviously has her own ideas.'

A smile danced over Lauren's red-painted lips. 'I think I'm going to like this Marguerite.'

Emily ushered Oscar and Lauren into the living room. 'Richard, you know Oscar Lansing.' Oscar put out his hand with a smile. Richard, who was standing next to the stereo with his hands full of Emily's CDs, merely raised one eyebrow and nodded. Oscar's hand hovered a second or two and then dropped, along with his smile.

'And this is Lauren Hsu. From Psychology.'

Richard turned to face Lauren and instantly became a different man. He put down the CDs and took her proffered hand in both his own. 'Delighted to meet you, my dear. How is it we haven't met before? I can't imagine how you could have escaped my notice.'

Lauren laughed and extricated her hand. 'Oh, we psych rats tend to stay in our own little maze. Basement of Eliot, you know. We sneak in and out in the middle of the night and no one ever sees us.' That might be true of some psych profs, but Emily doubted it was true of Lauren. She was much too vivacious to stay cooped up in the windowless nether regions of the psych labs.

No doubt casting about for an avenue of escape from Richard,

Lauren pounced on the cats, who were sitting in the bay window. 'Oh, you beauties!' she gushed. 'What are their names?'

'Kitty and Levin,' Emily replied. 'Levin's the bigger one, in case that's not obvious.'

'From *Anna Karenina*, right? Clever.' She proceeded to shower the two cats with more attention than they'd received since Emily brought them from Windy Corner.

Richard turned from the scene with a disgusted sneer. He sniffed dramatically and put a dirty handkerchief to his nose. 'Can't stand cats,' he muttered. Levin shot him a glare that made it clear the feeling was mutual.

With an interrogatory glance at Emily, Richard held up a CD of Ella Fitzgerald singing Gershwin. The CDs had belonged to Philip, Emily's late husband; being fond of silence and preferring live music over recorded, she rarely played them. But she did love Ella and Gershwin. She smiled acquiescence, and Richard put the CD in the stereo. At least they had one thing in common.

As the opening notes of 'Someone to Watch over Me' floated out of Louis Armstrong's trumpet and filled the room, Richard turned to face the others and frowned slightly. 'How do you two know each other?' he asked Emily and Oscar. 'You came after she left, didn't you, Lansing?'

'Yes, but—'

'It is all my fault,' Marguerite interrupted. 'Emily was looking for writers to fill her retreat center over Christmas, and Oscar was looking for a quiet place to work on his doctoral thesis. I put them together.'

'Retreat center?' Now Richard looked truly baffled.

Emily realized the transformation of her inherited Victorian mansion into a writers' retreat center was not yet common knowledge at Bede. She'd assumed Marguerite would have talked it up more generally.

'The house my aunt left me is way too big for one person, but I love it too much to let it go. So I decided to turn it into a writers' retreat center. People can come by invitation for a week or a weekend and donate whatever they can afford toward the food and upkeep.'

Richard smirked, no doubt searching for some sarcastic

remark to make about this inherently altruistic scheme. His eye fell on the dining table. 'So do you do the cooking and cleaning yourself? Somehow you never struck me as such a domestic type.'

Emily knew she'd been famous on campus for never bringing homemade food to departmental potlucks. 'No, I have an assistant who does all that. She's quite a marvel. Gourmet cook, brilliant manager, immaculate housekeeper, all while taking care of a young baby. I couldn't do it without her.'

'Nice for some.' Richard gave a tight smile.

Oscar took a long sniff of the odors emanating from the kitchen. 'Something smells delicious. Is that one of Katie's recipes?'

'Indeed it is. And it should be ready to eat. Shall we?' She led the way into the dining room and brought the casserole from the oven.

'I forgot to ask if anyone was a vegetarian,' she said, lifting the lid to reveal the top layer of ground beef bubbling in tomato sauce. By 'anyone' she really meant Lauren, as she knew all the others ate meat.

'Not me,' Lauren said. 'I'm an omnivore. If it's free, I'll eat it.' She looked ready to dip her fork straight into the casserole dish.

'Pass your plates, everyone. This is too hot to hand around.' Emily loaded up the plates one at a time as Marguerite passed the salad and bread. Everyone dug in.

'Mmm! This is delicious!' Lauren gushed after her first bite. 'This Katie person must be some cook.'

'Oh, she's amazing,' Oscar said. 'You should have seen the stuff she made over Christmas. I couldn't put a name to half of it, but every bite was to die for.'

Emily took up her cue. 'You'll have to come down at spring break, Lauren, and experience Katie's cooking firsthand. That is, if you don't have other plans.'

'I just made plans. I'll be there with bells on.'

Oscar gave Emily a significant look, and she said, 'You, too, Oscar, of course.' She darted a glance at Richard, hoping he wouldn't angle to be included in the invitation as well, but he was concentrating on his food. Something about the way he shoveled it in, swallowing so quickly he could hardly be tasting anything, made Emily shudder.

She took a moment as all were occupied with eating to ponder why her feeling toward Richard bordered on revulsion. As a rule she managed to get along with people, even difficult ones. She tried to remember that everyone had a backstory she knew nothing about and to make allowances accordingly. But Richard touched something visceral in her that was not amenable to reasonable argument. Perhaps on a subconscious level he reminded her of someone or something from her past that held more emotional power than did her actual relationship with Richard himself.

Emily shook off these unproductive thoughts and turned her mind back to her hostess duties. She'd meant the evening as an opportunity for Oscar to move forward with Lauren, but seeing how comfortable the two of them were together, she didn't think they needed her help. Marguerite had turned the dinner into a networking opportunity for Oscar, so they might as well make the most of that.

'How is your thesis coming along, Oscar?' Emily knew he hadn't made a lot of progress between Christmas and New Year's, due to circumstances beyond either of their control, but in the week before that things had seemed to be going well.

'Really well,' he said. 'I got so much done at Windy Corner, in spite of' – he glanced at Richard – 'in spite of being practically comatose from all that great food. I'll probably be able to finish over spring break, if all goes well.'

'That's terrific! So you'll have your PhD before next fall?'

He nodded. 'Finally.'

'And I've pretty much decided to retire completely, so there should be an opening in the department.' That was probably too blatant, but she couldn't take it back now. Richard still seemed focused on his food, though, so perhaps she hadn't done any harm.

'And I will definitely be applying for it.'

'I have heard good things about your teaching,' Marguerite put in. 'From your students, that is. You seem to have a good rapport with them.'

'That's probably because he never really grew up,' Lauren said with a teasing dig of her elbow. 'He's one of them.'

Oscar blushed. 'Well, I do try to speak their language. While maintaining a reasonable level of authority, of course.'

Richard finally came up for air and a long sip of Merlot. 'I expect we'll have a strong pool of applicants for the new position. I've been getting feelers from all over since September.' He smiled blandly at Emily. 'No one ever expected you to come back once you'd joined the leisured classes. Why put up with students and long hours and campus politics if you don't need the paycheck?'

Emily bit back the answer she would have liked to give, which would have hinted that some teachers were more dedicated than others. 'There was a time when I would have continued teaching just for the love of it. But I have to confess, I was getting a bit burned out by the end of last year. I'm grateful to have the opportunity to change direction. And finally write my Dostoevsky book.' She smiled brightly, hoping someone would pick up that topic and run with it.

Lauren obliged. 'You're writing about Dostoevsky? I love Dostoevsky! His novels are like a textbook on abnormal psychology.'

'That's one way to look at them, I suppose. I've always thought of him as simply an acute student of human nature. But his characters do tend toward the extreme, certainly.'

'You bet they do. I mean, look at Raskolnikov – classic paranoid schizophrenic. Dmitri Karamazov – complete lack of impulse control. And Rogozhin from *The Idiot*? Obsessive attachment. And Dostoevsky predates Freud! Incredible.'

'Well, Dostoevsky didn't attempt to categorize his characters or put names to their disorders – he simply observed and recorded them. And honestly, there's fair ground for saying that in most of his characters he took some element of his own personality and exaggerated it. He was an amazingly complex and conflicted man.'

'He was a Russian. Aren't they all like that?' Richard said. A glance told Emily he meant that for the conversation-stopper it was.

'Lauren, I'm afraid we're boring the others. Perhaps you

and I should continue this conversation another time. Marguerite, isn't there something wonderful in that white box you brought in?'

Marguerite rose with her and they served the dessert – a mocha torte – with coffee in the living room. Conversation drifted to more neutral topics, and soon Richard took his leave. The others relaxed in his absence like Victorian ladies who'd removed their corsets for the night.

'That didn't seem like a great success in terms of my career prospects,' Oscar said with a sigh. 'He as good as said I don't have a chance for promotion.'

Marguerite waved an elegant hand. '*Pas du tout.* That is merely Richard's way. It is against his religion ever to say an encouraging word. You will have as good a chance as anyone when it comes to the point.'

'Though perhaps not better,' Emily said. 'We still have work to do.'

'But how is such a man to be worked on?' Lauren's place in Emily's heart was cemented with that obscure reference to *Pride and Prejudice*. 'He seems impervious.'

'Oh, he has one weak spot, at least,' Emily said. 'Surely you noticed.' With these words one piece of the puzzle of her feelings toward Richard clicked into place; but there must be more to the picture.

Lauren dropped her eyes. 'Yeah, I noticed that.' She turned to Oscar. 'If there's anything I can do through normal channels to further your cause, I'll be happy to do it. But seducing Richard is too much to ask.' She shuddered. 'I'd rather kiss a cobra.'

Oscar turned beet red. 'I'd sooner starve than have you so much as flirt with that creep. And after all, Bede isn't the only school in the world. It isn't even the only school in Portland.'

'No,' Emily replied, 'but it is the best place to work, once you get your foot properly in the door. Don't worry, Oscar, we'll manage this somehow. Richard is only one vote, after all.'

FIVE

The next morning, Emily was already at work in the library when Daniel appeared – this time without Svetlana in tow. 'Good morning,' she said. 'No Svetlana today?'

Daniel's eyes went black. 'Her father's here,' he grunted.

No further explanation was necessary. 'Oh, I see. She didn't mention he was coming – is this a surprise visit?'

'Totally. He was in Seattle on business and decided to come down before heading back to Boston.' Daniel snorted. 'Doesn't trust Sveta to turn that D around on her own, I guess.'

'I see. But if he thinks he can intimidate Taylor Curzon into changing a grade, I'm afraid he's in for a rude awakening.'

'Try telling him that. Try telling him anything.'

Emily had not the least confidence in her own ability to 'tell him anything', but she was curious to see this apparent bully for herself. 'You don't happen to know where they are?'

'They were heading for the coffee shop a minute ago.'

She stood and grabbed her coat and purse. 'I feel a sudden need for a cup of coffee. Can I get you anything?'

Daniel returned her sly smile. 'Plain black, thanks. No rush.'

On her way out of the room, Emily passed Sidney, who greeted her with an ingratiating smile. 'Good morning, Professor Cavanaugh. I'm on my way to see if Daniel wants to go for coffee.'

'He's only just started to work. I'm getting coffee for him.'

Sidney's smile faded momentarily, then reasserted itself. 'In that case I'll say a quick hello and get on with my day.'

Emily resisted the impulse to turn the young man around and frog-march him out of the library. She wasn't Daniel's keeper, after all; she couldn't save him from every annoyance.

She entered the Paradox as if focused solely on getting a caffeine fix. Not until she'd placed her order did she look around and spot Svetlana sitting at a table by the window with a balding, pudgy middle-aged man. She caught Svetlana's eye and waved.

Svetlana looked like a falling trapeze artist who suddenly realizes she has a net. 'Professor Cavanaugh! Please, join us.'

The man who was presumably her father looked around and frowned. No doubt he expected, and preferred, a tête-à-tête with his daughter. But basic social training forced him to make way for Emily at the table.

'I can't stay long – I'm taking coffee back to Daniel, and I don't want it to get cold.'

Svetlana's face pinched with worry again – whether at the mention of Daniel or at the briefness of Emily's sojourn, she couldn't be sure. 'Professor Cavanaugh, I'd like you to meet my father, Saul Goldstein.'

Emily extended her hand and put on her brightest smile. 'It's a pleasure. Svetlana's told me so much about you.'

Goldstein's frown intensified as he gave her hand a cursory shake. 'She hasn't mentioned you to me.'

'Oh, that's because I've been gone for a while. I'm on sabbatical this year – just came back for Paideia to do some research. But I did have the pleasure of teaching your daughter in a lit class last year. She's an excellent student with keen insight.'

He snorted. 'That opinion does not appear to be unanimous.'

'Yes, she told me about the difficulty with Professor Curzon. What you need to realize, Mr Goldstein, is that Curzon is notorious for playing favorites. A poor grade from her is not necessarily any reflection on a student's ability or hard work – it's only a sign that Curzon has taken against her.'

Goldstein glowered at his daughter. 'What did you do to antagonize her?'

'Please, don't assume it's Svetlana's fault. Curzon's likes and dislikes are entirely capricious. And her favor rarely extends to the women in her class.'

The glower turned back to Emily. 'Are you serious? Why is such a person allowed to go on teaching here?'

Emily gave a rueful shrug. 'She has tenure. It takes a pretty serious accusation, backed up by solid proof, to get a tenured professor dismissed. And most of the students won't come forward for fear of retaliation.'

He pushed to his feet. 'We'll see about that. The law is on our side, and the name of Saul Goldstein has struck fear into worse offenders than her before this. Where's her office?'

Svetlana touched a tentative hand to his custom-tailored elbow. 'Papa, please. It's not that important. You'll only make things worse.'

'Not important? You know that one grade will keep you from getting into Harvard Law.'

Emily knew Svetlana's fear was more for Daniel than for herself. 'Your daughter may be right, Mr Goldstein. I'm sure you're well known in Boston, but I don't think your fame has spread to the West Coast. It takes an awful lot to intimidate Taylor Curzon.'

'She hasn't met Saul Goldstein yet. If you won't tell me where to find her, I'll figure it out for myself.' He slammed out the door, and a minute later Emily could see him through the window marching toward Eliot Hall.

Svetlana buried her face in her hands. 'Oh, Professor—'

'Emily, remember?'

'Emily. I'm so afraid she'll just take it out on Daniel. Why can't he back off and let me live my own life?'

'I hope I didn't make things worse by telling him what she's like. I was just trying to get him to let up on you a little.'

Svetlana shook her head with a small smile. 'Don't worry about that. He was bound to find out sooner or later.' She smoothed her hair with a deep sigh. 'I'd better warn Daniel.'

Emily glanced back toward the pickup counter and saw two cups that looked like her latte and Daniel's black coffee. 'I'll walk with you.'

As they left the building, Emily said, 'I wouldn't want to be actually in the room when your father confronts Taylor Curzon – it doesn't sound very safe – but I wouldn't mind watching it through a hidden camera. That could be a confrontation worthy of a Dostoevsky novel.'

Svetlana sighed. 'I wish I could be a million miles away. Though I couldn't be sure the fallout wouldn't reach that far. My father is a pit bull. Once he gets his teeth into something, he doesn't let go until he's torn it to shreds.'

'I hate to say it, but that could be a godsend in this case.

Someone's got to bring Curzon down eventually. He just might be the man to do it.' Emily gave a gallows chuckle. 'Who knows, he could end up inadvertently saving Daniel from her clutches. That would be irony for you.'

Svetlana burst out in a musical laugh that ended with a slightly hysterical edge. 'Saving the man he'll never let me marry. That might be enough to make him give up law for good.'

They had nearly reached the library when Svetlana's phone pinged. She glanced at it and stopped in her tracks.

'Daniel's gone to Curzon's office.' She shot a panicked look at Emily. 'He's bound to run into my father there.'

Emily gave a sly smile. 'I just remembered some urgent business with Professor Curzon. Would you care to join me or sit this one out?'

Svetlana hesitated. 'My being there might only make things worse, but I don't think I can stand to stay away. I'll wait in the hall in case I'm needed.'

They changed course slightly toward Vollum College Center. The two coffees Emily was carrying seemed superfluous now, so she set them down on a concrete pillar before they entered – free caffeine for some needy student. She and Svetlana climbed to the third floor. As soon as they reached the top of the stairs, they could hear raised voices from the direction of Curzon's office. The loudest among them, unsurprisingly, was Saul Goldstein's.

'Ha! Caught you in flagrante. I'd heard about your . . . proclivities, Professor Curzon, but I must admit I did not expect to walk in on you actually trying to force yourself on a student.'

Emily and Svetlana raced down the hall and arrived breathless in the doorway. They peered over Goldstein's hunched shoulders to see Curzon smoothing her jacket with a smug smile, while Daniel cowered purple-faced in a corner.

'You mistake me, sir. Whoever you are. I was merely conferring with Daniel over a difficult passage in his paper.' Curzon gestured toward the open laptop on her desk – the far side of the desk, facing toward her chair and away from where they all stood. The woman couldn't even be bothered to come up with a credible explanation for her behavior. Outrage arose in

Emily's blood – along with something in her throat that threatened to gag her.

Goldstein was clearly not taken in by this transparent ruse. He moved farther into the room and turned toward Daniel, so that Emily could see his face. 'And you – you weren't exactly fighting her off.' Recognition dawned in his eyes. 'Wait a minute – you're that Daniel my Svetlana's always going on about. Are you responsible for her getting a D?'

Daniel opened his mouth to protest, but Curzon cut him off. 'I assure you, Mr – Goldstein, I presume? – neither Daniel nor any other student has anything to do with my grading policy. "Your" Svetlana earned that D through consistently shoddy work in my class.'

'That is outrageous and untrue!' Goldstein shouted. 'I demand to see her work!'

Her smile turned derisive. 'And you're fluent in Russian, are you, so as to be able to understand a word of it?'

He sputtered. Emily swallowed down whatever was choking her and came fully into the room. 'Perhaps I could be of assistance as a mediator. I am fluent in Russian and could evaluate Svetlana's work as a neutral party.'

Curzon flared. 'Since when is one professor's grading policy open to scrutiny by another professor at this institution? Especially one who doesn't officially work here anymore?'

Emily had to admit she had a point. Disputes like this technically had to be resolved at a higher level. 'I suggest we take this to the head of the division. This isn't the first time a student has complained about your grading being unfair, Taylor. Mr Goldstein's interference may be . . . inappropriate, however well meant, but that doesn't mean his point is invalid. Svetlana would have complained herself if—' At the last moment Emily decided it would be unwise to finish the sentence: *if she weren't afraid you'd retaliate against Daniel.*

Curzon crossed her arms and leaned back against her desk. 'Fine. Will you call Richard or shall I?'

Emily hesitated. She had momentarily forgotten that the head of her division was unlikely to take her side in any dispute, no matter how obviously in the right she might be. But at least she could present the case without Taylor having a chance to put her spin on it. 'I will. I'll let you know what he says.' She turned to Goldstein. 'And now I suggest you let your daughter give you a tour of the campus. There's nothing more you can do here for the moment.'

Svetlana moved forward into her father's line of sight. He glowered, but capitulated for the moment. 'Come on, Svetlana,' he growled. 'I need some air.'

Emily turned to Daniel. 'And I think you and Professor Curzon could discuss your paper at another time. Perhaps in a more public place.'

Daniel shot her a look of pure gratitude and scurried out. Emily closed the door behind him and turned to face Taylor Curzon.

'Taylor, this has got to stop.'

'Parents interfering with my instructional methods? I fully agree.'

'You know what I mean. *You* interfering with your male students. Don't deny it – everyone on campus knows what you get up to. Only the students are too afraid to speak out, and the rest of us can't do anything without proof. Well, I intend to put a stop to it one way or another. Starting with Daniel.'

Curzon sneered. 'Oh, so you want him for yourself, do you? Can't say I blame you – so deliciously dark and disturbed, just like a character from your precious Dostoevsky.' She gave Emily the once-over, making her acutely aware of every wrinkle and extra pound which Taylor herself did not possess. 'But do you seriously think you're in with a chance?'

'I don't want to be. I'm happily engaged to a wonderful man my own age. But if I did want to try, my chances would be exactly the same as yours – zero. Daniel's heart is taken, and his integrity would never allow him to give in to you out of expediency. He'd rather flunk out of Bede completely.'

'Oh, come now, Emily. No one's as idealistic as that. What's a little harmless fun compared to his entire future career? No, I think you'll find Daniel will be quite amenable in the end. They always are.'

'Not this time, Taylor. Mark my words. Not. This. Time.'

SIX

Once she'd closed Taylor's office door behind her, the thing that had risen up to choke Emily when she first saw Taylor with Daniel came back in full force. She could hardly breathe. Still clueless as to what was causing this, she stumbled down the hall to Marguerite's office, seeking sanctuary.

Marguerite opened to her knock, and immediately her delicate brows contracted in concern. *'Chérie, qu'est-ce qui se passe?* You look like death.'

'I'm not sure. I need to sit down.' Emily staggered past her and dropped onto her small sofa. 'Water . . .'

Marguerite filled a water glass and handed it to her. 'You look as if you need a doctor.'

'No, no, I'll be all right. Just give me a minute.'

'Perhaps some brandy, then?'

'Yes, I will take that. Thanks.'

Marguerite handed her a snifter, then sat beside her and took her free hand. 'Your hand is like ice. If you are not ill, then something must have happened. Tell me.'

Emily took a few deep breaths punctuated by sips of brandy. 'I'm really not sure. I've just come from Taylor's office. It's a long story – other people were there – but we more or less walked in on Taylor making a move on Daniel. And it hit me like – I don't know – not just the outrage you'd expect, but something more visceral. It hit me like a punch in the gut.' She took another breath, battling the sensation that her chest was closing in.

Marguerite frowned. 'Perhaps it reminded you of what happened to Katie in the autumn?'

A few months ago, Emily had been just in time to rescue Katie from being assaulted again by the man who had raped and impregnated her more than a year before. That had been traumatic, but her concern had all been directed outward, toward Katie. This was different.

'I don't think so. This feels – more personal. As if it reminded me of something that had happened to *me*. Only . . .'

She was about to say, *Only I've never been sexually assaulted.* But was that true? Indistinct flashes of memory tugged at the corners of her mind. A blurry face, much too close to hers. A cloying smell. A wheedling voice that sickened her.

A knock came at the office door. Emily started, but Marguerite steadied her. '*Reste là.* I will send them away.'

Marguerite opened the door, and Emily heard Richard's voice. She didn't pick up his words, but the voice itself merged with her memory flashes and intensified them. Then, as Marguerite shut the door on Richard, a draft blew in, carrying a whiff of his aftershave. Suddenly all the flashes coalesced and she was sick.

Marguerite grabbed the wastebasket just in time, then wet a cloth and gently wiped Emily's face. '*Ma pauvre petite,*' she crooned, rocking Emily and urging her to take another sip of brandy.

At length Emily regained enough control over herself to speak. 'It *was* something that happened to me. Right here at Bede. Over thirty years ago. And I'd blocked it out until now.'

Her breath was still coming ragged. She willed it to steady as Marguerite stroked her hand. 'Old Professor Jenkins. He was gone by the time you came. By the time I came back as an instructor.'

She paused, and Marguerite put in, 'And he had a reputation like Taylor's?'

Emily nodded. 'I had him for Hum One Ten. He singled me out from the very first seminar, only I was too naive to realize what was going on. I thought he just appreciated my contributions to the discussions. I was used to being teacher's pet, after all.'

She took a breath and another sip of brandy. 'Then I had my first paper conference with him. First time I'd been alone in a room with him. His office was in the old Faculty Office Building. That was gone by the time you came, too. Terrible place, crumbling at the edges. Never meant to be permanent.'

Marguerite pressed her hand as if to recall her gently to the point. It was so much easier to talk about the derelict old building than about what had happened there.

'We discussed the paper first. I was expecting a positive review, given how encouraging he'd been in class. But he picked it to pieces. My first paper at Bede, of course it wasn't brilliant, but his criticism was harsh, unreasonable. I was in tears.'

Emily's hands began to shake as if the scene were being repeated here and now. 'He told me he was going to have to give me a D – unless I was really nice to him.' She snorted. 'I was so stupid. Even then I thought, what, bring him coffee? Carry his briefcase from class to class? I just sat there gaping at him, trying to figure out what was really going on.'

A shudder shook her from head to toe. Marguerite rubbed her back, murmuring unintelligibly in French. Emily forced herself to continue. 'Then he got this smile that even a nun couldn't misinterpret, and I got scared. He stood up, came around the desk, and pulled me to my feet. I tried to get away, but he was too strong. I started to yell, but he smashed his mouth down on mine. I thought I was going to suffocate. I struggled and kicked, trying to make enough noise to attract someone's attention outside. But he backed me up against the door and shoved his hands down my jeans, up my sweater.'

Marguerite gave a little cry, and Emily squeezed her hand. 'Thank God, that's as far as it went. Someone knocked on the door right then, and I kicked at it from my side so Jenkins had to let me go. He called out, "Just a minute!" and made signs at me to put myself right. Then he opened the door to whoever it was, and I hightailed it out of there. I didn't stop running till I got to my room.'

Marguerite gave her a minute, then said, 'What happened after that? Did you report him?'

'No. I was too ashamed. I felt I should have caught on so much sooner, never put myself in that position. For all I knew, that was how one got As at Bede. I didn't have a close female friend at that point, so I never told a soul. Until now.'

'And he never tried it again?'

'I didn't give him a chance. I transferred out of his section and never took another class with him, so I never had to be alone with him after that.'

'And all these years you did not remember this?'

Emily shook her head. 'I know it's common for people to

block out traumatic experiences. But you'd think what happened with Katie would have brought it back, wouldn't you?'

'Perhaps you needed to be in the same place – at least on the same campus – to trigger the memory.'

'I suppose. And Richard helped as well, when he came to the door just now.' Emily blinked in sudden understanding. 'Now I know why Richard bothers me so much. His voice is like Jenkins's. And he wears the same aftershave, too.'

'And has the same lustful tendencies. Though, as far as I know, he has never assaulted a student.'

Emily snorted. 'His one redeeming feature. Although I'm sure that's only because he would fear losing his job if he did.'

'*Sans doute*. You may feel your emotions have been accusing Richard unjustly, *mon amie*, but I would not let him off the hook because he is not Jenkins. He is Richard, and that is bad enough.'

After the stress of her revelations, Marguerite insisted on getting Emily something to eat. Since returning immediately to work was out of the question in her emotional state, Emily allowed herself to be led back to the Paradox and plied with a croissant and more coffee.

'Now that I'm thinking straight again,' she said after a few bites had dispelled her shakiness, 'I never told you about the whole scene in Taylor's office. What I was doing there in the first place.'

'*Non*, you did not,' Marguerite replied placidly. 'And I am burning with curiosity. But for your sake I restrain myself.'

'Daniel came into the library alone this morning and told me Svetlana's father was on campus. You know Svetlana? Daniel's girlfriend?'

'The dancer?' Marguerite sketched a chignon. '*Oui*, she is hard to miss.'

'That's the one. But if her father had his way, she'd never dance – or see Daniel – again. He's set on her going to law school, and he came to bully Taylor into replacing the D she gave Svetlana last semester with the A she probably deserves.'

'Bully Taylor? That I would like to see.'

'It would take a different kind of man from Saul Goldstein

to pull it off, if it could be done. But Svetlana and I followed him to Taylor's office once we heard Daniel was already there. That's when – well, I told you about that bit.'

Emily took a restorative sip of latte and went on. 'Anyway, trying to defuse the situation with regard to Svetlana, at least, I promised I'd talk to Richard about getting a review of her work for Taylor's class. If we could prove unfair bias there, it would help Svetlana directly and might give us the beginnings of a sexual misconduct case against Taylor.'

Again the aftermath of her flashback shuddered through her. 'But honestly, I don't think I can face Richard at this point; even though I know it isn't really about him, the memories he's connected to are too raw. I was hoping you might take care of it for me. Are you making any progress with him?'

'*Comme ci, comme ça.* He enjoyed your dinner party, though one would not have known it at the time. He is perhaps slightly, how would you say, softened up toward you and your concerns.'

'I suppose it would be pushing it to try to sway him in two directions at once. Getting rid of Taylor *and* promoting Oscar.'

'It would be easier if Taylor's position were one Oscar could move into. Then it would be two sides of one coin.'

'Yeah. Too bad Oscar's not qualified to teach Russian.' Emily licked the last flakes of croissant from her fingers. 'Would Richard have any natural sympathy with our cause against Taylor?'

'It is possible. I believe he fancies her, which would work against us, but as she has undoubtedly spurned him for her younger men, his resentment could outweigh his lust. I am to dine with him this evening. I will do some subtle probing.'

'Thanks, Margot. I'm going to owe you big-time after all this.'

'*Certainement.* Merely spending time in Richard's company, let alone buttering him up, is a sacrifice worthy of great reward. But do not worry, I will take it in the form of frequent visits to Windy Corner.'

'That's no sacrifice at all on my part. Win-win for me.'

'Which of course you do not at all deserve, since all of these efforts on your part are entirely for your own personal ends.' With a lift of a perfect eyebrow, Marguerite reached across the table and pressed her hand. 'We are friends, not bookkeepers. There is no need to balance the accounts.'

After this conversation and its accompanying sustenance, Emily felt calm enough to attempt to return to work. At least working would be preferable to brooding over the past. She had her area in the library to herself for the rest of the day, as Svetlana was no doubt kept busy by her father, and Daniel was too shaken to try to work without her.

Emily had been making good progress on her research despite the distractions, but the volume of her notes was becoming increasingly unwieldy. Her table overflowed with notebooks and index cards, and she was running out of sticky notes to mark all the spots in her books that she wanted to quote or remember.

As she tidied her things in preparation for leaving that afternoon, she cast a wistful glance at Daniel's side of the table. The surface was stained with coffee and littered with candy wrappers, but otherwise bare. He had taken his laptop with him, naturally, and apart from the books ranged on the shelf above the desk, he apparently needed nothing more.

Perhaps it was time to think seriously about taking the plunge into the deep and turbulent waters of the modern technological world. She'd have to talk to Luke about it. He, of course, would be in favor of plunging, so it would be a one-sided conversation, but perhaps he could help to allay her fears. And after today, she needed to talk to him anyway – though her triggered memories were not something she could imagine discussing over the phone.

At home, she fed the cats and heated a microwave dinner for herself. She was looking forward to continuing her current round of the A&E version of *Pride and Prejudice* – she was up to part four, where Elizabeth and Darcy rediscover each other at Pemberley – but first she needed to talk to Luke.

'Hey, beautiful,' he said. 'Caught me just about to veg out in front of the tube.'

'Same here,' she said with a laugh. 'But I bet you're not watching *Pride and Prejudice.*'

'Nope. *Terminator.* Can't watch that with you around.'

'Gather ye roses while ye may. *I'll be back.*' The last in a Schwarzenegger accent.

'Hey, I'm just passing the time. I'll take you over Arnold any day.'

'That's fortunate, because I was just about to ask if you'd like to come up for the weekend.'

'This weekend? I guess I could. Pete and Heather can cover for me. Got anything special in mind, or you just miss me too much?'

'I do miss you, of course. But I was also hoping you might help me buy a computer.'

She heard a jumble of noise, and a few seconds passed before he responded. 'You literally made me drop my phone. Lucky it fell on the carpet. A computer? You? Is this the real Emily Cavanaugh speaking?'

'It's really me. Trying to corral all my research on to a library desk has finally defeated me. You have my permission to drag me kicking and screaming into the twenty-first century.'

He laughed. 'Try to keep the kicking and screaming to a minimum, OK? Or my nephew on the Portland force might have to arrest you for disturbing the peace.'

'You have a nephew on the Portland police force? I shouldn't be surprised. Is there anywhere in the world you *don't* have a nephew?'

'A few places, outside of Oregon. This one's Colin, my brother Glen's boy. Just graduated from the academy a couple years ago and he's already in plain clothes. Real smart cookie.'

'You'll have to give me his private number. Good to know I have someone nearby to call if anything happens.'

'Happens? Like what?'

'God knows. But the situation up here is getting more explosive by the day. Given my history, it wouldn't surprise me if it erupted into something police-worthy before long.'

'Want to tell me about it?'

'Too complicated for the phone. I'll tell you when you come. See you by lunchtime on Saturday?'

'You just try keeping me away.'

She poured herself a glass of wine, collapsed on the couch, and lost herself in the trials and triumphs of the Bennet sisters for the next couple of hours. Not even Lydia's outrageous behavior could keep Darcy and Elizabeth apart forever. That was why Emily loved fiction – it was almost always resolved satisfactorily in the end. Unlike her entirely unpredictable life.

SEVEN

The next morning, Svetlana arrived in the library alone. Her usually pale face was pasty white except for the purple shadows under her eyes. She looked on the brink of collapse.

'Svetlana, what's wrong?' Emily asked. 'You look as if you haven't slept for a week.'

'It feels more like a month. But really it was only one night.' She ran a hand over her hair, brushing back the wisps that had escaped from her normally neat chignon. 'I was at the infirmary with Daniel.'

'Oh dear! Was he injured?'

'Not exactly.' She hesitated. 'Can I tell you something in confidence?' A little laugh escaped her throat. 'I don't know why I ask. I've already burdened you with all my other troubles.'

'Of course. Don't worry about it. I'm happy to help if I can.'

'The thing is . . . Daniel had a seizure. All that drama with Curzon must have brought it on. His epilepsy has been more or less under control for a while, but when he gets really stressed . . .'

'I see.' Emily's heart twisted in sympathy. She'd seen seizures before and knew how terrifying they could be. 'Is this the first time you've witnessed it?'

'Second. And I'm so afraid it won't be the last. Life is just not going smoothly for him right now.'

'Isn't he on any medication?'

She gave a sigh that seemed to come from her toes. 'He used to be as a kid, but now he can't afford it. He only has the school insurance, and that won't cover it. I've offered to help, but he won't accept it.'

Emily pondered. 'I can understand why he wouldn't want to accept help from his girlfriend. But do you think he'd accept it from me? I'm independently wealthy, you know. The cost would be nothing to me.'

Svetlana screwed up her eyes. 'I doubt it. He's so proud.'

'Well, maybe I can wangle it so it looks like it comes from the college. Then he couldn't turn it down, right?'

'I suppose not. That would be so wonderful if you could manage it.'

'I'll see what I can do.' Svetlana lingered, so Emily probed further. 'What kind of seizures does he have?'

'Convulsive. What they used to call grand mal. Last night's wasn't too severe, but when they're really bad they can leave him weak and disoriented for hours, days even. I hate to think what could happen if he had a bad one when no one was around.'

Emily shuddered. 'I'd send him my best wishes for recovery, but I'm guessing the confidence extends to not letting him know you've told me?'

Svetlana's eyes widened in panic. 'Oh, yes, please. For God's sake, don't breathe a word to Daniel. He'd die of shame if he thought anyone knew besides the infirmary staff and me. He would have hidden it from *me* if he could.'

Emily drew her finger across her lips. 'Mum's the word.' But that wouldn't prevent her praying for Daniel. His malady was already known to God.

When she broke for lunch, Emily stopped by the college infirmary on her way to the dining hall. Miriam Zimmerman, the doctor in charge, was out to lunch, so Emily left word she wanted to discuss something with her and continued on her way.

Absorbed in her own thoughts, as she joined the main path she collided with someone and dropped the book she was carrying. A deep, British-accented voice said, 'I beg your pardon,' and she looked up to see a tall man of about her own age whom she didn't recognize.

'I'm so sorry, I wasn't looking where I was going.' She smiled up at him.

'No harm done.' He stooped to pick up her book, then handed it to her, brushing her fingers in the process. He returned her smile, and their eyes locked for a moment. Emily felt a frisson she hadn't felt since first reencountering Luke the summer before, after their separation of thirty-five years.

She pulled her hand back a little too quickly. Luke was still Luke, and no frisson with a stranger could change that.

'Douglas Curzon,' he said. 'Are you a professor here?'

'Sort of. I'm on sabbatical, possibly on the verge of retirement. Just here for Paideia to do some research.' Then the name sank in. 'Curzon? Any relation to Taylor Curzon?'

He grimaced. 'Her soon-to-be-ex-husband. For my sins.'

Emily couldn't stop her astonishment being reflected in her face. 'Goodness! I had no idea she had a husband. Soon-to-be-ex or otherwise. She certainly—' Emily bit her lip.

'Doesn't act like it?' he finished for her with a wry smile. 'No. I'm not surprised. She never did, actually. Which is the main reason for the *ex*.'

Feeling her face flush, Emily was about to make a tactful retreat, but Douglas said, 'May I have the honor of your name?'

'Oh! I'm sorry, how rude. Emily Cavanaugh.'

He took her hand and held it a second rather than shaking it. 'Pleased to make your acquaintance, Ms Cavanaugh. I was just about to get some lunch. Would you by any chance care to join me?'

Emily was a bit startled by this forwardness, especially from an Englishman; she would have expected more of the famous British reserve. One instinct told her to flee from this budding attraction, which appeared to be dangerously mutual. But another whispered that this could be a golden opportunity to dig up more dirt about Taylor that could be useful in getting her fired – or at least officially cautioned.

She gave Douglas her best smile. 'Thanks, I'd like that.'

They continued the short distance to the Commons. Emily chose a premade salad so she could dash to the cash register ahead of Douglas, thereby averting any awkwardness that might potentially result from him offering to pay for her meal. Any suggestion that this was a date was to be strenuously avoided.

Once they were seated, she asked with all the innocence she could muster, 'So what brings you to campus?'

The grimace returned, self-deprecating but with an edge of resentment smoldering in his eyes. 'The settlement.' He paused and peered at her cautiously. 'You're not a particular friend of Taylor's, are you?'

'Heavens, no. I don't think she has any women friends.'

'No, she wouldn't. Then I may speak freely. Taylor is being stubbornly unreasonable. I would have preferred to leave everything to the lawyers, but on one particular point she won't budge. I'm certain she wants me to beg in person.'

Emily swallowed her astonishment with a bite of salad. 'It must be a point of great importance to you.'

'It is. Sentimental more than financial. She's holding out only to torture me. Honestly, I'd pay everything I have – which, between us, is considerable – to get rid of the woman if it were merely a question of money. Don't tell her that, though. She'd take me up on it.'

Emily approached her next point with caution. 'It wouldn't by any chance have anything to do with the icon hanging in her office, would it?'

'Icon?' Douglas's surprise was genuine. 'Oh, no. What she's keeping from me is a secular painting, a family heirloom. I don't know anything about an icon.'

'I only asked because it looks quite valuable. Medieval Russian, if I'm not mistaken. And it doesn't seem like the kind of thing she'd be attached to in any personal way.'

He snorted. 'Certainly not for religious reasons. And probably not for its artistic value, either. The only aesthetic objects Taylor seems to have any use for are handsome young men.'

'Yes, I've noticed that,' Emily said dryly. 'In fact, she's become rather notorious on campus in that regard.'

'Students?'

'At the moment she's after a student I take a particular interest in. A purely academic interest, you understand.'

He nodded.

'It's imperative we get her to leave him alone. Her pursuit of him is threatening not only his work but his girlfriend's academic career. Not to mention his own health.' She stopped herself before revealing any more. She hadn't mentioned Daniel's name, but Douglas might easily come to learn the identity of Taylor's current prey.

'Do you know anything that could help us get her sanctioned? Or, ideally, fired? It's almost impossible to get students to speak out, she has them so intimidated. And then it's only their word against hers. We need some hard evidence of misconduct.'

'Hmm.' He stroked his smooth-shaven chin with an elegant hand. 'Evidence of sexual harassment, I assume you mean? Not just a consensual affair with a student. These days that wouldn't be likely to lead to any consequences, unless the student was underage.'

Emily sighed. 'Bede is notoriously lax on the issue of consensual affairs between professors and students. But in this case, it is harassment, yes. Coercion by threat of academic consequences, primarily.'

'Right. I can't say off the top of my head. I know of such things in the past, certainly, but whether I can find hard evidence is another question. I'll have to give it some thought.'

'Thank you. I'd really appreciate it, and so would D . . . the student in question.'

He pushed a paper napkin toward her and produced an expensive-looking pen from his jacket pocket. 'May I have your number so I can let you know what I find?'

She hesitated, sensing an ulterior motive. But after all, if he did ask to see her in a more private setting, she need only refuse. He didn't seem like stalker material.

She wrote the number of her little-used cell phone on the napkin and handed it back to him, along with the pen. He gave her his number in return. 'Thanks again,' she said. 'And now I'd better get back to work.'

She scurried off before he could offer to accompany her.

At lunchtime the next day, Emily waited a few minutes after Daniel and Svetlana had left the library before she headed to the Commons, so she could sit alone without appearing rude. But when she entered the dining hall she saw Daniel, Svetlana, and her father sitting together – Goldstein looking angry as usual, Svetlana downcast, and Daniel both resentful and glum.

Svetlana caught sight of Emily and sent her a look of desperation. Emily felt herself being sucked into the vortex of their combined emotions as her feet pulled her in their direction.

'Good afternoon,' she said with forced brightness as she settled herself at the table. 'How is everyone today?'

Svetlana managed a weak smile. 'Better,' she said with a sideways glance at her boyfriend, which Emily interpreted to mean that Daniel was recovering, at least physically, from his seizure. Daniel himself neither spoke nor lifted his eyes; Goldstein merely scowled.

'Have you made any progress in your investigation, Mr Goldstein?'

'Interviewed some students. Couldn't get anyone to agree to testify, let alone bring charges, but a few would at least talk off the record.'

'What did they say?'

'Same story from all the boys. She tried to seduce them. If they went along, they got As in her classes. If they didn't, they failed.'

'Did you find any other women in Svetlana's position?'

'Not exactly. But not a single female student I talked to got above a B. Seems pretty suspicious. Subject like language and literature, you'd expect more girls to excel than boys.'

'That's been my experience as a teacher, yes.' It might sound sexist, but it was the truth. 'Though I have had some brilliant male students. Daniel included.' She shot him an encouraging smile, but he barely flicked his eyes in her direction.

Goldstein met her declaration with a deeper scowl.

'You'll keep digging, I presume?' she asked him.

'Goes without saying. Didn't get where I am by giving up that easily.' He contemplated his sandwich, then put it aside with a grimace. 'What about you? Did you talk to the head of the division about reviewing Sveta's work?'

Emily swallowed. 'Actually, I'm going to need a little more time with that. The division head, Richard McClintock, is not particularly well disposed toward me right now. I've asked my friend Marguerite Grenier from the French department to broach the subject with him. I hope to have an answer for you soon.'

'See that you do.' He spoke as if to an underling, but Emily suppressed her resentment; it would do Svetlana no good for her to stand on her dignity.

Goldstein rose abruptly. 'Got an appointment with another student. Sveta, meet me back here in an hour.' He stalked off, leaving his dirty dishes for his daughter to bus.

'Thank you for all you're doing, Prof— Emily,' Svetlana said when he was out of earshot. 'I don't care about the grade in itself, but if it could be a means of bringing Professor Curzon's activities into the light . . .'

'Of course. This is a matter of the good of the whole college. I'm committed to seeing it through.'

Daniel opened his mouth to say something at last, but before he could get out the first word, Sidney Sharpe appeared at the table, as if from nowhere. He seemed to have Jeeves's gift of oozing imperceptibly in and out of a room.

'Hello, my little chickadees,' he said in a poor imitation of W.C. Fields. 'How's tricks? And who was the angry gentleman who exited just now?'

'That was my father,' Svetlana said with icy dignity. Clearly she felt enough loyalty to defend her father against attack from a stranger, even though she had small enough cause to be happy with him herself just now.

Sidney's bushy eyebrows, which contrasted oddly with his slicked-back hair, rose in a mocking tilt. 'Bit of a helicopter parent, is he? Come all the way from Boston to make sure his baby girl's OK?'

Svetlana drew herself up, but Daniel spoke before she could muster a reply. 'Mr Goldstein's trying to make a case against Curzon. For sexual harassment and unfair grading policies.'

Sidney's eyes narrowed, and in that moment Emily could have sworn their pupils took on an elliptical shape like those of a cat or a poisonous snake. It must have been a trick of the light. In a second he returned to his usual slightly mocking demeanor.

'Making a play for you, is she, Daniel? Not surprising. You are the gloomy Byronic hero type women seem to go for. Though why that is I'll never understand.'

Daniel shot him a disgusted look but did not deign to answer. Sidney glanced from him to Svetlana, then leaned back in his chair.

'You know, I just might be able to help you with your problem,' he said.

'How on earth could you do that?' Svetlana burst out in spite of herself.

'I have my little ways. Don't you worry about a thing, chickadees. Sidney is on the case.' He fell to his lunch with a self-satisfied smile.

Daniel mumbled, 'The only thing that could help is for Curzon to die.'

'Oh, Daniel!' Svetlana exclaimed. 'Don't say that. I know she's a terrible person, but she's still a person. You can't wish her dead.'

'Why not? Look at all the lives she's ruined. We'd all be better off without her.'

'So we get her fired. Not killed.'

'And then she moves on to disrupt some other college in the same way. That's no solution. Why shouldn't one person die for the good of the community?'

'That's what the Sanhedrin said about Christ,' Emily said quietly. 'In fact, that's been the justification tyrants throughout history have given for getting rid of anyone who opposes them – even up to and including genocide.'

Daniel reddened. 'That's different. Jesus wasn't harming people; he was just undermining the Sanhedrin's authority. Same with all those tyrants and their victims. Curzon is a genuine menace.'

'I'm not disputing that. But our system of justice exists to remove people like that from society. We don't have to resort to vigilante killing to get rid of them.'

Sidney cleared his throat in that particular way that is meant to announce a communication of some profundity. 'I wouldn't say that one must die for the sake of the community. The community can take care of itself. But I would say that the inferior must give way to the superior. Daniel is a superior man, and a worm like Curzon should not be allowed to stand in his way.'

Svetlana's eyes went wide, and Daniel sat up straight for the first time. 'That's not the point at all,' he said. 'No one person has more intrinsic right to exist than another. We're all . . .'

He hesitated, and Emily finished the sentence she suspected he couldn't consciously endorse, though at his core he knew it to be true. 'We're all made in the image of God. Equal in his sight. That's exactly why no one of us individually has the right to decide whether another person lives or dies.'

Sidney snorted. 'God is dead. Nietzsche proved that over a century ago.'

'He asserted it. He didn't prove it. Nietzsche saw God as a social construct, and in that sense I'd have to say he's right: God as a social construct is dead because people are no longer willing to believe in him, or more precisely to follow him. But God himself is real and transcendent and infinite. He cannot die, because he is the source of life itself.'

Svetlana nodded agreement, while Daniel returned to slumping over his tray, presumably too conflicted in his own heart to either refute or support her argument. But Sidney simply smiled a smug, superior smile. 'How quaint to see an educated person in the twenty-first century embracing such outmoded ideas. I'm not surprised you're heading toward retirement, Professor.'

Emily bridled but forced herself to remain calm. 'I seem to remember some graffiti from the women's restroom in the library back in my day. I suppose they've replaced those stalls long ago. Someone wrote, *God is dead. – Nietzsche. Nietzsche is dead. – God.* I don't think it was meant seriously, but you do have to consider – two thousand years after Christ's death, the church he founded is billions strong all over the world, and Christians are still being martyred for their faith every day. Little more than a century after Nietzsche's demise, you'll find very few people who'd be willing to die for the ideas he propounded. I'd be surprised if you could find even one.'

'Of course no one would die for them, because the one who believes with Nietzsche is the one who deserves to live. The Übermensch.'

Emily knew an unpersuadable audience when she saw one. 'We're talking in circles here. The point is, we do need to get rid of Taylor Curzon, but we need to do that through the proper channels, by getting her fired. I would like to say for the record,

I'm sure neither of you is serious about taking the law into your own hands. Are you?'

Sidney gave a smarmy smile. 'Of course not. We're just having a philosophical discussion. That's what Bedies do.'

Daniel merely grunted, but when Svetlana pressed his hand he grudgingly shook his head.

'If it came to the point,' Svetlana said, 'I'm sure Daniel wouldn't actually be able to take another person's life. Would you, Daniel?'

'No,' he mumbled. 'Too much of a damn coward in the end.'

'It isn't cowardly to refrain from doing evil,' Emily said. 'Sometimes it takes all the courage in the world.'

EIGHT

Outside the Commons, Sidney turned eastward toward the far block of dorms. 'See you later, then,' he said placidly as he walked away.

Svetlana checked the time on her phone. 'I'm supposed to meet my father pretty soon. I'd better stay here.'

Daniel gave her a quick hug. 'Come to the library when you can.' He turned to Emily. 'Going that way, Professor?'

'Emily, please. Yes, I'll walk with you.'

She deliberately set a slow pace, glad to have this opportunity for a tête-à-tête with Daniel. She was growing increasingly concerned for his emotional well-being. 'What is it with Sidney, anyway?'

Daniel rolled his eyes. 'God knows where he's really coming from. That whole Nietzsche thing is just an act. He doesn't have the gumption of a snail to actually do anything. But the "superior being" bit . . . I'm not one, of course, but I think he may really believe I am.'

Daniel shivered and pulled his coat collar closer around his neck. The cold had intensified over the course of the week. Even at midday, frost crunched beneath their feet as they cut a corner across a small patch of grass.

'He's like a leech,' Daniel went on. 'Ever since we met in Russian Three Hundred last semester, he's been following me around like Colin Creevey trailing Harry Potter with his camera. Sidney's never had an original thought in his life, and he's trying to live off mine. Signs up for the same classes – God knows how he knows what I'm going to take – and every time a paper's due, he pumps me about what I'm writing and then comes up with some stupid pastiche on the same subject. Drives me round the bend.'

'How do you suppose he thought he could "help" with Curzon?'

'Maybe he's hoping to turn her attentions toward himself.'

'Good luck to him with that. Curzon has many faults, but poor taste in men isn't one of them. She always goes for the best.'

He snorted. 'You'd think she'd leave me alone, then. I'm hardly the healthiest specimen. Maybe if I told her—' He cut off abruptly, and Emily mentally supplied the rest of the sentence: *about my epilepsy.*

'What we need is a magic wand,' she said. 'We could do a *presto reverso* spell or something to make Svetlana's father love you – not in the same way, of course – and Curzon be indifferent to you.'

Daniel gave a dark, mirthless laugh. 'I'll write to J.K. Rowling. See what she can come up with.'

'Seriously, though, what does Saul Goldstein have against you? It can't be your Russian descent, since he's married to a Russian.'

'No, he's not one to obsess about the anti-Semitic history of Tsarist Russia. He would rather I were Jewish, of course. I think on some obscure level he feels guilty about marrying a Gentile and wants Sveta to make up for it by marrying a Jew. Not that it would do any good – his grandchildren would still be Gentiles, because Jewishness descends through the maternal line. But I don't think that's the most important thing to him. If I had plenty of money, or even the prospect of a solid, high-six-figure income, he'd be more than ready to overlook my ancestry.'

Emily sighed. 'You won't get to the high six figures as an

academic, that's for sure. If it's not too intrusive – what is your family's situation?'

'My parents were academics, too. Typical Russians – money is seen as some sort of abstract quantity that either comes to you or doesn't. So of course it doesn't. They were descended from the landed gentry, way back, but any crumbs of wealth my great-great-grandparents managed to salvage from the Revolution were gone before they made it to America. We've been scraping by ever since. And since my father died a couple of years ago – leaving no savings, no insurance, nothing – we've been scraping the bottom of the barrel.'

'I'm so sorry to hear about your father. Did he die while you were here at Bede?'

Daniel nodded. 'Sophomore year. I wanted to leave right then – go to work, bring in some money instead of racking up debt – but my mother wouldn't hear of it. Neither would my little sister. She should have started college last year, but she's waiting till I finish, and then it'll only be a state school. So I have to graduate this semester no matter what. I can't let them down.'

'And if Curzon fails you?'

'I won't have enough units to graduate.'

'That's a lot of pressure to be under.' No wonder his health was precarious. 'I suppose you're here on scholarship, then?'

'I have a small scholarship, plus a school grant. And a heck of a lot of student loans that I'll probably never be able to repay.'

Emily would have been in that situation as a student herself if not for Aunt Beatrice, who had paid her way through Bede. She longed to be able to do something financially to help this worthy young man, but she knew he would be too proud to accept it. Part of her legacy was earmarked to help future students like him, but she wanted to help Daniel himself. Maybe she could at least create an impromptu, anonymous scholarship to get him through his last semester without additional loans. She'd have to talk to the financial aid department. Even more important, though, was getting Curzon off his back so he could pass with his integrity intact.

But that could wait till Monday. She had enough on her plate right now, and she was already counting the hours until she would see Luke. She checked her watch. About twenty-two hours now. And probably another eight or so after that before she'd have the opportunity to shift on to his stalwart shoulders the burden of memory she'd been carrying for the last two days.

Late that afternoon, Emily and Marguerite met by appointment at Grounds for Debate, their favorite coffee shop just up the hill from campus. The snacks here were better and the atmosphere more private than at the Paradox, and the pithy quotes from famous pundits that lined the walls provided entertainment while waiting for one's order.

'How did it go with Richard?' Emily asked when they were seated.

Marguerite shook her head. '*Pas si bien*. He is perfectly aware of her proclivities but showed no inclination to do anything about them. In fact—' Marguerite broke off and, to Emily's amazement, actually blushed.

'In fact what?'

'He put the moves on me, and I refused him. Not emphatically, *tu comprends*, but playfully, as if I might give in another time – which, of course, I have no intention of doing. But he took my refusal seriously, and he said – *enfin*, I do not recall exactly what he said, but I believe his intention is to try his luck with Taylor before he agrees to any proceedings against her.'

Emily snorted in disgust. 'He is incorrigible. But if you think about it, that's likely to work in our favor. I mean, what are the chances he'd actually get anywhere with her?'

'Less than zero, I should think. He is about her own age, *c'est-à-dire* twenty years too old for her. And I cannot imagine he was ever in her league in terms of looks.'

'So all we need to do is bide our time until his ardor turns to resentment, and then he'll be just as hot to get her out as we are.'

'A foregone conclusion.'

They sipped their coffee pensively for a few minutes, then Emily said, 'I met someone yesterday who might be more to your liking than Richard.'

Marguerite was instantly alert. 'Who is this man?'

'Oddly enough, he's Taylor's ex-husband. But you'd never think to look at him that his judgment had ever been so poor. He's quite charming. And handsome. And British. And rich.'

'Already I like this man. When can you introduce us?'

'He's supposed to call me as soon as he finds some sort of solid evidence of Taylor's misbehavior with students. But I should warn you, you may not be his type – I got the distinct impression he was attracted to me.'

Marguerite waved a dismissive hand. 'You have Luke. You will not encourage this paragon, and he will move on. And I shall be there when he does.'

Emily was slightly offended by Marguerite's confidence that she could so easily divert any man's attention from Emily herself, but after all, she did not intend to encourage Douglas.

'What is his name, this *homme très intéressant*?'

'Douglas. Douglas Curzon. And they're not actually divorced yet, though they must have been separated for some time – he's in town to wrestle with her over their settlement.'

Marguerite made a disappointed moue. 'Then he will be angry. I do not care for angry men. They are *pas si amusants*. Perhaps I will leave him to nurse his wounds in solitude once you have sent him away.'

'Or maybe a miracle will happen and Taylor will let him have what he wants. He'll have some leverage over her now with disciplinary action in the air. Although that's bad for us if he agrees to withhold his evidence in exchange for her cooperation.'

'*Que será, será*. One way or another, we will bring her down.'

Marguerite dropped Emily back at the campus on her way home. Emily had planned to do some work before dinnertime, but she felt suddenly exhausted by all the drama of the last few days. It was Friday, after all. She decided instead to collect her things and head home to eat her dinner of deli takeout, finish watching *Pride and Prejudice*, and go to bed.

But as she approached the library, she saw Douglas Curzon walking toward her on an adjoining path. He held up an arresting hand, and she stopped to wait for him.

'Have you found anything?' she said by way of greeting, then felt ashamed of her own rudeness. But after all, she had promised herself not to encourage him.

'Nothing of significance quite yet, but I have some ideas of lines I might pursue. If you would do me the honor of dining with me, we could pool our resources and see what we can come up with.'

He made it sound so innocent, she was tempted to accept. After all, they were embarked on a joint venture of sorts, and they both needed to eat; what was the harm in combining a strategy session with dinner?

But then she caught the look in Douglas's eye and thought about how she would relate this event to Luke when he arrived in the morning. There was no spin she could put on it that would not bring a tinge of guilt to her recital.

'Thanks so much, but I'm afraid I'm done in. I need to put my feet up and zone out tonight.'

He looked crestfallen but quickly recovered. 'Perhaps tomorrow night? You will take Saturday off from your studies, I presume?'

'My fiancé is coming to town for the weekend.' There, she'd put herself out of harm's way in one stroke.

He closed his eyes with a deep breath. 'I should have known a charming lady like yourself would not be unattached.'

The pearl-and-emerald ring on her left ring finger might have provided a little clue as well, she thought. Perhaps he'd ignored it on purpose.

'We can touch base on Monday,' she said. 'Assuming you'll still be around?'

'Very well, Monday it is. I wish you a pleasant weekend.' He made her a small courtly bow and walked away.

It was a good thing Luke would be there in the morning. She needed him right now on so many levels – not least to keep the handsome, cultured, gentlemanly Douglas from turning her head.

NINE

After less than a week's separation, Emily was not expecting the intense rush of love and relief that overwhelmed her when Luke appeared at her front door. He had been with her through several periods of great stress in the past six months, and she had come to rely on him more than she knew. His solid presence – six foot three of muscle backed up by a natural air of steadiness and authority – had become her rock. She couldn't imagine how she'd gotten along without him during all the years they were apart. And now she was feeling especially vulnerable – but any discussion of that would have to wait until the business of the day had been accomplished.

Appropriately effusive greetings finished, he asked her, 'So what's the plan?'

'Lunch first – Baumgartner's up the road has great sandwiches – then the Apple Store downtown.'

'You already figured out you want a Mac?'

'I think so. Marguerite has a MacBook, and it's so sleek and compact, it seems like it would blend in at Windy Corner more than most of the other laptops I've seen. Plus, according to her, the what-do-you-call-it – interface? – is more intuitive than that of a PC. I've heard so many people whine about Windows over the years, I'd prefer to avoid it if possible.'

'Sounds good to me. We have PCs at the office, but my personal machine is a Mac. Only thing I can see in a PC's favor is the cost, and I'm guessing you don't care about saving a few hundred bucks.'

'Not if I have to pay for it in frustration. Learning the basics of computer use is going to be hard enough without having an inanimate object working against me.'

Over lunch they caught up on events in Stony Beach and at Bede. Stony Beach was usually quiet in the winter, the only drama for the tiny local population arising from the occasional fierce storms that rocked the coast. One of those had hit over

Christmas, but now the weather was calm. Luke had nothing to report beyond the fact that his grandmother, who lived in a rest home in Seaside, had contracted a nasty cold.

Emily had already told Luke on the phone most of what was going on in her circle, but she filled him in on the most recent developments. 'I see what you mean about an explosive situation,' he said when she had finished. 'That Curzon woman seems like the kind that would make trouble wherever she went.'

'And so far, without much in the way of consequences to herself. She's like the eye of a hurricane. But hopefully not for much longer. The hammer of fate is about to fall.'

'I just hope it doesn't fall too literally. Think any of these people would go so far as to take the law into their own hands?'

Emily shuddered. 'I hope not. And really I doubt it, unless every possible avenue of legal retribution turned into a dead end. These are civilized academics we're talking about, after all.'

'Yeah, but you know as well as I do what can happen to that civilized veneer when the stakes get high enough.'

'True. But enough of this morbid speculation. Let's go buy me a computer.'

They took a bus to the Apple Store, since parking downtown was always a problem. The storefront itself intimidated Emily, composed as it was entirely of glass with huge pictures of various Apple devices lining the center of the broad back wall. An employee met them at the door and entered Emily's name on an iPad. The young woman (none of the employees looked over twenty-five) asked what they had come for, and when Emily said she was there to buy her first computer, the girl made a visible effort not to gape at her in astonishment. Her impulse must have been to point at Emily and call out to the whole store, 'Look! A dinosaur!'

Even without that, Emily could have melted into the floor, she felt so self-conscious. Thank God she'd brought Luke along instead of Marguerite. He could provide the moral support she needed to survive the experience as well as the technical know-how to help her make the best decision. Marguerite would have been either oblivious to or dismissive of her anguish, feeling it served her right for being such a Luddite for so long.

So when Luke put a hand on the small of her back and

said, 'She's interested in a MacBook,' she was grateful that
he was speaking for her rather than resentful, as she might
have been in other circumstances.

'Great. Looks like about a ten-minute wait, then an associate
will be with you. Why don't you look around in the meantime?
The MacBooks are right over there.' The employee pointed
toward one of the long counter-height tables that ran the length
of the store, each holding a row of sample products for
customers to examine at their leisure.

They found an empty spot, and Luke showed her some of
the basics of computer use while they waited to be served. Just
as Emily felt her brain might explode from all the new information, a perky blonde came up to them. 'Emily?' she said. 'I'm
Caiden. I understand you're looking for a new laptop.'

With Luke as tech-to-English interpreter, Emily managed to
communicate what she needed out of a computer and determine
that a MacBook was in fact the best machine for her. She
chose the gold color, grateful for at least one decision she could
make on familiar aesthetic ground. Caiden walked her through
the setup and use of a few basic apps, and Emily signed up for
some classes that would help her get fully up to speed.

An hour after the ordeal began, Emily collapsed on to a bus
bench next to Luke with a minimalist white Apple box on her
lap. 'I'm not sure this is going to be as much help with my
book as I thought. It'll take me all the time I have at Bede just
to learn how to use it and get all my notes typed in.'

'Fair point. Any chance you could hire a student to help you
out? With the data entry, if nothing else? Then you could keep
researching while they get you caught up.'

'That's a thought. Maybe Svetlana could do it. She doesn't
seem to have a lot of work of her own; she's mainly just keeping
Daniel company.' She thought back to her conversation with
Marguerite about the whole computer issue. 'Margot told me
about this program she uses called Scrivener. Apparently it's
great for keeping all your notes and stuff in one place. Do you
suppose that's on here?' She stared at the box as if she could
see through to the inner workings of the computer and locate
the program there.

'Doesn't sound familiar, so I'd guess it isn't a native Apple app. When we get back to your place we can look for it on the Web. All programs are downloadable these days.'

'You're forgetting one thing. I don't have internet access at home.'

He shook his head at her with a fond smile. 'Oh, Emily. My favorite throwback. OK, how about a nearby coffee shop? Those usually have Wi-Fi customers can use.'

'Sure, let's try Grounds for Debate. I see people in there with laptops all the time, so I suppose they must have Wi-Fi.'

The bus let them off across the street from the coffee shop, and within half an hour Emily was refreshed with a latte and muffin and her laptop was equipped with Scrivener. One more thing to learn, and probably not included in the Apple Store classes. She'd have to get Marguerite to show her the ropes.

Her feet were dragging as they walked the block back to her house. She had intended to use this time with Luke to unburden herself of her newly recovered traumatic memories, but she felt at peace in this moment, comforted just by his presence. And she was too exhausted at this point to put herself through another emotional ordeal. Surely the recital could wait. She'd already been through it with Marguerite, and it wasn't anything that could affect her relationship with Luke – it had all happened so very long ago.

'I'm done in,' she said as she unlocked her front door. 'How about we order a pizza and veg out tonight?'

'Sounds good to me. I love being a vegetable with you.' He put an arm around her and kissed her cheek.

'Thanks for coming with me today. I couldn't have survived it without you.'

'Oh, sure you could. You're a strong and intelligent woman, Emily. You don't give yourself enough credit.'

'Well, I'm glad I had you, anyway. And I wish I could keep you around longer than tomorrow.'

'Me too, but I've got to get back tomorrow night. Pete and Heather are both overdue for some time off, since I made them work through Christmas.'

'True.' She paused, wondering how to phrase her next request. Might as well just come out with it. With Luke especially, direct was always best.

'Would you be willing to come to church with me tomorrow? I really need to go, and I'd like you to meet some of my friends there.'

'Sure, no problem. I'd like to see what this Orthodox thing is all about. It's part of you, and I need to know all of you if we're going to be one flesh.'

Emily offered Svetlana a ride to St Sergius, but she regretfully declined, saying her father had other plans for the morning. So Emily and Luke went alone.

Walking into the nave felt far more like coming home than had Emily's return to her little Tudor house. The church had not been taken over by strangers in her absence but had continued its own vital life. The people – both the parishioners and the saints in the icons that lined the nave – welcomed her back as if she had never been away.

Luke, of course, inspired a number of whispers and sly glances during the liturgy, and afterward in the coffee hour the curiosity about him became more overt. Her closer friends in the congregation, including Father Paul, knew about Luke, but none of them had met him or heard the very recent news of their engagement. Emily twisted the pearl-and-emerald ring on her left ring finger. She'd noticed several sly glances taking that in as well.

Father Paul came to sit with them in the fellowship hall and shook Luke's hand before offering his to Emily to kiss in the traditional priestly greeting as he blessed her with his other hand. With a pointed glance at her finger, he said, 'Do you have some news for me?'

Emily blushed, suddenly acutely conscious that she had entered into this engagement to a man who did not share her faith without her priest's blessing. 'Yes, Father. We got engaged at New Year's.'

Father Paul gave her an inscrutable look and said to Luke, 'I've heard a fair bit about you over the last six months – enough to feel confident you'll take good care of Emily. But one thing I don't know is where you stand in regard to faith.' He held Luke's eyes with an intensity that belied the casual friendliness of his tone.

Luke looked flustered for perhaps the first time in Emily's

experience. 'I believe in God, if that's what you mean. But I've never been inside an Orthodox church before today.'

'Do you attend any church?'

'Not regularly, no. I go to St Bede's Episcopal with Emily once in a while.' He shot her a rueful glance. 'Mostly for funerals, seems like.'

'Have you been baptized?'

'Yeah, I was dunked as a kid. Local Baptist church.'

Father Paul gave a brisk nod. 'They do at least baptize in the name of the Holy Trinity. What did you think of our service?'

'Different from anything I've experienced before, that's for sure. Little bit like the Episcopal service, I guess. But way heavier on the smells and bells.' He grimaced. 'Sorry. No offense meant.'

'None taken. That's a fairly accurate if succinct description of the sensory aspect of the Orthodox liturgy.' Father Paul's eyes twinkled. 'The real question is, were you attracted or repelled by the "smells and bells"? If Emily were out of the equation, would you ever come back?'

Luke pouched his lips in thought. Emily held her breath waiting to hear what he would say. Whatever it was, it would be the unvarnished truth, and it would have a huge impact on their life together from this point forward.

'I think I would. In the past I've always felt like God was closer on the beach or in the woods than he was in church. But here I felt like he was in the air all around me. Like if I prayed he would actually hear me.' He turned to smile at Emily. 'Yeah, I'd come back.'

Father Paul beamed. 'Splendid. Then I can marry you here. Have you thought about a date?'

'We were hoping for June first,' Emily said. 'It's kind of a special day for us.'

Father Paul dug his phone out of his pants pocket through a gap in the seam of his cassock and looked at his calendar. 'June first . . . That's a Saturday this year. The last Saturday of Pascha, in fact. We can work with that.' He smiled at Luke. 'We prefer to do weddings on Sundays when we can. It's an extra blessing. But having a wedding during the Pascha season is an even greater blessing. Not to mention you save on flowers because the church is already decorated.' He turned his smile toward

Emily. 'Not that you care about saving money these days, eh?'

'Not so much. But the Pascha flowers are so lovely. I always thought that would be the perfect time for a wedding.'

The perfect date for a wedding – and the perfect groom. Looking forward to that would get Emily through the next couple of weeks, stressful though they promised to be.

TEN

Emily said a reluctant goodbye to Luke later that afternoon, feeling she would be so much better able to face the current situation at Bede if she had his strong presence to come home to at the end of each day. Throughout their newly revived relationship, she'd wondered whether she could abandon her Portland life for a life in Stony Beach with Luke without regrets. Now she knew that home was neither at Bede nor at Windy Corner, but wherever Luke might be.

On Monday morning, Emily stopped by Vollum Center in the hope of catching Marguerite in her office so she could beg for computer advice. Marguerite's office was two doors down from Taylor Curzon's, and as Emily passed Taylor's slightly open door she heard a distinctive male voice – Daniel's. Until a few months ago Emily would never have dreamed of eavesdropping, but her experience as an amateur detective had softened her scruples in that regard. Daniel might be technically an adult, but he was a vulnerable person in a volatile situation and could easily need her help. She paused outside the door, holding her breath.

'Come on, Daniel,' Taylor's voice wheedled sensually. 'I'm not so repulsive as that, am I? I have a few years on you, yes, but you know what they say about older women. I could teach you things that aren't on any curriculum.'

'I didn't come here for that kind of education,' Daniel muttered.

At this point Emily had a brainwave which she attributed to either Luke's influence or a prompting from her guardian angel, because she would never have thought of it on her own. She took out her cell phone and set it to record, as Luke had taught her to do in case she ever needed to. The evidence she was about to obtain might not be admissible in court but it could still be enough to get Taylor sanctioned, or even fired.

'The best things in life are the ones we don't plan for.'

Emily could see nothing through the crack of the door, but she heard a loud bump that suggested Daniel had backed into a piece of furniture in trying to escape.

'Professor, please. I love Svetlana. Even if I did find you attractive, I would still be true to her.'

Taylor's husky tone took on a harder edge. 'You can help your precious Svetlana. You can make all her problems disappear – as well as your own.'

Daniel's voice rang clear and angry. 'In other words, if I sleep with you, you'll change her grade and pass me with flying colors. And if I don't?'

'Let's just say . . . you could both find yourselves out in the cold. In more ways than one.'

Emily jumped back as Daniel swung the door fully open. 'I'm so glad we understand each other. I'll see you in hell first.'

He stepped into the hall, slamming the door behind him, and started as he came face-to-face with Emily. 'Did you hear that?' he asked her *sotto voce*. 'She came out and admitted our grades depend on me sleeping with her.'

'I not only heard it, I recorded it,' Emily responded, holding up her phone. 'We've got her now.'

Having assured Daniel that she would take the matter from there, Emily continued down the hall to Marguerite's office and found her in.

'We've got her, Margot,' she said without preamble. 'I've just recorded Taylor threatening Daniel with failure for himself as well as Svetlana if he doesn't sleep with her. Richard can't weasel out of it now. She's going down.'

'Play it,' Marguerite demanded. When the playback was finished, she nodded sagely. 'It is true she did not say the actual words of the threat – Daniel said them – but her intention is clear. I believe you are correct. We have her now.'

'Should we get Svetlana's father involved?'

Marguerite considered with pursed lips. 'Perhaps not yet. This is an internal college matter, and Goldstein as a parent should not be involved. If Richard does manage to weasel out, as you put it, and we have to resort to the public courts, that will be the time to bring in a lawyer.'

'Right. Do you want to take this to Richard, or shall I?'

'I will do it. He might argue that since you are retiring you have no right to be involved.'

'OK. I guess I can live without this for a while.' Emily held out her phone.

'*Mais non, chérie*, you will simply email me the file.'

'Do what with the what?'

Marguerite rolled her eyes and swept the phone from Emily's hand. After a few mysterious passes of her perfectly manicured fingers, she handed it back. '*Ma chère amie*, when will you join the modern world?'

'I'll have you know' – she opened the padded compartment of her briefcase and pulled out her new laptop – 'I bought a MacBook on Saturday. And I'm going to take some classes in using it. But I need you to teach me Scrivener. Apple doesn't cover that.'

Marguerite put a theatrical hand to her brow and reeled back. '*Je suis époustouflée*. Flabbergasted. Emily Cavanaugh with a Mac? Is the world coming to an end?'

'Ha ha. I finally had to admit that keeping track of a book in progress will be much easier on a computer. Provided figuring out how to use it doesn't take up more time than it saves.'

'We are two women *très intelligentes*. With my help you will be up to speed in no time. But first, we must not lose one moment in getting this recording to Richard.'

Marguerite opened the door and set off to the right toward Richard's office, while Emily retraced her steps to the left toward Taylor's door. As she approached she saw an unfamiliar man just leaving the office and heard him say something to Taylor in Russian as he closed the door. She couldn't be sure, but it sounded like *Ne podvedi menya* – 'Do not fail me'. The verb form was familiar and the tone urgent, even threatening.

Emily's curiosity was piqued. She was almost certain this man had nothing to do with Bede. He appeared to be about her own age – thus too old to be Taylor's paramour – and his too-bright navy sharkskin suit with its slightly exaggerated cut was something no Bede professor or staff member would be caught dead in. The man's shaved head and bulky build suggested an underworld enforcer – the Hollywood version, at any rate. Emily had no experience of the real thing.

Her mind flashed back to the almost certainly contraband icon she'd seen in Taylor's office and made a connection that was hardly warranted by physical evidence but which she was intuitively certain was correct: Taylor was involved with the Russian mafia in importing illegal goods.

Getting Taylor sanctioned for sexual misconduct was one thing; taking on the Russian mafia was quite another. That was a matter for the police. The Russian mafia made the Sicilian version look like schoolyard bullies. Emily filed her speculations away in case they were needed later on, but for now, she told herself no action could be expected of her. After all, she had no real evidence that anything illegal was even happening, let alone that Taylor was directly involved.

She hung back a moment so as not to attract the Russian's attention, then proceeded down the hall. But as she approached the stairway, she met Saul Goldstein coming up. He scowled at her.

'I'm sick of this shilly-shallying,' he said. 'I'm going to confront your department head and get this thing settled once and for all.'

Emily put out a restraining hand. 'Just a moment, please, Mr Goldstein. There are developments you need to know about.' She explained about the recording. 'Marguerite's talking to Richard McClintock now. I really think it would be best if you let us handle this as an internal college matter. If we fail, then it will be time for you to get more involved.'

He hmphed. 'I want to hear this recording for myself. Come along if you like, but I'm going to McClintock's office.'

It was clear to Emily that there was no way she could stop Goldstein, so she contented herself with saying, 'Just please promise me you'll be a silent observer until we see how he reacts. Honestly, getting hostile with him at this stage will only make him more recalcitrant.'

Goldstein hmphed again and marched on down the hall. Emily

scurried to get to Richard's door ahead of him. She could hear Marguerite and Richard talking, so she walked in without bothering to knock.

Richard was holding forth in his best pompous manner. 'If you think this is going to change anything—' He broke off, spotting the incomers. 'What the heck? Emily, could you please mind your own business just this once? And who is this man?'

'This is Saul Goldstein. His daughter Svetlana is the one Taylor was making threats about. He also happens to be a lawyer.'

At the word 'lawyer' Richard's red face paled, and his tone went from commanding to groveling in nothing flat. 'Pleased to meet you, Mr Goldstein. As I was just telling Professor Grenier, we will naturally treat this matter with all the seriousness it deserves. It is an internal college matter, though. No need for you to be involved – either as a parent or as a representative of the law.'

'I'll be the judge of that,' Goldstein growled. 'If I see appropriate action within the next twenty-four hours, fine. If not . . .' He left the rest of the sentence to Richard's imagination.

Judging by his face, Richard's imagination supplied the most daunting possible conclusion to Goldstein's unfinished clause. 'I assure you I'll do everything in my power to bring this issue to a satisfactory conclusion for all parties.' He gave an unconvincing smile.

That was the mother of all diplomatically meaningless remarks. Any conclusion that was satisfactory to the reluctant cooperative of Emily, Marguerite, and Saul Goldstein could hardly be satisfactory to Taylor Curzon.

'Marguerite, you've emailed me that recording? Good. Now if you'll all excuse me, I think it best that I speak to Professor Curzon in private.' Richard reached for his desk phone with one hand while waving them all out the door with the other.

With her back to Richard and a significant look at Emily, Marguerite tapped on her phone and then slid it surreptitiously on to a shelf by the door. In a moment Emily felt her own phone vibrate in her pocket.

As soon as they closed the door behind them, Marguerite whispered, 'Pick up the call but say nothing.' Emily complied, and Marguerite shooed her and Goldstein into her office. As she pulled the door shut, Emily glimpsed Taylor emerging from her own office and heading across the hall toward Richard's door.

Marguerite took Emily's phone from her hand and did something to it. 'There. I have muted the sound from our end and set it to record the conversation.' She set the phone on her desk and beckoned the others close. Soon they heard Taylor's voice, sounding annoyed.

'What is it, Richard? I do have things to do, you know.'

'Oh, I think you'll find this is worth your time, Taylor.' They heard Emily's recording playing faintly from Richard's computer.

'Where did you get that?' Taylor's tone was dismissive, but Emily sensed fear underneath.

'Never you mind. The point is that it proves you've been sexually harassing Daniel Razumov.'

'It proves no such thing. *Daniel* said his and Svetlana's grades depended on his . . . cooperation. *I* never did.'

'Perhaps not, but you strongly implied it. At any rate, Svetlana's lawyer father seems to think your words are quite clear enough to warrant your dismissal.'

Goldstein's eyebrows went up and he opened his mouth, presumably to protest that he'd said no such thing – in fact, he hadn't even heard the recording yet. But Marguerite shushed him with a raised palm.

Taylor's confident voice wavered slightly. 'There's no way this would stand up in court. It was obtained without my consent.'

'We don't need it to stand up in court. All we need is for the college disciplinary board to accept it. And given your well-deserved reputation, I don't think there's much question that they will. Accept it – and act on it. Your career could be over, Taylor.'

Richard's tone shifted to one that made Emily's skin crawl. 'Of course, there is a way to make this go away.'

Taylor gave a derisive snort. 'Nice try, Richard. But there is no way you're ever getting into my bed, threats or no threats. I've got something worth two of that.'

'Wh–what do you mean?' Emily pictured Richard backing away and Taylor advancing in a travesty of a tango.

'That last article of yours in the *Journal of Modern Literature*? I happen to know exactly where you got it. And it certainly wasn't out of your own feeble little brain.'

'Nonsense,' Richard blustered. 'I dare you to find either the ideas or the words anywhere else, in print or online.'

'In print or online, no. But on your student Pacifique Morel's computer, yes. Practically word for word, and file-dated well before your article appeared.' Emily could almost hear Taylor's triumphant smile. 'Pillow talk is a marvelous thing. You should try it sometime. Oh no, I forgot – you have no one to share a pillow with. Nobody will have you, for love, money, or threats. Poor Richard.'

'You devious bitch,' Richard hissed. 'I'll get you for this. One way or another. Or Goldstein will. Now get out of my office.'

'Toodle-oo, dearie. Just remember – if I go down, you go down with me.' They heard footsteps, then the opening and closing of the office door.

Marguerite ended the call and the recording as Goldstein erupted. 'That spineless slimeball! Now you've got to admit it's time for me to take this into my own hands. I'm going to sue.'

Marguerite and Emily exchanged a defeated glance. 'You must do as you think best,' Emily said. 'And may God have mercy on us all.'

ELEVEN

'After that debacle, *chérie*, we need a distraction,' Marguerite said to Emily when Goldstein had stormed out. 'Let us have a Scrivener lesson.'

Emily agreed readily. As frustrating as learning new technology might be, it would still be a relief from the impossible Curzon situation.

They worked for an hour, after which Emily felt like the *Far Side* cartoon character who asks to be excused because his brain is full. It was time for coffee anyway, so she and Marguerite decided to adjourn to the Paradox. But as they left Marguerite's office, Emily saw Douglas Curzon entering the office of his erstwhile wife.

With a significant glance at Marguerite, Emily stole close to Taylor's door. If she was going to embark on a new career as an eavesdropper, she might as well make the most of it. She must be developing a suspicious mind – she couldn't help wondering if there was more to the situation between Taylor and Douglas than Douglas had led her to believe.

The door closed behind Douglas but then drifted open again. The latch must be faulty. That explained why the door hadn't been fully closed when Daniel was in with her earlier.

'Douglas,' they heard Taylor say, 'I thought we'd said everything we had to say.'

'You may have. I have not.'

Emily hardly recognized the normally urbane, courteous tones of Douglas's voice. It rang with an edge of barely controlled rage.

'Oh, come now, Dougie. Is that painting really so important to you?'

'You know it is. It's been in my family for generations. It was painted by one of my ancestors depicting another. You have no claim to it whatsoever – legal or moral.'

'But possession is nine-tenths of the law, sweetie. You know that.'

'Not in this case. The painting isn't legally under dispute. You simply stole it. And now you're holding it for ransom.'

'So sue me. Bring criminal charges against me. Go ahead. After all, you have nothing to lose.' Her voice dripped sarcasm. Could she have some hold over Douglas, as she did over Richard? Was this the way she got away with everything in her life?

Emily longed to see into the room, but her scruples would not bend that far. She pictured Taylor standing hand on hip, smiling provocatively, while Douglas's handsome face contorted with rage.

'Taylor, I swear to you, if you don't hand over that painting, I'll—'

'You'll what?' Her taunting voice suddenly dropped to a seductive whisper. 'Crush me in your passionate embrace? Rip off my clothes? Throw me over the desk and screw me silly?'

Emily could hear Douglas's rough and labored breath. Could

it be that he was still attracted to Taylor? Was he actually longing to do just that?

The taunt came back with a harder edge. 'You're not man enough, Douglas, and we both know it. You'd better just accept that I've won. The painting is my trophy, and I'm keeping it.'

Douglas did not reply. Sensing an end to the conversation, Emily and Marguerite darted back to the safety of Marguerite's doorway and peeked out as Douglas emerged. Emily watched him take a few deep breaths, no doubt willing his color to recede and his shaking hands to still. When he seemed more or less back to normal, the two women came into the hallway as if they had never suspected his presence.

Emily hailed him. 'Good morning, Douglas. Though from your expression I'm guessing your morning hasn't been any better than ours.'

'That woman is going to be the death of me,' he said with a failed attempt at lightness. 'Or vice versa. She refuses to budge an inch.' He collected himself enough to notice Marguerite. Men always did notice Marguerite.

Emily hastened to make the introduction. 'Marguerite knows all about our attempt to get Taylor fired,' she said. 'But I'm afraid we've had a major setback this morning, just when we thought we were on the cusp of victory.' She gave Douglas a thumbnail sketch of the morning's events without specifying the nature of Taylor's threat to Richard.

Douglas rolled his eyes and threw up his hands. 'Typical Taylor. She always makes sure to have something she can hold over anyone who might be a hindrance. In my case, it's this heirloom I want her to return. It looks like I'll have to choose between that and my entire fortune.'

Emily marveled at his ability to speak so lightly of a situation that had to all appearances driven him to the brink only moments before. Self-control was one thing, but she preferred Luke's transparent honesty.

'You should hire Saul Goldstein as your lawyer,' Marguerite said. 'I do not know if he does divorces, but he is out for Taylor's blood. If anyone could defeat her in court, I think it would be he.'

'That's not a bad thought,' Douglas said with a closer, more appreciative look at Marguerite. 'My current lawyer is an old family friend, and I half suspect Taylor has got her hooks into him. He doesn't seem to be giving me his all.'

Emily was having second thoughts about fixing Marguerite up with Douglas, but Marguerite was forewarned as well. She could take care of herself, and her flirtations had sometimes proved useful in the past. 'We were just going to the Paradox for coffee,' Emily said to Douglas. 'Would you like to join us?'

'I'd be delighted.' He turned toward the staircase and offered them each an elbow. 'With the two most charming ladies on campus on my arm, I can face down the world.'

Douglas insisted on paying for all the coffees, and they sat at one of the rickety tables. Marguerite always refused to sit on the Paradox couches as it was impossible to maintain a ladylike posture against their sagging seats and beaten backs.

Douglas and Marguerite soon became enmeshed in a happy if not very serious flirtation. Marguerite could flirt for France, even in a parka in a snowstorm surrounded by hungry polar bears. Emily allowed her attention to wander out the window. She saw Daniel approaching around the corner, and soon he entered the café.

He ordered his coffee, then turned and noticed Emily. He didn't approach but gazed at her with an intensity that told her he wanted to talk to her alone. She joined him on a couch. Douglas and Marguerite were too absorbed in each other to notice her move.

'Do you have any news?' he asked her in a low voice.

'Yes, but I'm afraid it's not all good. We played the recording for McClintock, and he agreed to confront Curzon. But she's got something on him that made him back down. Svetlana's father was there, and he's decided to go ahead and sue Curzon. It'll be hell for Svetlana, I'm afraid, but I don't see what we can do to stop him.'

Daniel dropped his head into his hands and pulled at his hair with both fists. 'I'm at the end of my rope,' he said. 'This is going to tear Sveta and me to pieces.' He dropped his hands and looked up at her with anguished eyes. 'If this goes to court, it'll kill Sveta. She's so sensitive, you have no idea. To have her personal business paraded in front of the world – it'll just kill her.'

Emily searched Daniel's face with concern. His haunted eyes darted around the room, and his hands shook on his cup, making his coffee slosh. She didn't know much about epilepsy, but she feared these might be signs of an oncoming seizure. Emily suspected Svetlana was actually the stronger of the two – much stronger than Daniel gave her credit for. It was Daniel whom this whole impossible situation might destroy.

'Perhaps Mr Goldstein will be able to avoid a trial, or at least avoid involving Svetlana. Surely he'd want to keep her out of it if possible.'

'But it's her grade he cares about. Curzon could coerce every male student in the whole college and he wouldn't care, as long as it didn't touch his precious little girl. No way will he keep her out of it. Or me. And when it's all over – if it's ever over – he'll find some way to separate the two of us. Take her back east, make her marry a Jewish lawyer. He probably has a junior partner all picked out for her already.'

Emily covered his shaking hand with her own, her voice gentle. 'Daniel, this is twenty-first-century America. No parent can force his daughter to marry someone she doesn't want to marry. Nor can he prevent her from marrying the person of her choice – you're both of age. You may have to run away together, but you wouldn't be the first couple to do that.'

He shook his head, clinging to his despair as if it were his only friend. 'You don't know Sveta. She loves her dad in spite of everything. She'll never go against him.'

'I think you underestimate her love for *you*. I'm quite sure it's you she'll hang on to at all costs.'

Daniel merely heaved a sigh and struggled to his feet, wavering as if he were tipsy – but Emily knew it was stress and illness that caused his instability. 'I've got to get to work. Even if I can't have Sveta, I still have to get my degree. My mother and sister are counting on me.'

Emily stood and caught his elbow as he seemed about to fall. 'Daniel, I'm begging you, get some rest. You really don't look well at all. One afternoon off won't ruin your thesis.'

'No.' He shook his head slowly, eyes half-glazed, hardly

seeming to take in her words. 'Got to work.' He staggered out in the direction of the library.

Emily called Svetlana's cell to warn her to look out for Daniel, but she didn't answer. Probably in the midst of being harangued by her father. She left a message, then said a prayer for Daniel. His guardian angel would need to work overtime in the days and weeks to come.

TWELVE

Emily had arranged with Marguerite for another Scrivener lesson first thing Tuesday morning. At eight o'clock she walked down the hall toward Marguerite's office. Noticing Taylor's door ajar, she had the sudden mad notion of making one more attempt to plead with her to see reason and give Svetlana and Daniel – and even Douglas, while she was at it – a break.

She knocked and called, 'Taylor?' but there was no response. Emily pushed the door open halfway and poked her head in.

Immediately she wished she hadn't. The sight of an inert form sprawled on the Persian rug in front of the desk gradually overcame Emily's instinctive disbelief and resolved itself into the shape of a woman, dressed as Taylor had been the day before in a revealing purple dress, one black spike heel kicked off under a chair. Emily assumed the woman was Taylor, but the face was unrecognizable, the head covered in blood. No need to check for signs of life. The blood was dull as if congealed, not shiny and wet. Given that and her day-old outfit, it seemed safe to assume Taylor had been dead for some hours.

With shaking hands, Emily pulled out her phone and called Luke. 'What was the name of your nephew on the force again? I'm going to need him.' She took a gasping breath and said the word. 'Body.'

'Oh, crap. It's Colin. Colin Richards. Want me to call him and introduce you?'

'Please. Then have him call me right away.'

'Roger. Call me back after you talk to him and fill me in. You know I'll be up there like a shot if you need me.'

'Thanks, but I'll be OK. I will call you back, though.'

Emily hung up and attempted to gather her wits as she looked around. She knew better than to touch anything or even to walk on the rug, where her shoes might disturb any traces left by the murderer. She made her way gingerly around on the cement floor, avoiding spilled blood and looking for a weapon or anything that might present a clue.

She got the call from Colin just as she glimpsed a heavy bronze statuette that had rolled a short distance from the body. It was caked in blood, but something about it looked familiar. She had no time to figure out what before answering Colin's call.

'Emily Cavanaugh.'

'Detective Colin Richards here. My uncle Luke said you needed the police?'

'Yes. I've just discovered a dead body.'

The young voice on the other end of the line squeaked up an octave. 'A body?' He cleared his throat, and his voice returned to its normal pitch and deliberately official tone. 'What is your location?'

'The Bede College campus, Vollum College Center, room three-fifteen.'

'You're in luck. That's in our precinct, just, and our team is next up. Stay right where you are and don't touch anything. We'll be there as quick as we can.' As an afterthought, he added, 'Better notify some college authority. They could get sticky if we come on campus without notice.'

Sticky like the blood. Emily fought down nausea and called campus security, then Luke again, just to fill him in on what had happened and to promise an update later in the day. Meanwhile her unconscious chugged away trying to identify the bloody statuette. For some reason her mind connected it with Daniel.

Of course. It was Daniel's Bronze Horseman. She'd seen it on his desk in the library. Daniel looked on it as some sort of talisman. In Pushkin's poem, the original beyond-lifesize statue came to life and hounded a man to his death. Perhaps as Daniel's talisman this statuette had taken the initiative to eliminate Daniel's greatest enemy all on its own.

She shook off that nonsensical thought. The shock of discovering Taylor's body must be affecting her reason. Temporarily, she hoped. No, the statuette could not have gotten here unless someone – possibly Daniel himself – had brought it.

Emily went cold, remembering the state in which Daniel had been when he left her the day before. Despite their discussion last week about personal justice, she did not consider him capable of murder under ordinary circumstances. But what if he'd had a severe seizure and was disoriented, as Svetlana had said could happen? Would he be capable in that state of something he would never normally do? He'd certainly had sufficient provocation. Still, she was reluctant to believe it.

Her first impulse was to take the statuette and get rid of it somehow. But how? There was no handy body of water she could throw it into, nor did she have time before the police arrived to contrive a hiding place. Besides, she'd learned through experience that trying to protect an innocent party by deceiving the authorities could lead to nothing but trouble for both herself and the suspected person. In fact, it could quite easily backfire and delay or prevent the arrest of the actual culprit.

Not to mention that if the statue had acted on its own, it might choose not to stay hidden.

Again she shook off the fantastical thought. She would have to have faith – both that Daniel was in fact innocent and that Colin and his colleagues would be smart enough to figure that out.

Emily had grown accustomed to murder as dealt with by the skeleton sheriff's department in Stony Beach, so she was overwhelmed when the Portland police arrived in full force with several uniformed officers, a medical examiner, half a dozen crime scene technicians, and three or four plainclothes detectives, of whom Colin turned out to be the most junior.

The lead detective looked around and spotted Emily being guarded in a corner by the campus security officer she'd called. Emily felt the officer was being a trifle overzealous in fulfilling his duties, but then the campus didn't see a murder, or indeed any serious crime, every year. His caution was understandable.

The detective introduced himself as Sergeant Jonah Wharton. He was a heavy-set, middle-aged black man who looked as if he had perpetual indigestion. 'You the one who found the body?' he asked without ceremony.

'Yes. Emily Cavanaugh.' Something about his attitude impelled her to add, '*Professor* Emily Cavanaugh.' As if her title would somehow put her above suspicion, or at least gain her a little respect.

He glanced over his shoulder, then turned to point at a young man she guessed must be Colin, since he looked like a blond version of the young Luke. 'You. Richards. Interview her.'

The young man scurried over to her. 'Detective Colin Richards,' he said unnecessarily. He gave her a deprecatory smile and a handshake, as if apologizing for his superior's rudeness and acknowledging his own connection to Emily in one gesture. He asked her where they could talk, and she suggested Marguerite's office. Marguerite was glad to oblige in exchange for Emily's whispered promise to fill her in on the whole scoop once she was free.

Colin took the visitor's chair while Emily sat on the small sofa. He wrote down her full name and contact information, then asked, 'Can you take me through finding the body?'

'Starting when?'

'Start with entering the building. What time was that, and why were you here?'

'I entered the building at about eight o'clock. I was on my way here, to this office, to keep an appointment with my friend Marguerite. As I passed Taylor Curzon's office, I noticed the door was ajar, which seemed odd as she usually kept it locked. I knocked and called, but she didn't answer. I had a feeling something might be wrong, so I pushed the door open. That's when I saw her.'

'She was exactly like we found her?'

Emily nodded.

'Did you call us immediately?'

'Well, I called your uncle Luke first, as you know. He'd told me he had a nephew on the force, so I thought it would be nice to start with someone I had a connection with instead of just calling nine-one-one.'

'Right. I got that call at' – he flipped back through his notebook – 'eight oh five. Pretty quick after you found the victim. Did you check to make sure she was dead?'

'No. I could see the blood had congealed, and it seemed pretty obvious she'd been dead a while. That dress is the same one she was wearing yesterday. I didn't want to disturb anything by checking needlessly.'

'Good call. Did you touch anything at all in the room while you were waiting?'

'Not that I can remember. Only the door when I came in. I did walk around a bit, but only on the clean cement floor, not on the rug or' – she swallowed – 'in the blood.'

Colin gave her an appreciative glance. 'Sounds like my uncle has you pretty well trained.'

The verb grated, but she brushed that off and smiled. 'We've been through a few murders together. I know the drill by this time.'

'We'll need to take your fingerprints for elimination. Have you been in the office previously when you might have touched something?'

'Oh, yes. I was in there a couple of times last week, and probably on other occasions back when I was still teaching here. I couldn't say for sure what I may have touched. Except I know I touched the icon.'

'Icon?'

Of course, to Colin an icon would be a picture on a cell phone screen. 'The large painting of the Virgin Mary and Jesus hanging over Taylor's desk.'

Colin nodded and made a note. Then he paused, tapping his pencil on his notebook, a gesture Emily recognized from Luke. 'What was your relationship with the victim?'

'We were colleagues. Not friends. She wasn't the sort of woman to have female friends.'

He raised one eyebrow. 'Any bad blood between you?'

'In a sense, yes. She was harassing a young couple I'm rather fond of. Some others and I were in the process of trying to get her sanctioned, or preferably fired, for sexual misconduct.'

'Tell me more about that.'

'She had a series of affairs with her male students. Not entirely consensual. She coerced them with grade manipulation. And sometimes their girlfriends got punished as well.'

'You have proof of this?'

'It's one of those open campus secrets that everybody knows. But so far the students have been too intimidated to come out and testify against her, so we haven't been able to bring her down.'

'I'd say she's down now.'

'Yeah.' Emily grimaced. 'A bit more permanently than we had in mind.'

'Did you have a personal animosity against her?'

'No, not really. I hate everything she represented on general principles, but it wasn't *personal*. I had no grievance strong enough to make me want to – harm her.'

'How about other people? Like the students she harassed. This young couple you mentioned, for example? Would they want to harm her?'

Emily sighed. 'If you're asking who might have wanted to kill Taylor Curzon, I'm afraid the answer is just about anyone who knew her. She was simply an infuriating sort of person. She was out for herself and didn't care who stood in her way.'

'All right, then, let me ask this: who knew her particularly? I mean beyond just a casual association.'

She sighed again, hating to be the one in the position of potentially implicating people whose lives she valued far more than she valued Taylor's. At least they would have safety in numbers; she needn't emphasize one over all the others. 'All her colleagues, especially those in the Lit & Lang division. Not too many of us are on campus at the moment, though. Marguerite Grenier, whom you just met, and Richard McClintock, the department head, had the most to do with her. Besides me.' She hesitated to disclose the secrets about Richard she'd discovered by unethical means – not because she had any desire at all to protect Richard, but because she was rather ashamed of her own and Marguerite's electronic eavesdropping. Perhaps Marguerite would mention it. She had fewer scruples, and she had masterminded it, after all.

Thank heavens neither Oscar nor Lauren had any direct

contact with Curzon – she'd hate for Oscar to be targeted in yet another murder investigation. The fact that he could potentially profit from an opening in the department was something the police could ferret out for themselves if they felt the need.

'Then there are her students. Again, not many on campus now. The two I mentioned before are Svetlana Goldstein and Daniel Razumov. Oh, there's also Sidney . . . Sidney something. Svetlana or Daniel could tell you. He hangs around them – he sort of worships Daniel – but I don't know that he had any personal connection with Curzon. Then there's Svetlana's father, Saul Goldstein – he was planning to sue Taylor because Svetlana had suffered on account of her unfair grading practices. He interviewed some other students who had been her victims, but you'd have to get those names from him.'

'Where can I find him?'

'I don't know for sure, but I'd start with the most expensive hotel in town. Oh, and one more person – Taylor's soon-to-be-ex-husband, Douglas Curzon. He's been trying to negotiate a settlement with her. I do have his number.' She found it on her phone and rattled it off.

'So this Douglas Curzon would be the next of kin?'

'I suppose so. But as I said, Taylor and I weren't close. I really know nothing about her family.'

'Right. Backing up a bit. When did you last see the victim alive?'

She did a mental calculation. 'Actually saw her? Yesterday morning – say, around nine thirty. Just glimpsed her going out of her office as I was coming in here.'

'Actually saw her? As opposed to what?'

'Well, I heard her for a bit after that. I know she was alive until at least eleven a.m.'

Colin gave her a quizzical look but did not pursue the matter, to Emily's relief. Especially in retrospect, she felt all her eavesdropping the day before had been justified, but she was not proud of it.

'I expect someone else will be able to narrow it down closer than that.' He glanced back over his notes, then looked at her thoughtfully. 'Uncle Luke did just have time to mention that in addition to being trustworthy, you're a pretty astute observer.

While you were waiting for us, did you happen to notice anything that might be helpful?'

Although she had talked herself out of hiding the apparent murder weapon, Emily did not feel her responsibility to the police extended as far as identifying the person she believed to be its owner. After all, she couldn't be certain. There could be another Bronze Horseman statuette on campus besides Daniel's. It could even have been Taylor's own.

But there was something else she could mention. 'This isn't something I noticed this morning, but there is another area you might want to look into. It's pretty vague – nothing more than a feeling, a suspicion, but . . .'

'Let's have it. Uncle Luke said you have good instincts.'

'All right. I have a feeling Taylor may have been involved with the Russian mafia in smuggling contraband artifacts from Russia.' She explained about the icon and the thuggish Russian-speaking visitor. The words sounded outlandish as she heard them come out of her mouth – like something that would happen in a movie rather than in real life.

'Hmm. Kinda sounds like the proverbial intruder from outside that everybody blames because they don't want to think it could be one of themselves. But we'll look into it.'

'Right. I don't think it deserves more than that.'

He stood. 'OK, thanks for your help, Mrs – can I call you Emily? 'Cause I guess you're going to be one of the family pretty soon.'

'Absolutely. Thanks, Colin.' She hesitated, then said with a smile, 'Can I ask you to keep me informed? I know I'm just a civilian here with no special privileges, but if I know what's going on I might be able to be of some kind of help. I promise I won't get in your way.'

He hesitated in turn, then grinned a grin so familiar it made Emily's heart turn over. 'Sure. I'll do what I can. What I can get away with, that is. My boss is kind of a stickler. He wouldn't like it if he knew.'

'Kind of a grouch, too, from what I saw. I don't want to get you into any trouble.'

'You let me worry about that.'

* * *

Emily hung around campus the rest of the day – not in the library, since she couldn't focus on her work for a moment, but in more public spots, hoping to hear something further about the murder investigation. But either it was still too early or Colin hadn't had a chance to check back in, because by dinnertime Emily had heard nothing but rumors. For example: Curzon had been strangled in broad daylight. Curzon had been set upon by a gang of thugs in a dark corner of campus at midnight. The murderer had already been caught. The murderer was so clever he or she would never be caught. Curzon hadn't been murdered at all but had committed suicide. Curzon had suffered a fatal accident. Curzon had been abducted by aliens. Emily was amazed at the ability of even an exceptionally intelligent collection of people such as the Bede community to come up with any story, no matter how absurd, to fill the hole when the truth was unavailable.

At last she gave up and trudged home. She had been scheduled to attend a class at the Apple Store that night, but she'd never be able to concentrate while in this state of suspense. She waited all evening for a call from Colin, then finally called Luke. He'd heard nothing from Colin and thus had no news for her, but she filled him in as far as she could.

'Hard to make any kind of guess without knowing more about the rest of her day,' he said when she'd finished. 'Who do you like for it?'

The word that popped out of her mouth astonished her with its vehemence. 'Richard.'

'Richard McClintock? I haven't met the man, but from what you've told me, he seems like too much of a wimp.'

Emily took a shaky breath. 'You're right, he is. I'm not quite sure why I said that.' She paused to collect herself. 'Well, yes, I do know. It's because I have an irrational antipathy to the man. He's done plenty to earn my dislike on a rational level, but beyond that . . .'

She couldn't finish her sentence without telling Luke about her memories of being harassed. And that would have been so much easier to do in person. Why had she chickened out when she had the chance?

No getting around it now. 'There's something I haven't told you. I meant to tell you when you were here, but . . . well, once I had you near me, it didn't seem that important. But I guess it isn't the kind of thing that just goes away.'

His voice softened. 'Em, you know you can tell me anything. There's not a thing in the world that could change my love for you. You do know that, right?'

She nodded, then remembered he couldn't see her. 'Yes. I do know that. And it isn't – wasn't even my fault. It's something that happened years ago, when I was a student. Only I'd forgotten all about it until last week.'

She paused again, and he helped her out. 'I take it this was the blocking-out-trauma kind of forgetting, not the slipped-your-mind-'cause-it's-inconsequential kind?'

'Yes.' She took a deep breath and rushed the sentence out on the exhale. 'One of my professors put the moves on me and threatened to fail me if I didn't give in.'

'Shit, Em. No wonder this whole thing's got you riled.'

'Yeah.'

'What happened? You didn't give in, did you?'

'No. Not that he was waiting for permission. But I got rescued on that occasion and then managed to avoid him after that. Dropped the class.'

'I'm so sorry you had to go through that, sweetheart. Men like that should be taken out and shot. Figuratively speaking, you understand. But what's Richard got to do with it? He's about our age, isn't he? He couldn't have been the professor?'

'No, that prof is long gone. He retired before I came back here to teach. Sure to be dead by now. But Richard reminds me of him. Same attitude, same aftershave, same . . . I don't know, aura, I guess. When I'm around him I get the same hideous feelings all over again.'

Luke was silent a minute. 'I wish you had told me when I was there. I'm guessing you could use a hug about now.'

'Yeah. Stupid move on my part. But I thought I'd be going home soon and could tell you then. I didn't know Taylor was going to get herself murdered and bring it all to the surface.'

He gave her another minute, then said, 'Are you able to put those feelings aside for now and look at Richard as a suspect on a rational level?'

'I'll try. As you said, he is a wimp, but I could almost imagine him lashing out if sufficiently provoked. And he did have motivation beyond the fact that Taylor had rejected his advances. She had proof that he had plagiarized a student's essay and published it as his own.'

Luke whistled. 'That's pretty serious, isn't it?'

'Grounds for dismissal. Even for a tenured prof.'

'Sounds like he's in the running, then. And he had opportunity?'

'His office is down the hall from hers. I don't know if he was there last night, though. That'll be for Colin to figure out.' She swallowed. 'But I guess I'd better tell Colin about the plagiarism.'

'You didn't tell him that? How come?'

'Because of the way I found out. Marguerite recorded a conversation between Richard and Taylor without his knowledge. She used my phone and I didn't stop her, so that makes me complicit.'

'You better tell Colin. They'll need physical evidence to arrest someone anyway, so that recording being inadmissible shouldn't be a game-changer.'

'OK. I'll tell him when he calls.'

'So, Richard aside, who's your second choice?'

'Heavens, I don't know. I'd *like* it to be Saul Goldstein, because he's so obnoxious and it would help Svetlana and Daniel to have him out of the way. But that doesn't mean he's any more likely to be guilty than anyone else. Less, probably, because his weapon of choice is the law.'

'Good point. Third choice?'

She gave a half-laugh. 'The Russian mafia enforcer. Except then I'd have to give evidence against him, and his buddies would come after me. So I don't actually want it to be him.'

'I notice Daniel is not in your top three.'

'No. He had the most motive of anyone, but I can't believe it of him. Well, I don't want to believe it. He has his whole life ahead of him. Why would he throw it away by taking such a risk? And using his own statuette to do it? Daniel is many things, but he isn't stupid.'

'OK. And the ex-husband? You ruling him out too?'

'Not ruling him out, exactly.' In fact, her estimate of Douglas's potential as a killer had been raised significantly by the encounter she'd overheard on the morning before Taylor's death. 'I guess I'd have to put him in fourth place. Before yesterday, I would have said Douglas was too civilized to kill in that bloody, violent way. He hated her, certainly, but I would have said he'd go for poison, maybe, or stage some sort of accident. But since that quarrel Marguerite and I overheard – well, like Richard, he could have been provoked to violence on the spur of the moment. Even to the point of risking getting blood on his custom-made suit.'

'Sounds like whoever did it must have been pretty well spattered with blood. That's bound to be useful unless the murderer's a lot cleverer than any murderer I've ever met.'

'Yeah.' She sighed. 'This waiting to hear what's happening is killing me. I've been spoiled, being in on every detail with you.'

'I'm sure Colin will get in touch as soon as he can. Bound to have been a long day with not a minute to himself.'

'I'm sure you're right.' She felt her phone vibrate. 'Oh, maybe that's him! Can I call you back?'

She hit the button to accept the incoming call. It was Colin.

'Hey, Emily. Just calling with an update like I promised.' His voice dripped exhaustion. 'We're holding Daniel Razumov.'

THIRTEEN

'You're holding Daniel? Why?'

'The murder weapon has his fingerprints and no one else's, for one.'

Ouch. So much for the idea that it could have been a different statuette belonging to someone else.

'You know for sure what the murder weapon was?'

'The ME says the wounds to the skull have a distinctive shape. Only one thing fits. Plus it's pretty much covered in blood.'

'But were Daniel's fingerprints *in* the blood, or under the blood?'

A pause as Colin presumably consulted his notes. 'Under the blood, apparently. Or on spots not covered in blood. None actually in the blood.'

'So then all it proves is that the statuette belongs to Daniel. It doesn't prove he's the one who wielded it. The murderer must have worn gloves.'

'Wait a minute – I never said it was a statuette.'

'Oh, well, I saw it at the scene this morning and it was pretty obvious that was the weapon. Didn't I say?'

'No. You did not.'

'I just figured you'd see it, as I did. It's not like it was hard to find.' She knew her tone was too bright, artificially bright, but she couldn't seem to control it.

'Or you recognized it and didn't want to implicate Daniel.'

Dang, this kid was smart. Possibly even smarter than his uncle.

'Or maybe that. But after all, you did figure it out with no help from me.'

'Is there anything else you didn't happen to mention?'

She swallowed. 'Now you bring it up, I did remember one thing. A possible motive for Richard McClintock.'

'Oh? What's that?'

'Taylor had evidence that he'd plagiarized a student's essay and published it as his own. I don't think he realized anyone else knew, so he could have killed her to shut her up. I'm not saying he did, mind you. But it is a motive.'

Colin asked the question she'd been hoping he wouldn't ask. 'So how did you find out about this?'

'Marguerite and I sort of eavesdropped on a conversation between Richard and Taylor. We weren't just being nosy – we'd insisted he confront Taylor about her harassment of Daniel, but we didn't trust him not to let her off the hook. So Marguerite set up our two phones to listen in and record what they said.'

'And Curzon threatened McClintock with exposure?'

'It was a counter-threat – if he pursued sanctions for her behavior, she'd get him fired for plagiarism.'

'I think I need to listen to this recording. It wouldn't be admissible in court, but I might be able to confirm the information another way.'

'Sure. If you track me down tomorrow, I'll play it for you.'

'Can't you send me the file?'

At least Emily knew what that meant now. But she still didn't know how to do it. 'I'm afraid I don't know how. I'm a newbie where tech stuff is concerned. But I can get Marguerite to show me in the morning.'

'Oh, right, Uncle Luke mentioned you were kind of a Luddite. OK, please do that first thing.' He paused, presumably making notes. 'Anything else you've remembered since we talked?'

Her conscience compelled her to come clean. 'I did happen to overhear one other conversation. Not recorded, though. Between Taylor and Douglas Curzon. Her office door was ajar when I was passing by.'

'And? What was said?'

'I couldn't tell you word for word, but it was pretty heated. There's some family heirloom of Douglas's that Taylor had essentially stolen and was refusing to give back. She was taunting him. It got kind of . . . personal. So I guess that gives him a stronger motive as well.'

Colin huffed. 'You really should have told me all this earlier, you know.'

'I'm sorry, Colin. I should have said. Honestly, I was embarrassed about the eavesdropping, and I didn't want to be the one to implicate a potentially innocent person. But since you're holding Daniel – I just can't believe he's guilty. Is the weapon all you have on him?'

'No. His name is down in her appointment book for ten-thirty last night. Well, his initials, and we don't know of anyone else connected with the case who shares them. Plus we have a witness who puts him at the scene within an hour of the probable time of death.'

'What? Who? And when?'

'Sidney Sharpe saw Daniel enter the floor where the office is located at ten-fifteen p.m. The ME figures time of death between eleven and midnight.'

'If Sidney saw Daniel there, that means he was there himself.'

'Yeah, but he was leaving at that point. He's vouched for at that coffee shop, the Paradox – funny name for a coffee shop – from ten-thirty to eleven. Besides, he has no motive.'

'True.' Unless he was trying to help Daniel and Svetlana. But surely his doglike devotion would not extend to murder. Emily could not imagine that his Nietzschean pretensions could ever be translated into action. 'OK, so Daniel was in the building. So what? There must have been other people there too.'

'Not that we've been able to find out. Except the victim herself, of course. Unless everybody's lying. Of course there are no security cameras.'

'Do the others have provable alibis?'

'Haven't got as far as proving them yet. We're looking at a big field here. You said yourself, to know her was to hate her.'

'Yes, but surely not everyone is equally likely.'

'Presumably not. We're working on opportunity, but you're better placed to identify motive since you know them all. You've given me a couple of good ones already. Anybody else you'd say is more or less likely, motive-wise?'

Emily hated to sit in judgment on her friends and colleagues, but she could hardly get out of it now. 'Let's see . . . I told you who was directly involved with Taylor. Of those, you can rule out Marguerite Grenier. She had no personal axe to grind with Taylor; she was just working for the good of the department.'

'Check.'

'And I'd say you can rule out Svetlana. She's a gentle soul, and she's deeply in love with Daniel. I doubt she could ever kill anyone, but if she did, she certainly wouldn't let Daniel take the blame.'

'Early days on that – we haven't even arrested him yet. And her love gives her motive. I'm keeping her on the list for now.'

'If you must.' Emily was confident Colin would ultimately see the justice of her views on Svetlana. The girl's innocence was palpable. 'So besides Richard McClintock and Douglas Curzon, that leaves Saul Goldstein. He was angry enough with Taylor to do just about anything. Plus our putative Russian mafia guy.'

'So four, maybe five suspects with known motive. That's a small enough field to dig deeper on. I may need you to come in and look at some photos, maybe work with our sketch artist, for the Russian guy.'

'No problem. And will you release Daniel in the meantime?'

'Not unless we get something solid on one of these four.'

'But you have to get more evidence against Daniel to actually arrest him, don't you? Everything you have is circumstantial.'

'Except that Razumov has sort of confessed.'

'*Sort of* confessed? How can you sort of confess?'

'He says he doesn't remember the night at all. Had some sort of blackout. But he says he wanted her dead, so he probably did kill her.'

'*Probably* is not a confession. If he doesn't remember, he can't confess.'

'We did also find blood on some of the clothes in his laundry.'

'Is it Curzon's blood?'

'Don't know yet. Have to wait for the lab on that one.'

Emily huffed in frustration. 'I just can't believe your boss is being so precipitate.'

'If Razumov's memory doesn't return and if the lab doesn't come back positive on Curzon's blood within forty-eight hours, we will have to let him go. Doesn't mean we'll stop looking at him, but we will have to get something solid before we can arrest him.'

'Thank goodness for that. May I visit him in the meantime?'

'Not while he's in the holding cell. No protocol for that. After his arrest, yeah, I can arrange it.'

A massive yawn came over the line. 'Listen, Emily, I've got to get some sleep. Call me if you have any more ideas. Tomorrow, that is. Not tonight.'

'No. I'll sleep on it tonight.'

But whether she could sleep knowing Daniel was in jail was another question. The more she thought about it, the more certain she became that he was innocent – and that she would have to be the one to prove it. She could not allow Taylor Curzon to continue to victimize Daniel from beyond the grave.

Emily thought she might see Svetlana in the library next morning, even without Daniel. But she had the place to herself. Working on her book seemed pointless and selfish when a young man's life hung in the balance. She set off in search of Svetlana.

Halfway across campus she met the girl walking the other way. 'Oh, Emily,' Svetlana gasped, running up to her and grabbing her hands. 'They've arrested Daniel!'

'Not exactly arrested,' Emily said gently. 'They're holding him. That's not the same thing.'

'But they think he did it! It isn't possible, Emily. Really it isn't. He may talk like he thinks murder is justifiable, but he doesn't really believe that. He couldn't actually *do* it. You do believe me, don't you?' Svetlana gazed at Emily as if her whole world depended on her answer.

'As a matter of fact, I do tend to believe Daniel is innocent,' she said cautiously. 'And the evidence they have against him is all circumstantial. They don't have enough to charge him yet. The problem is they have nothing at all on anyone else.'

Svetlana wrung her ungloved hands, which had a bluish tinge. The thermometer had not risen above freezing this morning. Emily feared that between her emotional brittleness and impending frostbite the girl might shatter. 'I was just going for coffee. Come with me and we can talk inside where it's warm.'

They scurried to the Paradox. Emily ordered plain coffees, for the speed of it, while Svetlana collapsed on to a couch.

The girl received her coffee gratefully but barely sipped it; she needed it more as a hand-warmer than as refreshment. 'I want my father to represent Daniel, but he refuses. He thinks he's guilty. Can you imagine? My own father believes I could love a man who was capable of murder.'

'I'm sure he doesn't see it in those terms. And anyway, would your father be able to practice in Oregon? I assume he's licensed in Massachusetts.'

'Oh. I guess that's true. But the way he said it, it sounded like he wouldn't consider doing it even if he could.'

Emily squeezed Svetlana's hand. 'I understand your father's attitude is an extra burden when you really need his support. But it doesn't change anything for Daniel.'

The girl shook her head mournfully. 'You don't understand. My father won't let me visit him or even write to him. He wants me to leave Bede and transfer to Harvard or Radcliffe. Never see Daniel again.'

'And you can't just decide to stay, because he's paying the bills.'

She nodded. 'I don't even have a part-time job. I've kind of made Daniel my job. If I refuse to go home with my father, I'll have nothing to live on at all. And then how can I help Daniel?'

Emily made a snap decision. 'I can give you a job, at least for the next couple of weeks. You can be my research assistant. I just bought a computer, and I need someone to help me input all my notes.'

Svetlana looked up, her face brightening slightly. 'I could do that,' she said. 'I'm a good typist. And I can do OCR on my phone, too, so if you wanted a passage from a book I wouldn't have to type it in by hand.'

'OCR?'

'Optical character recognition. You take a picture of the page, and the app translates it into text you can edit, copy, whatever.'

That sounded like a small miracle. 'Great. You're hired.'

'Only . . . if my father withdraws me from Bede, I won't be able to stay in the dorm.'

'Good point. I can offer you my spare bedroom until my tenants come back at the end of Paideia, if that would help.'

'That would be perfect! By then I'll be able to figure something else out.'

Emily had a sudden vision of Saul Goldstein's reaction to this plan. 'Best not to tell your father until the last minute, though, OK? I mean, you'll have to tell him you're not going, but I'd appreciate if you'd leave me out of it. If you can.' Emily felt like a coward, but she didn't see how diverting Goldstein's anger toward herself would help Svetlana.

'He's planning for us to leave tomorrow. He's only giving me today to pack.'

'Has he cleared that with the police? I'd think they'd want everyone connected with the case to stick around until they've closed it.'

'I don't think he's thought of that. He doesn't see himself as being connected.'

'I'm afraid the police would disagree. He had a definite

grievance against Curzon. They can't rule him out automatically.'

'Good news and bad news, then. I have to put up with him longer, but he won't officially withdraw me from Bede until we're able to leave town. It would mean an extra hotel bill.'

'Your father cares about a hotel bill? I thought he was wealthy.'

'He is, but he's also kind of tight. He'll spend when he needs to, but he can't stand anything he sees as wasteful spending. The dorm's already paid for through Paideia, so he'll want to use it.'

'That works in your favor, then. At least for right now.'

Svetlana turned her still-full cup in her hands. 'Emily . . . I hate to ask one more thing of you, when you're already doing so much. But . . . well, I heard a rumor that you've been involved in solving some murders in Stony Beach. Is there any way you could help Daniel? Try to figure out who really did it?'

'I'm already planning to. As it happens, I have a police connection here, and he's promised to keep me informed about the case. He's consulted me about background, too. So yes, I'll be doing what I can.'

'Bless you!' Svetlana grabbed her hand and kissed it.

Embarrassed, Emily gently pulled her hand away. 'You can help me too. The first thing I need to know is exactly what Daniel did on Monday. As far as you know it.'

Svetlana buried her head in her hands. 'That's just the trouble. I don't know. Or only up to a point.'

'Let's reconstruct his day as far as we can. I saw him myself at around eleven a.m. here at the Paradox. Did you see him after that?'

She nodded. 'He met me at the library, but he was looking so ill I made him go back to the dorm. I went with him and made sure he went to bed. Then . . . well, I wish now I had stayed with him, but I was afraid my father would get the wrong idea about me being in his room, so I left. I didn't see Daniel again until dinnertime.'

'Curzon wasn't killed till late evening, so accounting for the afternoon shouldn't be crucial. How was Daniel at dinnertime?'

'Even worse. He didn't look as if he'd slept at all – he was gray and shaking. Honestly, I expected him to fall into a seizure at any moment.'

'Did you stay with him?'

'I couldn't. My father showed up and insisted I go out to dinner with him. I made Daniel promise to go back to bed, but I don't know if he did.'

'What about later in the evening?'

'I got back to campus around nine o'clock. I went straight to Daniel's room, but he wasn't there. I looked in the library and everywhere else I could think of, but I couldn't find him, and he didn't answer his phone. Eventually I gave up and went to bed.'

So Svetlana could not alibi Daniel, either for the time of the murder itself or for the time Sidney claimed to have seen him in Vollum Center. 'Did you run into Sidney, by any chance?'

'Sidney? No, why?'

'Oh, nothing. It's not important. What about yesterday morning? Did you see Daniel then?'

'He didn't show up for breakfast, so I went to his room. He was asleep, sort of. Sort of passed out. I managed to wake him up, but he was completely disoriented. He didn't remember anything he'd done after seeing me at dinnertime the day before. We figured he must have had a blackout seizure.'

'A blackout seizure? What's that?'

'I guess it's kind of like a fugue state. The person can function more or less normally, but they're sort of . . . not all there. And they don't remember anything about it afterward. So neither of us has any idea where he was or what he was doing during the evening, or what time he got back to his room. That's what makes it so scary – he can't vindicate himself because he doesn't remember.'

'Did he say anything about having an appointment with Curzon Monday evening?'

'An appointment? No. He was determined to avoid her as much as possible. He certainly wouldn't deliberately be alone with her. Not after what happened that morning.'

'Odd. He's down in her appointment book for ten-thirty. Unless there's someone else with the initials DR.'

Svetlana shook her head. 'No one I can think of.'

Emily hesitated to ask her next question. 'The police said . . . there was blood on some of his clothing. Did you notice that?'

She nodded. 'He'd cut his head somewhere along the line, and it bled quite a bit. He was a mess when I found him. I cleaned him up and put his clothes in the laundry.' An anguished look crossed her face. 'If I'd known at that point what was going to happen – I could have just washed his clothes and the police would never have been the wiser. Why didn't I?'

'It probably wouldn't have mattered. They had other reasons to suspect him, so they would have collected his clothing anyway. And it's almost impossible to remove every tiny trace of blood.'

'But they'll find out it's his blood, won't they? Not hers?'

'They'll analyze it, yes. I think they're doing that now. If none of the blood is hers, that will be a point in his favor, but it won't clear him completely.'

'Why, what else do they have on him?'

'A strong motive, for one. Probably stronger than anyone else's – he wanted to protect you as well as himself. Plus they have a witness that puts him at the scene – not exactly, but close enough. And the weapon belongs to him. His statuette of the Bronze Horseman. Naturally it's covered in his fingerprints.'

'Oh my God . . . oh my God . . .' Svetlana crossed her arms over her belly and rocked herself on the couch. 'It's hopeless, isn't it? We'll never be able to clear him.'

Emily rubbed her back. 'Be of good cheer, my dear. With God nothing is impossible. And I have a few tricks up my sleeve as well.' If only she could figure out how to play them to win.

FOURTEEN

At Emily's urging, Svetlana went to her dorm to rest. Emily ordered a latte and stayed on for a thinking session. One question that was high on her list was how – in terms of actual physical possibilities, not nightmare fantasies – the Bronze Horseman statuette could have ended up in Curzon's office. Assuming Daniel had not taken it there himself intending to use it as a weapon.

Partly to keep the nightmare fantasies at bay, Emily began writing down all the possibilities she could think of.

1. *Daniel took the statue to Curzon's office at some earlier time, before the night of the murder.* Query: Why? Why would he want to give up his talisman, and to Curzon of all people?

2. *Svetlana took the statue to Curzon's office.* Again: Why? The statue didn't appear to be particularly valuable, but perhaps it was rare and Curzon coveted it to add to her collection of contraband Russian objets d'art. Perhaps either Daniel or Svetlana hoped to use it to bribe Curzon to keep away from Daniel. A stretch, but more believable than the fantasy of the statue coming to life.

3. *Some unknown person stole the statue from Daniel's shelf at some unknown time and carried it to Curzon's office with the intent of using it to kill her.* But who had even known the statue was in the library? Emily herself, Daniel, Svetlana, Miranda the librarian. Of course, anyone might have wandered by the table at any time, but why would they take the statue? Surely they could have found some more convenient weapon.

4. *Curzon herself had stolen the statue, perhaps in order to use it as leverage against Daniel.* Seeing it in her office, Daniel had flown into a rage and . . . No, no,

she was trying to find ways for Daniel *not* to be guilty. That option wouldn't fly.

5. *Curzon had stolen the statue (see above), then the killer had opportunistically grabbed it and used it as a weapon.* That was the most appealing option, but not necessarily the most likely – and it did nothing to narrow down the killer's identity.

How could she possibly discover which of these, if any, was the truth? She could start by figuring out when the statue disappeared from Daniel's desk. She couldn't call Daniel at the police station, and she didn't want to disturb Svetlana's rest. She racked her own memory, but the books ranged on her side of the library shelf obscured the contents of Daniel's side; she couldn't positively remember having seen the horseman since the very first day she'd set up there.

Maybe Miranda would have noticed something. Emily gulped the rest of her coffee and went back to the library.

She found Miranda patrolling the stacks near her own and Daniel's table. Today the librarian was wearing a symphony in brown – a full pleated skirt of camel wool, a cream-colored tailored blouse, a waistcoat of tooled caramel leather, a chocolate corduroy blazer, and a brown tweed newsboy cap, all anchored by a pair of tan cowboy boots. Only a woman with Miranda's tall, rangy figure and unique sense of style could make such an outfit work. Emily was a tiny bit envious.

'Miranda, I need you to put your photographic memory to work.' This was not a joke; Miranda actually did have the ability to observe and remember a scene in full Sherlockian detail, though she seldom bothered to make the accompanying deductions. At least not consciously.

'Anything I can do to help. Does this have to do with the murder? I was devastated to hear about that – not so much for Taylor's sake, though nobody deserves such a death, but for Daniel's. Is it true he's been arrested?'

'Not arrested yet, but they are holding him for questioning, and it looks pretty bad. One big thing against him is that the murder weapon was his Bronze Horseman statue. That's what I wanted to ask you about.'

'Oh! I see. What exactly did you want to know?'

'Can you remember when you saw it last? Or had you noticed it being missing?'

Miranda squinted at the ceiling. 'Let me think . . . I don't go by there every day, you understand. But I do remember noticing that Daniel's books were falling over, which would mean his bookend was gone. I propped them back up again. Now when was that?' She tapped a finger against her lips, eyes closed.

Suddenly her eyes flew open. 'Sunday. It was Sunday. I remember because that's the day I always do my walkabout, just scanning for anything amiss or out of place. Of course the statue could have been gone before that, but it was definitely gone by Sunday afternoon around three.' She gave Emily a triumphant smile.

Emily sighed in relief. 'Excellent. That makes it much less likely Daniel took it himself intending to use it as a weapon. Because why would he take it more than twenty-four hours ahead of time? It must be quite a heavy thing to carry around.'

'True. The question is who did take it?'

'Can you remember seeing anyone else in here around that time? Or before? Besides Svetlana and me, that is.'

Miranda went into recall mode again, but this time she ended up shaking her head. 'No. Sorry. I don't remember seeing anyone else. This isn't a busy room this time of year.'

'OK. Well, knowing when it went missing is much better than nothing. Thanks so much, Miranda.'

'I'm happy to help. Will you be visiting Daniel at some point?'

'If he's arrested, God forbid. They won't let me before that.'

'Well, if you do, give him my regards and tell him the library staff is rooting for him.'

'Thank you. I'm sure that will mean a lot.'

Emily betook herself to the front lobby of the library, where there were several large nooks with built-in padded benches to lounge on. The room was deserted except for a couple of students at the main circulation desk on the level a few steps above.

Emily called Colin's private number. 'I have a piece of information for you.'

'Just a sec.' She heard muffled background noises, then, 'OK, shoot.'

'Daniel kept that statuette on the shelf at his thesis desk in the library. It was his lucky talisman. He was very protective of it, and it's heavy, right? So he wouldn't just carry it around for no reason.'

'I suppose. What of it?'

'I just talked to Miranda Brooks, the librarian. She has a photographic memory, and she's certain the statue was gone by Sunday afternoon around three. Could have been earlier, but she doesn't go by that area every day.'

'OK. I still don't see where you're going with this.'

'You don't? It seems perfectly clear to me that someone stole the statuette from Daniel's desk. Whether they saw it and thought, Hey, that would make a great weapon, or whether they did it deliberately to implicate Daniel, I couldn't say, but it shows premeditation, right? They would have had to take the statue on Sunday, or earlier, and stash it somewhere until they took it to Curzon's office on Monday night to kill her.'

'But why couldn't that person have been Daniel?'

'Why *would* it have been? He could have moved the statue at any time, so why do it more than twenty-four hours before he was going to need it?'

'I'm still not convinced. All it does for me is prove premeditation. Or strongly indicate it, anyway. Which of course makes Daniel's situation worse.'

Emily's heart sank into her shoes. What had she done? She should have left well enough alone.

'Unless your total-recall friend has some idea who else might have taken the statue.'

'No. Unfortunately she doesn't. I did have another brainwave, though – Curzon could have taken it herself. If she knew how much it meant to Daniel, she might have thought she could use it as leverage to get him to sleep with her. Then the killer could just have seen the statue in her office and grabbed it to use as a weapon.'

'Doesn't seem terribly likely. And again, no reason that killer couldn't have been Daniel. Besides, in that case Curzon's fingerprints would be on the statue. She wouldn't bother wearing gloves to steal it if she wasn't going to conceal her theft or use it as a weapon.'

'It's cold out, though – she could have left on her outdoor gloves if she went into the library just for that purpose.'

'Boy, you have an answer for everything, don't you? But this is all total speculation. You're going to have to come up with something solid if you want to do Daniel any good. Like, for instance, finding someone else who had the opportunity to take the statue, or who even knew it was there.'

Emily sighed. 'All right. I'll talk to Svetlana. She might have some idea.'

'You do that.'

'What's happening on your end?'

'The good news for Daniel – bad news for us – is that none of your three possibles (not counting the Russian) has a totally solid alibi for the time of the murder. Goldstein says he was in his hotel room alone from about nine-thirty. Front desk remembers him coming in, but that doesn't mean he couldn't have left again. Same with Douglas Curzon, except he came in at nine. They're both staying in swanky suites at the Benson, funnily enough. Wish I had that kind of money. And McClintock says he was asleep alone in his apartment.'

'So the field is still open.'

'Yep. Can you see any of those guys stealing Daniel's statue in order to implicate him?'

'Richard doesn't seem terribly likely,' she admitted with some reluctance. 'He may have known Daniel slightly, but he wouldn't have had anything against him except that Taylor fancied Daniel and not him. Douglas could have been jealous of Daniel, but Taylor had so many boy toys, there wouldn't be much point in taking revenge on just one. But I could see Goldstein trying to implicate Daniel. He not only wanted Taylor out of the way, he wanted Daniel out of his daughter's life. He could have killed two birds with one stone. Or statue, as the case may be.'

'Fair point. I'll look into it.'

'OK. That's all I ask.' She was about to end the conversation, then remembered. 'What about the blood? Have the results come back?'

'Not yet. Should be in by this evening.'

'Call me when you hear?'
'Will do.'

By this time Emily thought Svetlana might have gotten a sufficient nap, so she called her cell phone. Svetlana answered on
the third ring, sounding groggy, and Emily regretted being so
precipitate.

'I'm sorry, did I wake you up?'

'No, actually my father woke me up a few minutes ago.
Complaining because the police won't let him leave town, just
like you said. What's up?'

'I'm trying to figure out who might have taken the statue
from Daniel's desk in the library, and when. Miranda Brooks
remembers seeing it was gone on Sunday afternoon. Do you
remember it being missing before that?'

'Gosh, I don't know. My father kept me busy all weekend;
I wasn't in the library at all. Before that – I'm sorry, I really
don't remember. I guess I'm not the most observant person. Or
at least I observe people rather than things.'

'That's OK. We have some idea of the when, thanks to
Miranda. What about the who? Do you remember anyone
coming by the table who might have noticed the statue and
come back later to take it?'

'Let's see . . . My father came by there a few times looking
for me. But he has tunnel vision when he's angry, which he
usually is. I doubt he'd have noticed anything to do with Daniel.
And of course Sidney's always hanging around, but he's known
about the statue being Daniel's talisman for ages. He teases
him about it, like, "One day that's going to come to life and
impale you." That kind of thing. But Sidney idolizes Daniel.
He wouldn't do anything to hurt him.'

'No . . . There is still my other theory, that Curzon could
have taken it herself. Do you have any reason to think she knew
about it?'

'Hmm, I don't know . . . We did study the Pushkin poem in
her class. Daniel may have mentioned something about it. And
it wouldn't surprise me a bit if she stalked him to his thesis
desk when I wasn't there and saw the statue. Taking it to tease
him sounds like just the kind of thing she might do.'

Emily's heart lifted at the increased probability of this theory, then fell again at the realization that it could hardly be proved – nor did it necessarily vindicate Daniel. She still favored the idea that Saul Goldstein had taken the statue in order to implicate Daniel, but she could hardly voice that thought to Svetlana. The girl would never believe her father capable of murder, no matter how much evidence stacked up against him – and they had no real evidence yet.

Maybe she could feel him out in some subtle way. As a lawyer he'd be alert to conversational traps, but he had treated Emily dismissively up to now, so he might be less on his guard with her than with the police. 'Do you expect to see your father today?'

Svetlana gave a yawn that was half a groan. 'He's on his way over here now to take me to lunch.'

'Could you plead exhaustion as an excuse to eat on campus? I'd like to horn in and have a chat with him.'

'Sure. It wouldn't be a fib, either. I definitely don't have the energy to go farther than Commons.'

'Good. See you there in a few. Just don't let him know I'm in on the investigation at all, OK? Because I'm really not supposed to talk about it.'

'Right.'

Now to figure out how to cross-examine a lawyer without letting him know he was being cross-examined. Piece of cake.

FIFTEEN

S vetlana and her father were already seated in the dining hall when Emily entered with her tray. Svetlana waved her over before her father could object.

In deference to the injunction not to let her father know about Emily's unofficial role in the investigation, Svetlana asked Emily how her work was going.

'It was going reasonably well before . . . well, before yesterday.' She smiled brightly at Saul. 'I'm working on a book about Dostoevsky. Are you familiar with him at all?'

Saul shook his head, mouth full of sandwich.

'How about other Russian writers? Tolstoy? Pushkin?'

He finished chewing (mostly) and said, 'Nope. No time for that nonsense. Takes all my reading time just to keep up with the law journals.'

'I just thought since your wife is Russian you might have an interest. Didn't you meet in Russia?'

He shook his head again. 'Never been there. Met when she was on tour over here. We fell in love and she never looked back.'

Svetlana's expression suggested that this might be a slightly romanticized version of the actual events.

If Saul had neither visited St Petersburg nor read Pushkin, the chances of his recognizing the Bronze Horseman statuette for what it represented were slim. But that didn't mean he couldn't still have noticed it, taken it, and used it to implicate Daniel.

'I've never been to Russia either,' Emily said, 'but through the literature I do feel as if I know it to a large extent. All the landmarks in Moscow and St Petersburg seem familiar, like St Basil's Cathedral, the Hermitage, the equestrian statue of Peter the Great on Senate Square.' She watched Saul narrowly, but no flicker of recognition passed over his features. She decided to risk being a little more open. 'Svetlana, doesn't Daniel have a miniature copy of that statue? I think I've seen it on his desk.'

Svetlana's eyes widened momentarily in alarm, but her voice was controlled when she answered. 'He did, but it's gone missing. I have no idea what happened to it.'

Still Saul ate doggedly on with no reaction. As a lawyer he would naturally have cultivated a poker face, but it must be an awfully good one if he did actually know anything about the statuette. He gave every appearance of being clueless as to the significance of what they were discussing.

She took another tack – a back-door approach to his alibi for Monday night. 'I understand the police want everyone connected with Curzon to remain in town until they close the case. I hope you have a comfortable place to stay.'

'Benson. Good hotel. Damned inconvenient having to stick around, though. Work to do at home.'

'You could make it a vacation. Sample the Portland nightlife, for example.'

He gave a derisive snort. 'Not a nightlife person. Work best in the morning. Early to bed, early to rise, that's my motto.'

She couldn't approach that subject any more directly without tipping her hand. Apparently what happened at the Benson was going to stay at the Benson, at least as far as Saul Goldstein was concerned.

Emily was racking her brain for some neutral topic to bring up when Sidney approached the table. She felt enough at a loss to be almost glad of his presence. At least she could count on him to take over the conversation.

'Greetings and salutations, all,' he said in his nasal voice as he sat down, uninvited as always. 'Svetlana, would you do me the honor of introducing me to this gentleman?'

Her face pinched, Svetlana complied. 'Papa, this is Sidney Sharpe, a classmate. Sidney, my father, Saul Goldstein.'

Sidney extended his hand with a sycophantic smile, but Saul ignored it, both hands on his sandwich. Sidney blinked and dropped the hand but not the smile. 'Pleasure to meet you, sir. Have you come to support your daughter through this difficult ordeal?'

Saul bridled. 'Ordeal? What ordeal? Sveta has nothing to do with the murder.'

'No, of course not. Far be it from me to suggest such a thing. But I hear our Daniel is being held for questioning. And I'm sure that's a terrible worry to you, dear Svetlana.' Sidney put on an exaggeratedly sympathetic face.

'Sveta has nothing to do with that miscreant Daniel, either. At least she won't have from now on.' Saul glared at his daughter, who averted her eyes, her cheeks flushing.

Saul shot a sidelong glance at Sidney, taking in his sportscoat, tie, and slicked-back hair, all so weirdly formal for a Bedie, with something that looked like tentative approval. 'I'm a lawyer. Came to bring suit against that slut Curzon, and now that she's out of the way, the damn cops won't let me leave. What's your line?'

'What a coincidence! I'm a combined Russian–computer science major, but I plan to go on to law school. Hopefully Harvard, if I can make the grade. My uncle Moishe went there, and he says it's the best.'

The thawing of Saul's attitude was tangible. 'Good man. Couldn't do better. Best lawyers in the country come out of

Harvard.' He gave Sidney a closer once-over. 'I know people there. Let me know when you're ready to apply and I'll see what I can do.'

Svetlana's look of panic escaped her father's attention but not Emily's. This was the first she'd heard of Sidney being either a prospective lawyer or Jewish, as dropping his uncle's Hebrew name was clearly meant to imply. Could he be putting on a front just to gain Goldstein's approval? A Jewish lawyer was exactly what Goldstein wanted for his daughter. Could Sidney possibly be putting himself forward as a potential suitor for Svetlana's hand?

Surely not. Sidney was Daniel's friend, or at least his follower. He wouldn't take the first hint of an opportunity to cut Daniel out with his beloved. Daniel hadn't even been arrested yet, let alone convicted. Chances were good he'd be free and cleared within days, and his future with Svetlana would go forward in spite of any obstacle her father could throw in their way.

Provided, that is, that Emily could accomplish her task of finding some evidence that would clear Daniel and/or implicate someone else. So far, that wasn't going terribly well.

Having no idea how to proceed with her investigation at this point, Emily took Svetlana back to the library with her after lunch and got her started on the task of inputting notes while she attempted some further research. But Svetlana's fingers were slowed by exhaustion, and Emily's concentration had gone the way of Daniel's missing memory of Monday night. She was relieved when she got a call from Colin. Asking him to hold a minute, she sent Svetlana to her dorm to rest and stepped outside to take the call.

'I hope you have lab results for me.'

'I do, but you're not going to like them. Based on blood type – DNA will take longer – the blood on Daniel's jacket looks like a mixture of his and the victim's.'

Emily's heart sank. 'Was it only the jacket that had blood?'

'No, the shirt did too. Shirt was all his own.'

She pondered. 'Does that make sense to you? If he had killed her, wouldn't her blood be on both?'

'Not if he had his jacket zipped up when he did it.'

'Then how would he have gotten his own blood on his shirt?'

'His head wound must have happened at a different time. When he wasn't wearing the jacket.'

'But if that were the case, why would his blood be on the jacket? It was on the outside, right, not just on the lining where it would have transferred from the shirt?'

'Yeah. So he put the jacket on right after, while he was still bleeding. I don't know. Why does it matter? The point is *her* blood was on him. That means he came in contact with the body.'

'I suppose. But that still doesn't necessarily mean he killed her. He could have come in right after the murderer left and bent over her to see if she was dead, or even tried to revive her.'

'*Could* have, *might* have, *maybe*. What it comes down to, Emily, is that you're grasping at any straw to clear this guy when the fact is that every single piece of evidence we have points straight to him. There may be a reasonable doubt, but that will be for a jury to decide. We're arresting him.'

So she had failed. Svetlana would be crushed, and Daniel would most likely spend his life in prison. Probably a short life, as he was not the sort of person who could survive in there for long. She shuddered to think what could happen to a good-looking, sensitive, emotionally and physically fragile young man surrounded by hardened criminals.

But what if he was guilty, after all? She didn't want to believe it, but that didn't mean it couldn't possibly be true. What if he had wandered into Curzon's office in the midst of his blackout, maybe hoping to persuade her once and for all to leave him alone? What if she had assaulted him again, or had taunted him with his stolen statue and he had simply snapped, grabbed the statue, and struck out, without necessarily intending to kill? It wouldn't have taken much to break him even in the state he'd been in on Monday afternoon, let alone in the aftermath of a seizure. Maybe Emily should give up kicking against the goads and bow to what appeared to be the facts.

But she couldn't do that without at least talking to Daniel. 'May I visit him, then?'

'Tomorrow. Come in tomorrow morning at nine, do the ID thing on your mafia guy, then you can visit him. I'll set it up tonight.'

Tomorrow. Emily sent up an earnest prayer that Daniel's memory would come back to him overnight – if blackout memories could ever come back at all.

SIXTEEN

Promptly at nine Thursday morning, Emily walked into the Central Precinct police station downtown and asked the officer at the front desk if she could speak to Colin Richards. Within minutes he was by her side. He ushered her through a large room full of desks and activity, into a cubicle with a table and a couple of chairs.

Colin laid a large binder on the table and sat down. 'I borrowed this from the organized crime unit. Take your time and flip through it. Let me know if you recognize the man you saw leaving Curzon's office.'

Emily turned page after page of mug shots and other photos. The faces in them were of all shapes, sizes, ages, and ethnicities, but they had one thing in common – a kind of deadness behind the eyes. She fervently prayed she would never have to encounter any of these men face-to-face.

At last she came to one photo that looked familiar. Middle-aged, stocky, powerful-looking. Completely shaved head with a bit of white stubble on scalp and chin. Fleshy face, thick neck, flabby lips, bulbous nose. Bushy eyebrows over tiny piggy eyes.

'That's him.'

Colin turned the binder to face him. 'Are you sure?'

'Pretty sure. It's always hard to go from a living technicolor person to a static black-and-white headshot, but it is a distinctive face. And in the circumstances he made an impression.'

'Right. That's great, Emily. I'll get this to the boss pronto and we'll follow it up.' He pulled the photo out of the binder and stood. 'But first, let's get you in to see Razumov.'

She followed him into the open office, but before they could pass through the room, Sergeant Wharton yelled from a few desks away. 'Richards! Hold it right there!'

He stalked up to them, frowning at Emily. 'What's she doing here?'

'I asked her to come in to identify a suspect.'

'What suspect? We've interviewed them all.'

'Not quite all, sir. Professor Cavanaugh mentioned seeing a suspicious person come out of the victim's office a few days ago. He doesn't belong to the college, and we haven't been able to track him down.'

Wharton's frown deepened. 'We've got a suspect in custody. What are you doing wasting your time on some alleged random guy?'

'Well, sir, the evidence against Razumov is all circumstantial. I didn't think it could hurt just to find out if this person is known to us. And he is – Professor Cavanaugh identified this photo. Ivan Bordetsky.' Colin showed the photo to Wharton.

Wharton's eyes widened. 'Bordetsky? Russian mafia?' He rounded on Emily. 'What the hell would Russian mafia be doing at Bede College?'

'Taylor Curzon was a professor of Russian with Russian connections. I saw an icon in her office that I suspect may have been imported illegally. She may have been working with the Russian mafia to smuggle religious artifacts.'

Wharton stared at the photo again. 'No shit. Well, that's a wrinkle.' He handed the photo back to Colin. 'Better have it checked out, Richards. But leave it to the organized crime guys – they'll know how to handle it. These Russians are dangerous buggers.'

He looked at Emily with a new respect. 'Where are you headed now? That's not the way out.'

'I'm taking her to visit Razumov, sir.'

Wharton hmphed. 'Don't give him any ideas about being let go. We've got too much on him, Russian mafia or no Russian mafia.' He turned and stalked off.

Colin turned to Emily. 'Oh, on the subject of things not to say to Daniel – we haven't talked to him about the murder weapon at all. We're saving that in case he gets his memory back and confesses for real – so we can be sure it's a true confession.'

'OK, I won't let the horse out of the bag.'

Colin led Emily down several hallways and through a couple of doors that required him to scan his ID. In a small room that held only a table, a uniformed officer instructed Emily to leave her outer clothing, purse, and the contents of her pockets in a locker. After this, they passed through one final door into a room with several small metal tables, each equipped with two plastic chairs.

'I'll be right back,' Colin said, and a couple of minutes later he reappeared holding Daniel by the elbow. Daniel's head was bowed, his hands cuffed in front of him; he barely shuffled along. Colin sat him down at the table and backed away out of earshot. Daniel slowly raised his head.

Emily was shocked by the change in him. Deep shadows ringed his bloodshot eyes; his skin was a pasty gray and seemed to sag over his sharpened facial bones with no supporting muscle. His eyelids and mouth drooped hopelessly. Emily caught her breath.

'Daniel? Are you all right?' A silly question, because obviously he was not; but she wanted to know how deep the damage went.

'I've been better.' He attempted a tiny smile.

'Are you being well treated?'

'Not bad. It's not the Ritz, but they're not going out of their way to be nasty. The food isn't much worse than Commons.'

'I'm sorry I didn't think to bring you anything. I'm not sure they'd let me, anyway.'

'Yeah, cakes with files in them are kind of frowned on. Really passé.'

She leaned forward. 'Svetlana sends her love. Her father's keeping a pretty tight rein on her right now – he won't let her visit.'

He nodded slowly. 'Figures. I'm sure he's convinced I'm guilty.'

'He may be, but I don't think anyone else on campus is. They're all rooting for you, as far as I can tell.'

'Good of them. I wish I could root for myself.'

She wanted to touch him, comfort him, but knew that wasn't allowed. 'Have you been able to remember anything more about that night?'

He shook his head, letting it fall like a dead weight from side to side. 'Not a damn thing. It's a complete blank from seeing Sveta before dinner to when she woke me up the next morning.'

'I guess that means you had a seizure. I'm sorry, Svetlana told me about your condition. I wasn't supposed to let on, but circumstances have changed since then.'

'Yeah. Compared to being in jail, having you know about my epilepsy doesn't seem like such a big deal.'

'Do you have any idea how likely it is you'll ever remember?'

'Not really. Prolonged blackouts aren't that common with epilepsy. I've never had it happen like this before.'

'Well, even if you don't remember, there's bound to be some evidence somewhere that points to the real killer. I'm determined to find it and get you cleared.'

His head drooped again. 'The thing is I'm not sure I deserve to be cleared.' His voice sank to a hoarse whisper. 'I'm terribly afraid I might have done it.'

She spoke gently. 'What makes you think that, Daniel?'

He shrugged listlessly. 'I wanted her dead. Not just out of the way, fired or whatever. I hated her like poison, and I really wanted her dead. Awake and normal, I had the usual inhibitions about actually killing someone, but in that blackout state – who knows? I've heard inhibitions are lowered, your basest instincts come to the fore. I can totally see myself going to her office and strangling her.'

'Wait – strangling her?'

'That seems like the appropriate end for a woman like that, don't you think?'

Emily's mind changed gears rapidly. If Daniel was being sincere, he did not even know the actual weapon or method of the murder. Surely that must count for something. If he had truly beaten Curzon over the head with a statue, wouldn't that leave some kind of residue in his mind that would slip out, even unconsciously?

'So when you say you can see yourself, you don't mean anything like an actual memory. You just mean you can imagine it.'

'Yeah. In fact I did imagine it, over and over. Before it

happened. Kind of like I was psyching myself up to actually do it, but also kind of like I was deliberately titillating myself with the horror of it. Like when you're a kid and you see how far you can stick your finger into a candle flame.'

'And that's why you think you might be guilty.'

'That's about the size of it.'

'It sounds like you were playing a pretty dangerous psychological game, Daniel. One that might ultimately have led to your committing murder. But the desire, even the intention, is not the fact. It doesn't mean someone else may not have gotten there before you. She did have plenty of other enemies, you know.'

'So why haven't they arrested any of them? Obviously the police believe I'm guilty. So I probably am.'

'The police do make mistakes, you know. I think in this case they're in danger of settling for the easy solution. It's true the evidence they have so far points to you. But it's all too pat, too consistent. I'm convinced there's more behind it. And I am a terrier when it comes to ferreting out the truth. Or I guess that makes me a ferret, doesn't it? I like terriers better. Anyway, you know what I mean.'

That speech elicited a tiny smile from Daniel. 'All right, Professor, I'll take whatever scrap of hope you want to offer me. Now is there anything else I can help with? Besides the stuff I don't, and probably won't, remember?'

'There are a couple of things. Did you make an appointment with Curzon for ten-thirty Monday night?'

'An appointment? Are you joking? *Oh, Professor Curzon, put me down in your book for ten-thirty. I'm going to stop by and kill you.*' He gave a hollow laugh.

'It's just that your initials are in her book for that time. Never mind, it's not important. But the other thing could be.' She'd have to tread carefully here so as not to violate Colin's proscription, but she felt compelled to ask. 'You know that Bronze Horseman statue you had in the library?'

'Yeah, of course. My talisman. What about it?' His tone and expression revealed no consciousness of the significance of the question.

'Do you remember it going missing at any time?'

'Missing? No. And I would remember, because I touch it every time I sit down to start work.'

'When was the last time you worked at that table?'

'I don't know, the days are running together in my mind . . . I guess Saturday? Yeah, that's right. I was there till closing time Saturday night. Then I spent Sunday at a Russian film festival downtown. They were showing a miniseries of *The Idiot*. And Monday I was too out of it to work.'

So the statue must have been stolen on Sunday, not before. Surely there was some way to find out who had been in the library that day. She grasped at this straw of progress.

'Why are you asking about the statue, anyway?' he said.

She cast about for an excuse that wouldn't give the game away. 'I just happened to notice it was missing and wondered what became of it. Nothing to worry about – I expect Svetlana took it for safekeeping.' She'd better extricate herself before she said too much. 'I need to get back. But you've given me more to go on than you realize.'

He shrugged; his mouth quirked in bafflement. 'If you say so. Glad to be of service.' He grimaced. 'What I really mean, of course, is thank you. I don't know why you're taking such an interest in me, but I do appreciate your faith in me. Really.'

He stood, and Emily stood also. 'Give my love to Svetlana. And tell her . . . if I never get out of here, tell her to get on with her life. Not to let her father bully her into settling. Tell her to be the dancer and the amazing woman she was meant to be.'

'There won't be a need. You'll be able to tell her yourself. Just have faith. Not in me, but in God. He will not allow you to be falsely convicted.'

'Sure. Whatever you say.' His defeated half-smile tore at Emily's heart. If only he really did have some sort of faith to carry him through. She would have to have enough for both of them.

A uniformed officer led Daniel out, and Colin came back to the table to meet her. 'Did you get what you wanted?'

'I got something very interesting indeed. We need to talk.'

Colin took her back to the room where she'd looked at the photos. 'What do you have to tell me?'

'I was asking Daniel if he could remember anything at all, and he said no. But he told me, as he told you, that he'd wanted her dead. Then he said he could see himself going to her office – and *strangling* her. Not bashing her over the head with a statue – strangling her. I even asked him about that specifically, and he said he thought strangling was a fitting end for a woman like her.'

Colin frowned. 'OK, but that could just be him foxing. Maybe he actually does remember doing it, but he's trying to make it look like a false confession.'

'You're getting too convoluted. I really believe his memory loss is sincere. He's so open about his thoughts and whatnot before the blackout time. And on top of that, I asked him about the statue – only when he last remembered seeing it, nothing connected with the murder – and he looked at me as if I'd completely lost the plot, as if there could be no possible connection between the statue and anything we'd been talking about. I wish you could have seen his face. A complete blank.'

'Yeah, I wish I could have seen his reaction for myself too.' He frowned at her in reproach. 'So what did he say? About when he last saw the statue?'

'It was Saturday. He stayed till closing time, and he hasn't been back to the library since. So that means it had to have been taken on Sunday.'

'Presuming he's telling the truth, yeah. Well, all this is very interesting and suggestive and all that, but it still isn't evidence of either Daniel's innocence or anybody else's guilt.'

'I know. I'll keep ferreting. Especially about who could have taken the statue.'

'I don't suppose there are any security cameras in the library?'

'No. Bede's on an honor system. Bedies are too independent to stand for that.'

'Of course.' Colin sighed. 'These Bede people seem like a different species sometimes. But I shouldn't say that – you're one of them, and you're relatively normal. I mean – at least I can understand what you're talking about most of the time.'

Emily smiled. 'You should hear me when I get going about Dostoevsky. But I'll spare you that for now.'

SEVENTEEN

Given the absence of security cameras in the Bede library and her own lack of psychic powers, Emily could not immediately think of a way to find out who had been in the library on Sunday before three o'clock. She went back to consult Miranda again.

She found the librarian in her office. Today she was wearing royal blue leggings and a white T-shirt topped by a knee-length, handkerchief-hemmed black vest adorned with huge, brightly colored appliquéd flowers. A black beret, blue bandanna neckerchief, and fuchsia flats completed the outfit.

When her eyes had adjusted to the blast of color, Emily said, 'I need your help again, Miranda. Daniel was working here until closing time Saturday night, and he knows the statuette was there the whole time. So it must have been taken on Sunday before you did your walkabout. Can you think of any way to find out who was in the south stacks during that time?'

Miranda pouched her lips in thought. 'Not the south stacks in particular, and not everyone who was in the library. But we could start by seeing who checked anything out that day. If none of them looks likely, you could ask them all who else they saw while they were here.'

Emily's heart sank at the possible enormity of that task. Talking to random people she didn't know was right up there on her list of dreaded activities along with attending crowded sports functions and killing spiders. But professional detectives had to do it all the time, so an amateur sleuth would have to accept the burden at least occasionally. 'OK, if that's what we've got, I'll go with it.'

Miranda led her to the front desk, where she commandeered a computer and typed for a minute before producing a printed list. 'This would normally be confidential information, but I haven't listed what materials each patron checked out, and since it is a murder inquiry . . . well, hopefully they'll understand.'

'Thanks, Miranda. I owe you one.'

'No, you don't. I'm doing this for Daniel.'

Emily sat at a table and perused the list, which filled about half a page. Naturally neither Saul Goldstein nor Douglas Curzon was on it, since they were not affiliated with the college and did not have borrower's privileges. She looked closely for any mention of Taylor Curzon, Richard McClintock, or any other staff member or student associated with the case. She came up blank on that, but she did see the name of one faculty member she was at least acquainted with – Teresa Rivera, the Spanish professor. She headed over to Vollum to see if she could find Teresa in her office.

Teresa's door was open, and she sat at her desk facing the doorway. Teresa was a sociable sort who liked to be accessible for her students and keep up with what was going on. In fact, Emily was rather surprised she hadn't made her presence felt in the whole to-do surrounding Taylor in the last couple of weeks.

She knocked on the open door, and Teresa raised her tousled gray head. 'Emily! How lovely to see you! Come in.' She piloted her electric wheelchair out from behind the desk and came to meet Emily, free hand outstretched. 'It has been far too long. How are you?'

'Well enough myself, thanks. But I'm kind of in the middle of this murder inquiry. In fact, that's why I'm here.'

'You? In the middle of a murder inquiry? But why? How?'

'It's a long story. I was working with some other people to get Taylor sanctioned for all her sexual misconduct, and the young man who's been arrested was a kind of protégé of mine. I'm convinced he's innocent, but the detective in charge doesn't want to "waste" resources continuing to investigate when he already has the man he thinks is guilty.'

'I see.' Teresa clucked sympathetically. 'I would not like to think any of our students – or professors – could be guilty of murder. But that which is important is the truth, no? What can I do to help?'

'I'm trying to figure out who was in the south stacks on the main floor of the library on Sunday before three p.m. It's probably best if I don't say why.'

'Of course. I did go to the library on Sunday, right after lunch. But I was not in those stacks, and I did not stay long.'

'Did you happen to see Richard or Taylor there?'

'Mmm . . . no, I do not think so.'

'Any students you recognized?'

'Only my thesis student, Anna Gomez. I stopped by her desk to check on her.'

'Where is her desk?'

'South stacks, lower level.'

'What about a couple of men you wouldn't recognize as belonging to Bede? Both middle-aged, probably wearing suits. One short, pudgy, balding, dyspeptic-looking, the other tall, suave, and handsome.'

'Together?'

'No, either one separately.'

Teresa screwed up her eyes in thought. 'I think I may have seen the first one. The dyspeptic one. He pushed by me in a hurry, bumped into my chair and made me drop my books. He did not even apologize, let alone offer to help me pick them up.'

That sounded like Goldstein. Emily's pulse raced. A lead at last. 'Was he headed in or out at the time?'

'Out, I think. I had just checked out my books and was heading for the exit, and he came up from behind me. But I stopped to pick up my things, so I did not see where he went from there.'

'Did you notice whether he was carrying anything?'

'Ahh . . . yes, I think he was carrying a briefcase. In fact, that is probably what he bumped me with.' She shook her head. 'What a boor.'

Emily tried to picture Saul Goldstein's briefcase and Daniel's statuette. Would the statue fit inside the briefcase? The height would probably fit, but she couldn't be sure about the width of the base. But still, it was a lead. She'd pass it on to Colin and let him take it from there.

'Thanks, Teresa. You've been a great help.'

'Any time. But you know, that is not what I expected you to ask about.'

'No?'

'I keep thinking someone is going to ask me about what I might have seen here in Vollum on the night of the murder.'

Emily started. 'The police didn't ask you that?'

Teresa shrugged. 'I was out that morning, when you discovered the body. That is when they went around and talked to everyone. I thought they would come back to question me later on, but they never did.'

Emily set her lips. She'd have a word or two to say to Colin when she talked to him next. Although it was probably Wharton's fault more than his. 'Did you see anything interesting?'

'Most certainly, yes. I saw a man go into Taylor's office. In fact, it may have been that other man you mentioned – the suave one. I expected him to go to Marguerite's office – he looked like her type. A great deal too old for Taylor.' She gave a wry smile.

An *embarras de richesse*. Surely Goldstein and Douglas couldn't have been in on it together? As far as Emily knew, they hadn't even met. 'What time was this?'

'Oh, dear. Almost never do I look at the clock. But I was just getting ready to leave, so maybe . . . eleven?'

That sounded very incriminating indeed. No wonder Douglas had lied about his alibi if he was here within the exact time window determined for the murder.

'Did you see the man come out again?'

'No. I left within five minutes. But I heard raised voices as I passed the door.'

'This is incredibly important, Teresa. You're going to have to report that directly to the police. I'll be talking to one of the junior detectives – should I tell him to call on you?'

'Certainly. I can check "being interviewed by the police" off my bucket list.' She laughed, then sobered. 'Seriously, though, I am so happy you came by. I never realized I had such important information.'

Emily thanked her again and left, marveling at how Teresa could have failed to come forward by this time with her knowledge about Douglas. But then, not everyone had been close to a murder before, as Emily had. Maybe Teresa didn't even watch detective shows.

*   *   *

Emily found a quiet corner in the faculty lounge and called Colin. 'I found a witness for you.'

'What sort of witness?'

'One you should have found for yourself, actually. She was in Vollum the night of the murder. And she was also in the library on Sunday afternoon.'

'Holy cow. I thought we'd interviewed everyone in Vollum.'

'She wasn't there on Tuesday morning when your people went door to door. And apparently no one ever thought to get back to her.'

Colin groaned. 'I wanted to check back to see if we'd missed anyone, but Wharton said it was a waste of time since we had Daniel. Who is this witness? What did she see?'

'Teresa Rivera, the Spanish professor. She saw two things that don't necessarily fit together. On Sunday after lunch, she saw a man who looked like Saul Goldstein leaving the library in a hurry carrying a briefcase.'

'He could have just been looking for his daughter.'

'Svetlana said they were together all weekend. Obviously not every minute, since she wasn't with him right then, but it didn't sound like he'd have had to go looking for her in the middle of the day.'

'OK, I'll follow up on that. And Monday night?'

'This is the really interesting part. Teresa is not big on keeping track of time, but just as she was getting ready to leave for the night – which she thinks was around eleven – she saw a man matching Douglas Curzon's description go into Taylor's office. She left a few minutes later, and she could hear raised voices as she passed the door.'

'Well, well, well. That is very interesting. So our Douglas did not go to bed early like a good little boy. I will definitely be looking into this.'

'And you will talk to Teresa yourself, won't you? She's looking forward to it. Says it's on her bucket list to be interviewed by the police.' Emily rolled her eyes, which of course Colin couldn't see.

He snorted. 'Right. I'll go see her right away. What are you going to do now?'

'I feel like I'm kind of at a dead end with regard to the murder, unless you can think of anything else I should do.'

'Not really.'

'Then maybe I'll tackle a matter of internal college business I've put on hold. That plagiarism accusation against Richard McClintock.'

'If you're going to talk to McClintock, I should be there. In case it turns out to be related.'

'No, I'm going to talk to Marguerite, see if we can verify Taylor's claim. I'll let you know what we find out.'

EIGHTEEN

Emily needed Marguerite as her ally in dealing with the plagiarism accusation, but she thought it would be better to discuss the matter away from campus and its possibly prying ears. She stopped by Marguerite's office on the way out of the building.

'Have you had lunch yet?'

'Not yet. I was just going.'

'Come to Baumgartner's with me. We need to talk' – she lowered her voice – 'about Richard.'

Marguerite nodded sagely, and they set off. As they walked, Emily filled her friend in on the investigation, which they had not yet properly discussed.

'*Chérie*, I know you are fond of Daniel, but do you not think all this evidence is convincing? I do not see how you can still insist on his innocence.'

'If you'd been there when I talked to him in jail, you'd understand. He was genuinely clueless about the actual method of murder.'

'But if he does not remember . . .'

'He doesn't, but he imagined it over and over beforehand, and he imagined it completely differently. He was going to strangle her.'

Marguerite shrugged. 'That is suggestive, but – up against

everything else, I do not think it is conclusive. All the actual evidence falls into line.'

'Yes, don't you see? It falls in too neatly. If it were genuine, it would be messier. I'm convinced it's all been staged. Someone is setting Daniel up. I think it's Goldstein.'

'Even though Douglas was seen in her office that night?'

'That does need to be accounted for, certainly. After that scene we overheard I could see him killing Taylor, but he would have no reason to implicate Daniel. Douglas as the murderer wouldn't make sense of everything else – the statue, the blood, the appointment book, Daniel being seen in the building. But someone trying to frame Daniel could have arranged all of that. And Goldstein's the only one with a motive to do it.'

'Hmm. You may be right. Many people hated Taylor, but Daniel no one hates. Though I personally find him annoying. I do not care for that self-martyring type.'

'But you have to admit, martyrs are rarely murderers.'

'*C'est vrai.*'

They'd arrived at the restaurant, so they got their food and adjourned to a table. 'Now, what shall we do about Richard?' Marguerite asked as she forked up a bite of salad.

'I guess the first thing to do is to talk to the student whose work he supposedly stole. What was his name again?'

'Pacifique Morel. I know him. He has taken one or two French lit classes. He is an intelligent young man, a good writer, with original ideas. His work would be worth stealing.'

'And he's had classes with Richard?'

'*Bien sûr*, he majors in English. Why, I do not know, when he could so easily do French, but . . .' She gave an eloquent shrug.

'Is he on campus for Paideia?'

'*Je ne sais pas.* I have not seen him, but I do not frequent the student haunts as much as you do.' Marguerite's disdain for Commons food was well known. She would skip lunch if necessary rather than stoop so low.

'And then we'll also need a copy of the journal in which the article appeared.'

'I believe there is one in the faculty lounge. Unless Richard has removed it.'

Emily put down her lox-topped bagel with a sigh. 'I feel like I'm wallowing in a mud puddle. Just when we get out of having to prosecute Taylor, since she's dead, now we have to deal with Richard. Thank God I've decided to retire.'

'There is always the option of letting it go, of saying nothing. No one knows but us and Goldstein, and I do not think he cares as long as his precious Svetlana is not affected.'

Emily's gorge rose at the thought of letting Richard of all people get away with such a heinous offense. 'Pacifique Morel knows. He probably trusted Taylor to do something about it – more fool him. But he needs a faculty member to stand up for him, or it'll go nowhere.'

'*C'est vrai*. And to say the truth, *chérie*, one way and another, I have put up with Richard for as long as I care to. I will not be sorry to see him go when there is such a good reason to take him down.'

They went by the faculty lounge first to look for the issue of the *Journal of Modern Literature* in which Richard's article had appeared. It was nowhere to be found.

'That is suspicious in itself,' Marguerite said. 'No doubt Richard has removed it lest anyone else should suspect.'

'Probably. But we should be able to find a copy in the library.'

They checked the library's periodicals reading room, but that particular issue of the journal was missing from the shelf. Nor was it lying on any of the tables or abandoned under a chair. Journals could not be checked out. It was conceivable someone could have taken it to another part of the library and neglected to bring it back, but under the circumstances this absence was even more suspicious than the first.

'Can we find the article online?' Emily asked.

'*Bien sûr*,' Marguerite replied, leading the way to one of the library's public computers. 'Richard cannot hide the entire internet.'

Marguerite navigated to the website and downloaded the article, 'The Idea of Order in Wallace Stevens's Middle Period'. Writing credit was given solely to Richard McClintock, PhD. She printed the article on the library printer, and Emily skimmed it.

She was out of practice interpreting poetry and had always found Stevens obscure, but the arguments in the article seemed cogent and well expressed. 'Yeah, I doubt Richard could write this well.' She handed the pages off to Marguerite.

Marguerite read a few paragraphs and nodded. 'Richard's writing is invariably pedantic and abstruse. This is clear and easy to read. It is definitely not his own work.'

'Right. Let's go find Pacifique.'

A glance at the campus directory revealed that Pacifique had a room in MacNaughton, one of the three dorms built in sixties-modern style with no sensitivity to the stately dignity of the original college buildings, from which they were fortunately set some distance apart. The group of dorms was not-so-affectionately known as 'God's revenge on Tudor Gothic', and being assigned a room there was often considered to be a punishment for some egregious wickedness in a former life.

Pacifique Morel proved to be in residence. His handsome if somewhat careworn face registered astonishment at seeing two professors at his door. '*Bonjour*, Pacifique,' said Marguerite. 'This is Professor Cavanaugh. May we have a few moments of your time?'

He glanced into the cluttered interior of the room, which contained but a single hard desk chair. 'Of course, but . . . may we talk in the social room?' His rich bass voice held a slight Caribbean lilt.

'*Certainement*. But bring your laptop.'

Looking confused, Pacifique grabbed his computer, unplugged it, and led the way to the dorm's social room. Following his tall, sculpted ebony form down the stairs, Emily could understand what Taylor had seen in him. But she would content herself with admiring him from a distance.

The three of them sat around a rickety table. 'May I get you anything?' he said, standing and looking blankly around. 'Perhaps some tea?'

'Thank you, no. We have just eaten.'

He sat back down. 'What is this about? Am I in some sort of trouble?'

'*Pas du tout*. But it has come to our attention that you have a grievance against another professor, and we have come to look into the matter.' Marguerite produced the printed copy of the article and laid it in front of Pacifique.

He recoiled. 'Oh. That.' Then he looked up at them, baffled. 'But how did you find out about it? I never told anyone except . . .'

'Except Professor Curzon? We learned of it – indirectly from her. How exactly is not your concern. But we would like to know if it is true that this article is in fact your own work.'

'Oh, yes, it is true. I told Tay— Professor Curzon, and I thought she was going to do something about it. But she never did.' He stared at his folded hands. 'Then she . . . moved on, and I did not want to bring it up again.'

'Can you show us the original article on your computer?' Emily spoke for the first time.

'Of course.' He opened a directory window and highlighted the file name. 'Look – it says here, created eleven/fifteen/ seventeen, last modified twelve/ten/seventeen. And that journal issue did not come out until October 2018. So I could not possibly have copied it.' He opened the file. 'Here. Read it for yourself.'

He turned the screen toward them. Emily compared the wording of the first few paragraphs with that of the printout. They were virtually identical, with only a word changed here and there – all changes for the worse, she noted.

'Did you write this for McClintock's class?' she asked.

Pacifique nodded. 'It was my final paper for Modern Poetry.'

'May we take a copy of the file?' Marguerite asked. 'I have a flash drive. But first make sure the file properties show you as the author.'

Pacifique took the tiny device Marguerite handed him, which to Emily looked like a miniature cigarette lighter, and stuck it into a port in his laptop. A minute later he handed it back.

'What will happen now?'

'Now we will show these to the academic review board. They will take the matter from there.'

'Will I have to . . . testify or something?'

'Possibly. But it should not be necessary for you to confront Professor McClintock directly.'

'Good,' Pacifique said. 'I do not know if I could control myself if I did. Do you know he had the gall to fail me in that class? He claimed I never turned in a final paper at all. Just wiped it out of existence. Until it turned up in that journal, that is.'

'I think you may be sure that Professor McClintock will have his comeuppance now, Pacifique. And you should have a brilliant career ahead of you. It is a terrible thing to have one's work plagiarized, of course – but it is a great compliment as well. Especially from professor to student.'

Pacifique allowed himself a small smile. 'I do not know how you got involved in this, Professor Grenier, and I do not want to know. But thank you. *Merci bien.* Thank you both very much.'

As they walked back from MacNaughton toward Vollum, Emily said, 'Revealing Richard's plagiarism may be the only good thing Taylor ever unknowingly and unintentionally did.'

'*Oui, c'est ça.* It goes to show that no life is wasted, *non?*'

They allowed themselves a small laugh over that.

NINETEEN

On the way across campus, Emily and Marguerite encountered Douglas, who was coming out of Eliot Hall. He nearly passed them completely, looking preoccupied and almost dazed, oblivious to his surroundings. Emily hailed him, and he blinked like one coming out of a dream.

'Oh, hello, Emily, Marguerite. How are you this afternoon?' His courtesy was ingrained but Emily sensed no real attention behind it.

'Fine, thanks. How are you holding up?' Emily realized with a jolt that she hadn't seen him since discovering Taylor's body.

'Me? Oh, you know. I couldn't say I'm exactly grieving for Taylor – not as she was lately – but there was a time when we loved each other. Or at least when I loved her. Her death brings up such memories and at the same time makes it absolutely certain that those days can never return.' His eyes grew misty, and Emily wondered if she should have said nothing.

'What brings you back to campus?'

He waved his hand to include all of Eliot Hall, where the administrative offices of the college were housed. 'Business. The ugly business of death.' He grimaced. 'It seems wrong, unkind, that one should have to deal with such emotional upheaval and such petty practicalities all at the same time.'

Emily had the thought that at least he did not have to plan a funeral just yet, since the police would not be releasing Taylor's body right away. But she didn't think Douglas would find that especially comforting.

Marguerite put in unexpectedly, 'This is not a time when you should be alone, I think. Come to dinner this evening. Both of you. We will drink wine and eat real French food and all your troubles will be washed away.' She flashed Douglas her most winning smile.

He brightened. 'Thank you. That would be lovely.' He blinked and smiled from one woman to the other. 'I feel better already.'

Marguerite gave him her address and a time, and they continued on their separate paths. 'That was very kind of you, Margot,' Emily said. 'I don't think I've ever known you to be so spontaneously hospitable. Usually you want at least a week to plan.'

Marguerite put a finger to her lips. 'I am not being kind. I am being cunning. We will ply him with drink and disarm him with our charm, and then we will winkle his whole story out of him. You will see.'

At Marguerite's insistence, Emily put on her green velvet Christmas dress with its slightly daring V neckline and swooshy mid-calf-length skirt over the highest heels she owned, which did not quite attain three inches. She arrived at Marguerite's modern, mostly white apartment a few minutes before the stated time of seven o'clock so she could help with last-minute preparations. But Marguerite had everything in hand. Her table was set with sparkling china and crystal and adorned with a single blue orchid in a sinuous white porcelain vase.

Marguerite's white Persian, Colette, greeted Emily with a leg rub and a purr, decorously demanding the attention that was her due. Emily obliged, picking the cat up and scratching her head as she talked to Marguerite in the streamlined white-and-stainless-steel kitchen. Marguerite's slim red silk sheath stood out like a splash of blood against the spare background.

'Do you have a definite plan for winkling information out of Douglas, or are we going to wing it?'

'We will improvise according to the opportunities of the moment,' Marguerite replied as she tossed the salad. 'You will notice I have put on some jazz to sharpen our improvisational skills.' Emily heard Stéphane Grappelli and Django Reinhardt in the background.

'Good. The best-laid schemes gang aft agley anyway.'

'What means this "gang aft agley"? Monsieur Burns is so obscure with all his Scottish words and peculiar grammar.'

'I think it means "'go oft awry". But as we are neither mice nor men, perhaps it won't apply.'

Marguerite laughed. 'No. We are two attractive women entertaining a susceptible man. We are sure to succeed.'

But at what cost, Emily wondered. Never mind; if Douglas did get a little too amorous, Marguerite would be sure to divert his attentions solely to herself, and she would be able to handle them.

The doorbell rang, and Emily deposited a slightly huffy Colette on the couch as she went to answer it. Douglas stood on the threshold with a bottle of wine in one hand and a bunch of white roses in the other.

Coals to Newcastle on both fronts. But Emily smiled graciously and let him in, closing the door behind him.

'Margot, Douglas has come bearing gifts,' she called. 'I'll take the flowers and put them in water.'

'Douglas brought wine,' she whispered to Marguerite in the kitchen. 'What shall we do with it?'

'Let him uncork it. It will not hurt to have two wines with dinner. Is it a decent wine?'

'I didn't see the label, only that it's red. He could afford something good, though, assuming he knows how to pick it.'

'Red is wrong for the meal, but *ce n'est rien*. We can linger over it with the cheese.'

Marguerite finished the salad and carried it to the dining area, where the other dishes stood ready: individual servings of coquilles

Saint-Jacques on chargers at the three places, and platters of chicken cordon bleu, potatoes au gratin, and braised asparagus with hollandaise sauce waiting on the sideboard. Marguerite must have been busy since the moment they parted.

Douglas cast an appreciative eye over the spread and the two hostesses. 'You ladies are a vision of loveliness, and this meal is worthy of *Gourmet* magazine. This is just what I needed to soothe my wounded soul.'

He pulled out their chairs for them one by one, then sat and unfolded his linen napkin from the flower shape Marguerite had created. 'How on earth did you manage all this on the spur of the moment? It's like a five-star restaurant.'

Marguerite smiled mysteriously. 'We Frenchwomen have our ways.' She filled his glass with the white wine she had chosen, a mid-range Sauvignon Blanc. 'We will keep your wine for the cheese course.'

Douglas took a long sip and addressed himself to his coquilles St Jacques. 'Delicious,' he said after the first bite. 'We don't get seafood like this in Chicago.'

'You live in Chicago?' Emily asked. 'I assumed you were from England.'

'Many years ago, yes,' he replied. 'But I've been in America most of my adult life.'

'Do you ever miss your native land?'

'I miss certain things about it. The gardens, for instance. The cool summers. The village pubs. But honestly, England is no longer the country of my childhood. The population has exploded, and its face has changed completely. Ethnic Brits are practically the minority now. Not that I'm racist, but the influx of other cultures means the old traditions are dying out. Especially in the cities.'

'America is at least equally diverse, surely,' Emily said.

'Yes, but – pardon me – you never had the centuries-old traditions to begin with. Your culture has always been in flux. So it's less disturbing here. Besides, there are many things I prefer about America. The openness and friendliness, for one. It's possible to have too much of the famous British reserve.'

That accounted for his forwardness when they first met, Emily thought. And it boded well for this evening's conversation also.

'What about you, Marguerite?' Douglas asked. 'I assume you're from France originally. Do you miss it?'

'*Mais oui*. The French do everything better – food, wine, fashion, to name a few. But France also is changing. I visit every summer, see family, do some shopping, and that is sufficient to assuage my homesickness.'

Marguerite rose to clear the starter plates and bring the other platters to the table. Emily helped her and refilled Douglas's glass.

'Where did you and Taylor meet?' she asked Douglas when they'd filled their plates, hoping to steer the conversation in the desired direction.

'Chicago. My business is based there, and she taught at the University of Chicago before she came here. We met at a fundraiser for the university.'

'How long were you together?'

'Only five years. We weren't starry-eyed teenagers; we'd both been married before. But in the beginning I deluded myself that it could work. She was less . . . restless then. The itch seemed to grow on her as she got older, strangely enough.'

Marguerite and Emily exchanged glances as Marguerite filled Douglas's glass, which was already empty again. The two women were still on their first glass each.

'It is not so strange,' Marguerite said. 'It was *peut-être* her form of mid-life crisis. When a woman who has always relied on her sex appeal starts to lose it, sometimes she tries to reassure herself by pursuing younger men. Hormones can also play a role. It is not so different for many men.'

'True. But for my own part, I have always valued the wisdom and experience of women *d'un certain âge*. I suppose that was my mistake – marrying a woman a decade younger than myself. The experience was there, in spades, but the wisdom was rather lacking.'

'Age doesn't necessarily equate to wisdom,' Emily said. 'Some never acquire it, while others have it from a relatively young age. Svetlana, for instance. She's quite an old soul.'

Douglas turned an inquiring face to Emily. 'Svetlana?'

'A student of mine. The female half of the young couple I mentioned whose lives Taylor was making rather difficult.'

'Ah. And that young man they've arrested – Daniel? – is he the other half?'

Emily nodded. 'Only I'm sure he's innocent.'

Douglas spoke carefully. 'He had sufficient provocation, surely.'

'Yes, but I just have a feeling about it. Everything doesn't quite seem to add up.'

Douglas finished his chicken and dabbed at his mouth. He took a last long drink of wine and looked longingly at the empty bottle of Sauvignon Blanc.

Marguerite took the cue and cleared the plates, even though Emily was not quite finished. Emily rose and helped her to serve the cheese – an assortment of Brie, Gruyère, and Camembert – and open the wine Douglas had brought, which proved to be a fairly pricey port. '*Parfait*,' Marguerite whispered to Emily as she opened it. 'He will be most relaxed after drinking this.'

Emily let Douglas get halfway through his port and cheese before returning to the subject of the murder. 'You say Daniel had sufficient provocation. But so did several other people. You must admit Taylor was a provocative sort of woman.'

Douglas rolled his eyes with a slight head-wobble. 'She was that. I myself' – he stopped for a tiny hiccup – 'I have been provoked by her many a time.'

'I got that impression,' Emily said. 'In fact, I must confess, we happened to be passing her office and overheard a tiny part of one such confrontation.' She need not admit that they had deliberately stopped to listen.

Douglas's fair cheeks had already begun to redden from the wine; now they turned purple. 'That time we met in the hallway and went for coffee.'

Emily nodded. '*Oui, c'est ça*,' said Marguerite. 'But, *vous comprenez*, we did not hear about what you were arguing. Only the angry voices.' Marguerite was more comfortable with outright lying, whereas Emily could usually go only as far as omitting parts of the truth.

Douglas's consternation visibly faded. That conversation had been compromising to his manhood, whether or not he had anything to do with the murder. Emily did not blame him for hoping it had been kept private.

'However, it was our impression that Taylor had won the argument,' Marguerite said. 'If I were you, I would not have been content to leave it there. I think I might have gone back later to try to have the last word.'

'I did,' Douglas mumbled. 'Go back, that is. Late that night. But she still had the last word.' The wine-fog seemed to lift for a moment, and he gazed at them intently. 'I didn't kill her, if that's what you're thinking. She was alive when I left her.' He closed his eyes with a tiny shudder. 'Very much alive.'

The two women gave him a moment to recuperate as they cleared the cheese and made coffee, to be served with a chocolate torte. 'I think he's telling the truth,' Emily whispered. 'How about you?'

'*In vino veritas*,' Marguerite replied. 'It is dangerous to assume, but yes, to me he seems sincere. She broke him, but he did not kill her. You have yet a mystery to solve.'

TWENTY

On Friday morning, as she was walking to campus, Emily finally received a call back from Miriam Zimmerman, the doctor at the Bede infirmary. She'd nearly forgotten her intention to work out some sort of health insurance for Daniel or else pay for his medication directly. Now that he was in jail, she wasn't sure how much point there was in pursuing it. But she would have to trust that he would be free and back at Bede before long.

'Miriam, thanks for getting back to me. I wanted to ask you about getting some medication for a student – a type that isn't covered by the regular college plan.'

'You know I can't disclose anything about a student's medical records, right?'

'Of course. I already know his condition and that he isn't being treated. I don't need to know the name of the appropriate medication.'

'Who's the student?'

'Daniel Razumov.'

'Ah. Terrible business. I've seen plenty of health catastrophes resulting from people not taking their meds, but this is the first time I've seen it lead to murder.'

'Don't jump to conclusions, Miriam. Just because he's been arrested doesn't mean he's guilty.'

'No, of course not. Sorry. Anyway, I'm happy to work with you on that. I've been racking my brains for some time trying to figure out how to help Daniel. But he's too proud to accept a handout from anyone.'

'I know. That's why I want to be sneaky about it. Would it work for me to pay for the medication and you pretend to him that the insurance has changed and started covering it?'

'Hmm. The coverage wouldn't be likely to change just randomly. But we do renew the policy each semester, so conceivably it could change at that time. Assuming he's able to come back for the spring semester.'

'I'm determined to see that happen.'

'All right. If you can get him released, we'll have the meds waiting for him. And I'll send you the bill. It isn't cheap, you understand.'

'I know. But it's worth it. Daniel has a lot of potential, and proper treatment could make the difference between him achieving it or not.'

Emily was approaching the entrance to the library when Sidney appeared out of nowhere, doing his Jeeves imitation again. She started, then put on a smile. 'Hello, Sidney.'

'Professor Cavanaugh. Just the person I was hoping to see. May I have a moment of your time?'

'I suppose so. But let's go inside. It's freezing out here.' The temperature was literally below freezing, and the air felt heavy with impending snow. It might not hit today, but it would hit soon, and hard.

They sat on one of the benches in the library lobby, and Emily removed her hat and gloves. Sidney was wearing neither but didn't appear to feel their absence. 'What can I do for you, Sidney?'

'I was wondering if you could tell me anything about how the investigation is going. You do have a sort of "in" with the police, don't you? And I'm so terribly worried about poor Daniel.' He put on a sad-puppy-dog expression.

'I have been talking with one of the detectives, yes,' Emily cautiously replied. 'He's my fiancé's nephew. But he hasn't really told me much about what's going on. The police like to play their cards pretty close to their chest in these matters.'

Sidney gazed at his puffy hands closed around the strap of his messenger bag. 'Oh dear. I was hoping to hear they had some other suspect besides Daniel. I feel so very badly about being the one to place him in Vollum that night.' He lifted pained, anxious eyes to meet hers.

'As far as I know, they aren't looking seriously at anyone else. Though of course they are open to other suggestions. At least, Colin Richards is. His boss, not so much.'

'One of the old school, is he? A stickler for procedure?'

'Somewhat. Or just stubborn, maybe even a little lazy. He has a suspect in custody and isn't interested in pursuing any others.'

'That's so sad. But you will do everything in your power to help the police see sense, won't you? And let me know if there's anything I can do to help? I just can't bear the thought of dear Daniel rotting in prison for the rest of his life.'

Interesting choice of words. Not I can't believe he's guilty, *just* I don't want to see him rot.

'Of course. I'm convinced Daniel is innocent, and I'm doing everything in my power to prove it. Unfortunately, not that much actually is in my power. The police hold all the big cards.' She regarded him thoughtfully for a moment. 'There is one thing you could do. I understand you told the police you saw Daniel near Curzon's office at ten-fifteen on Monday night?'

He nodded. 'That's right. Ten-fifteen. I was on my way out.'

'Did you see anyone else there at all? Any office doors open, even?'

Sidney frowned in concentration, fingers to his temples. 'I didn't actually see anyone else, no. But I think I did notice a door that was open a crack, with a light on. Across the hall from Curzon and down a few.'

That sounded like Richard McClintock's office. So Richard

was fibbing about his alibi as well. Emily's heart gave a little leap. Her primary goal of course was to prove Daniel innocent, but if Richard turned out to be guilty instead, an old raw place within her might finally be appeased. 'Thank you, Sidney. That could be very helpful.'

He smiled brightly at her and took his leave. Emily debated whether to pass the information directly to Colin or confront McClintock herself. She decided she'd like to see Richard's face when she put the question. Emily wasn't a vindictive person in general, but it would give her some satisfaction to see Richard McClintock squirm.

Emily knocked on Richard's door and heard his cautious, 'Who is it?' He didn't sound like a man with a clear conscience and not a care in the world.

She pushed the door open while announcing herself so he couldn't dismiss her too easily. 'It's Emily. May I have a moment of your time?' She realized after the fact that she'd borrowed her wording from Sidney. Not something she'd want to make a habit of.

'Oh . . . uh . . . hi, Emily.' He cleared his throat. 'What can I do for you?'

That was a step up from his usual growled *What do you want?* He was definitely nervous, afraid of being found out, but whether for murder or only for plagiarism she couldn't be sure. She'd keep him guessing for the time being.

'I just wanted to check on something. As you may know, I'm working to prove Daniel Razumov's innocence.'

'I think I heard something to that effect.' He frowned, clearly disapproving of someone from his division – or nearly retired from his division – colluding openly with the police.

'Perhaps you've heard they have a witness who saw Daniel in this corridor on Monday night.'

His grunt was neither negative nor affirmative.

'I just wondered if you might be able to corroborate that or dispute it. Since you were here too.' She gave him her brightest smile.

Richard visibly paled. His hands shook as he capped and uncapped his pen. 'Wh–what makes you think I was here?'

She moved a step closer to press her advantage, then recoiled from the smell of his aftershave, intensified by the sweat that was beading on his brow. She fought down a wave of nausea. It wouldn't do to let the memories take over and dictate her actions in the present.

'That same student says he saw your door open with the light on.' A bit of a stretch, as Sidney hadn't named the exact door – but Richard didn't need to know that.

His hands relaxed slightly. 'Oh, that.' So it was his door after all. 'I, uh – I think I went to the restroom right before I left for the night, and then I must have forgotten to go back to turn off the light and lock the door.'

Emily looked at him quizzically. 'Even though you had to pass your door between the restroom and the stairs? You must have been quite preoccupied.'

He cleared his throat again. 'I was. I, uh – I was anxious to get home. I was expecting company.'

'Oh, really? But didn't you tell the police you spent the evening alone in your apartment?'

His nostrils flared as he glowered at her. 'My guest didn't show. Got sick at the last minute. Didn't get the message until I got home.'

She was sure he was lying, but pressing him beyond this point was a job for the police. 'I see. I guess you can't help me then. Thanks anyway.'

'Any time.' He made a painful attempt at a smile.

She turned toward the door, then back again. 'Oh, by the way – Marguerite and I had a chat with Pacifique Morel yesterday.'

This time his face completely drained of color. His voice shook when he uttered, 'Oh? What about?'

'I think we'll keep that to ourselves for the time being. But it was an interesting chat. A very interesting chat indeed.'

She left him picking his jaw up off the floor. She hadn't learned anything substantial about the events of Monday night, but she had learned one interesting thing – Richard feared an accusation of plagiarism more than he feared one of murder.

Emily found her quiet corner in the faculty lounge again and called Colin. 'I have a couple of things to report,' she told him.

'OK, shoot.' She heard paper rustling and the click of a pen.

'First of all, Marguerite and I had a talk with Douglas Curzon last night. Have you gotten around to re-interviewing him yet?'

Colin cleared his throat. 'Not yet. I couldn't reach him yesterday, and I'm just digging my way out of the paperwork this morning.'

'You may still want to talk to him, but I doubt it's going to lead to much. Marguerite invited him to dinner, and, well . . . we sort of got him drunk. Tipsy, anyway. He admitted going back to Taylor's office Monday night, but he swears she was alive when he left her. And I'm inclined to believe him.'

'Why, exactly?'

'As Marguerite said, *in vino veritas*. And besides, it was so humiliating for him to admit he was even there, I think he would have denied that if he had actually killed her.'

'Hmm. I'm not sure that's quite logical, but OK. I will interview him myself, though. Assuming I can find him in.'

'I expect he'll be nursing a hangover for most of the morning, so your chances are good.'

'You said you had a couple of things?'

'Yes. The second was entirely fortuitous. Sidney Sharpe stopped me outside the library this morning to ask me how the investigation was going. I wasn't sure how much you'd pressed him about whether he might have seen anyone else in Vollum that night besides Daniel, so I asked him – not only whether he saw anyone in person, but whether he saw lights on or doors open in any of the offices.'

'Oh, I didn't think about that. What did he say?'

'He said he saw Richard McClintock's door ajar with the light on.'

'And this was at ten-fifteen, same time he saw Daniel?'

'Yes.'

'So McClintock was lying about his alibi too. Ten-fifteen isn't in the murder window, but the fact that he lied is suggestive in itself.'

'That's what I thought. So I confronted him with it.'

'You did *what*? Emily, my uncle would kill me if he found out I let you put yourself in any danger.'

'You didn't let me – I did it all on my own. And I would hardly consider Richard a danger.'

'But if he's killed once—'

'Yes, but if he did that, he must have been in a rage. He couldn't kill in cold blood, simply out of fear. He's too much of a wimp. And anyway, I've learned a thing or two from Luke about self-defense.' Luke had indeed taught her one or two moves, mostly designed for escape from a threat rather than for retaliation. 'And there were other people in the neighboring offices. I would only have needed to scream and someone would have come running.'

'I hope you're right. Well, you're talking to me now, so obviously he didn't attack you. But what did he say?'

'He claimed he left earlier and forgot to turn off his light and lock his door.'

'Did you believe him?'

'Not for a second. He was sweating so hard he must have gone home by now to change his shirt.'

'Still, it's a damned hard thing to prove or disprove, unless somebody else saw him. Or went into the office and saw he wasn't there. Of course, that could also mean he was in Curzon's office murdering her.'

'And I will very graciously leave figuring all that out to you.'

'Gee, thanks.' He gave a grim chuckle. 'You're something. I bet you keep Uncle Luke on his toes.'

'I certainly try.' Emily was assailed by a wave of missing Luke. She'd have to call him soon, maybe even get him up for the weekend again.

She signed off with Colin and decided to call Luke then and there. She gave him an update, then asked if he could possibly get away in the next couple of days.

'I wish I could, but Pete and Heather were on last weekend, and we're kind of busy with the weather still being bad. I can't leave them on duty alone again.'

She sighed. 'I suppose not. We'll just have to muddle through as best we can.' She didn't tell Luke, but she had an eerie feeling things were soon going to become far more muddled than they had been yet.

TWENTY-ONE

That evening, since she was going to be on her own for the weekend, Emily attended a concert in the college chapel – a lovely wood-paneled room at one end of the second floor of Eliot Hall, where the vaulted, beamed ceiling created excellent acoustics. The chapel had once been a place of worship but now hosted concerts, films, and the very occasional wedding. Tonight the Collegium Musicum, Bede's chamber ensemble of vocalists and Renaissance instruments, performed motets, chansons, and madrigals by Thomas Tallis, Josquin des Prez, Monteverdi, and Palestrina. The women's voices finished off the concert with an a cappella chant by Hildegard von Bingen.

As the final pure, high notes of the chant echoed through the rafters and deep into Emily's soul, she felt a peace and serenity that had eluded her all through the last two weeks. People filed out all around her, but she remained seated with her eyes closed, holding the music in her heart, unwilling to end the moment and return to ordinary life.

'Emily?' She came back from a great distance to register that a familiar voice was calling her name. She turned to see Oscar and, behind him, Lauren. She'd been so preoccupied with matters surrounding the murder that it hadn't even struck her that she hadn't seen either of them since the night of her dinner party a week and a half – or maybe a lifetime – before. Oscar shared a hole-in-the-wall office in a different part of the library from Emily's table, so she had not run into him either there or in Vollum.

'Oscar! Lauren! How lovely to see you. I was just trying to prolong the moment here. But I guess I'll have to admit it can't last forever.'

'We were thinking about going out for dessert,' Lauren said. 'Would you like to join us?'

Emily glanced from one to the other, gauging the sincerity

of the invitation. Both looked as though they genuinely wanted her company, so she said, 'I'd love to. If you're sure I won't be in the way.'

The night was clear and lovely, if cold; the clouds that had threatened snow had dissipated without delivering on their promise, though Emily suspected they would return. She was pleased to note the way Oscar and Lauren clung to each other's hands as the three of them walked up the hill to Baumgartner's. The deli stayed open late on Friday and Saturday nights to serve the post-event crowd with luscious concoctions such as blackberry cheesecake, mocha torte, and flourless chocolate cake. Emily chose the torte, Lauren the cheesecake, and Oscar the chocolate cake, and they settled into a booth in a back corner.

'Wasn't that concert heavenly?' Lauren said, snuggling much closer to Oscar than the size of the booth warranted. 'At moments like this I can believe Dostoevsky's assertion that beauty will save the world.'

'You know, he didn't really say that directly,' Emily responded. 'A character in *The Idiot* more or less accuses Prince Myshkin of having said it – giving it as evidence of his imbecility – but he denies uttering those precise words.'

'Don't you think Dostoevsky believed it, though? I bet he was just sneaking in his own pet theory in a form in which no one could challenge it.'

'That's possible. Maybe he didn't want to take the trouble of defending the idea in the novel, so he didn't give the characters a chance to debate it.'

'I wish he had. I'd have been interested to hear what they'd say,' said Oscar.

'Me too. I'd be inclined to think Dostoevsky himself did believe it, if you look at it the right way.'

'What way is that?'

'Assuming he accepted Keats's assertion, "Beauty is truth, truth beauty", I think Dostoevsky would identify both beauty and truth with Christ. And in that sense, absolutely, beauty will save the world.'

Oscar and Lauren exchanged an uncomfortable glance, and Emily realized she was talking to people for whom Christ was a historical figure, a moral teacher, a philosophical construct, perhaps, but not the Son of God and Savior of the world.

'But you can look at it on a more human level, too,' Oscar said. 'The beauty that people create goes a long way toward saving both those who create it and those who partake of it.'

'I sure felt saved tonight,' said Lauren. 'I've always believed that if you could get people to genuinely perceive and appreciate beauty, they'd be healthier psychologically and far less prone to antisocial behavior.'

'That sounds reasonable to me,' Emily replied. 'I've had a really tough time lately, and that concert just washed all the turmoil right out of me. I felt peaceful for the first time in weeks. Imagine if mental patients could live in a beautiful natural setting, in comfortable, orderly, well-designed buildings, surrounded by great art and music and literature. Surely that would go a long way toward facilitating their cure.'

'I see you share my opinion, ma'am,' Lauren quoted, reproducing Wickham's intonation to Emily's delight. 'That's been my vision ever since I started studying psychology. Maybe someday we can build a clinic together.'

'That sounds like a marvelous plan.'

Oscar said, 'Lauren will be the brains – the expertise, I mean, not to disparage your brain, Emily – and I guess Emily will be the moneybags. But I'm not sure where I could fit into this scheme.'

'You could introduce the residents to literature,' Lauren said. 'And do readings. You're great at reading aloud.'

'I second that,' Emily said, remembering Christmas Eve at Windy Corner. 'You were terrific when we read *A Christmas Carol*. And I hear you're an excellent teacher. I nominate you for official Literary Resident of our clinic. What shall we call it?'

'"Saved by Beauty",' Lauren pronounced. 'I can see it already.' She giggled. 'Of course, it's really just a pipe dream, isn't it? I mean, how likely is it to actually come about?'

'As likely as we want it to be, I think,' Emily replied. 'When the current kerfuffle is over, let's get together and talk about it seriously. I'm pretty tied up with this murder at the moment. I can't give a lot of thought to anything else.'

'Oh, the murder,' groaned Oscar. 'What do you have to do

with that? Or do you naturally end up sleuthing every time a murder happens in your general vicinity?'

'I was involved with a group of people who either were Taylor's victims or were trying to save others from her. So I know the whole gaggle of suspects and what was going on with them, more or less. The young man who's been arrested was a kind of protégé of mine.'

'I'm sorry,' Oscar said in a small voice. 'I didn't know.'

'No reason you should.'

Lauren had been following the conversation avidly, growing increasingly excited. 'You mean you actually solve murders, Emily? What fun! How did you get into that?'

Emily grimaced. 'It wasn't by choice. My great-aunt was murdered, but nobody knew it at the time. I ended up helping to figure that out. And since then murder seems to follow me around like a particularly nasty and unwelcome stray dog. I can't get away from it, so I do my best to get it off my back as quickly as possible. It isn't exactly what I'd call fun.'

Lauren looked abashed, but only momentarily. 'Well, no, not *fun* per se. But isn't it satisfying in some way? Digging for clues, chasing down the truth, bringing criminals to justice?'

Emily frowned. 'I might feel that way if I weren't always personally involved to some extent. In two cases I've been a target myself, and in another my housekeeper was a prime suspect.' She glanced at Oscar, silently querying whether she might mention his involvement in the last murder she'd faced at Windy Corner. He nodded almost imperceptibly. So he and Lauren had shared their closet skeletons, and she was still around. This relationship was looking more hopeful by the minute.

'And most recently, it was a murder that brought to light the fact that Oscar and I are siblings. This time around it isn't quite so close to home.' She paused, recalling the one aspect of the current situation that had hit extremely close to home. But her memories of past abuse were not intrinsically connected with the murder, and she didn't want to go into them with Oscar and Lauren. 'But I still care about the people involved. It isn't like being a policeman and dealing with a bunch of strangers.'

'No, I guess not. Well, these people are strangers to me,

pretty much, and it sounds thrilling. Do let me know if I can do anything to help.'

Oscar stared at Lauren in something like horror. 'You actually want to be involved with a murder investigation? Are you out of your mind?'

'Why not? I won't drag you into it if you don't want me to. But I'm interested in forensic psychology. If we don't build that clinic, that's probably what I'll go into. I don't want to be an academic forever.'

He shuddered. 'Better you than me.' He appealed to Emily. 'Just don't let her get in over her head, OK?'

'I won't if I can help it,' Emily said with a fond glance at Lauren. 'But I have a feeling she's likely to dive right into the deep end.'

On Saturday morning, while she was still at home, Emily was a little surprised to get a call from Colin. 'Do you guys work twenty-four seven?' she asked.

'During a murder investigation we do,' he said. 'Not all of the twenty-four, usually, but definitely seven. Anyway, I heard back from the organized crime guys about your Russian mafia dude.'

'Oh, really? So Wharton was right about him?'

'Absolutely. Ivan Bordetsky. He's not a hit-man or an enforcer, though. He's head of a smuggling ring.'

'Aha! I knew it! Did they look into that icon on Curzon's wall?'

'Yep. It's shady, all right. Looks like you were on target about Curzon being involved with the ring in smuggling it out of Russia. Our guys have confiscated the icon and are looking into getting it returned to Russia eventually. In the meantime, it may help get Bordetsky and his gang put away for a while.'

A part of Emily was glad to hear that, but another part mourned that she would never be able to venerate that beautiful icon in the way its creator intended, in a place of worship. But someone would – many someones – and that was the point. It wouldn't be hidden away in the office of one woman who saw it only as a valuable art object.

'So do you think Bordetsky's a viable suspect?'

'OC says not. For one thing, he's got a pretty good alibi – he was seen at a nightclub by more people than he could realistically have bribed to lie for him. And for another, the method is wrong for that kind of hit. Mob guys use guns, occasionally knives, but not opportunistic weapons like that statue. And they kill dispassionately, not in a rage. I didn't tell you this before, but Curzon had multiple head wounds – the killer struck half a dozen times. He was frenzied.'

Emily winced. 'I didn't know the number, but I always did figure rage was involved. I guess because Taylor was that kind of person.'

'Yeah. Sorry to kill your pet theory.'

'Oh well, I never gave it all that much credence. Any other developments?'

'We got some DNA results back. Daniel's DNA is on Curzon's clothing. Apart from the blood.'

'That's easily explained. She tried to force herself on him that morning.'

'The morning of the murder? Why did you never tell me that?'

'I guess the classic answer – you never asked. I told you about the general situation between them.'

'Yeah, but – stuff like that can be important. There's other DNA we can't identify. Do you know of other people she may have touched?'

'I do, as a matter of fact. She also had confrontations with her husband, Douglas, and with Richard McClintock. I only heard the conversations, I didn't directly witness them, so I don't know how much touching went on, but if I were you I'd swab those two. Then if you still have unidentified DNA left over, that will be really interesting.'

'It certainly will. I'm on it.'

He hung up, and Emily was left wondering what to do with her day. Of course, the library was open and there was nothing to prevent her from continuing her research. But she felt divorced from it at this point.

She could always visit Daniel again, just to offer him moral support. He must be badly in need of that. She called Colin back.

'Today? I guess so. I'll fix it up and call you back.'

She puttered around the house and played with the cats, who had been pestering her nonstop, until he called back. 'Can you be here by eleven?'

'No problem. See you then.'

TWENTY-TWO

E mily had an hour before she needed to be at the police station, so she stopped by the library to pick up some books for Daniel. Svetlana sat at his table, trying to type in some handwritten notes on the laptop Emily had left with her. But she was visibly flustered by Sidney hovering over her. 'Just let me help,' he wheedled as Emily approached. 'I can scan stuff while you type. Then we can finish faster and go for coffee.'

'Professor Cavanaugh is paying me to do this work. I can't let you do half of it. Besides, she pays me by the hour, not the job. If I finish artificially fast, I won't earn enough money to—'

'To what?'

'Never mind.' Emily assumed Svetlana did not want to disclose to Sidney her plan to circumvent her father's designs on her immediate future. That was probably wise.

'Good morning,' she said, making both students jump. 'Sidney, would you mind leaving us alone? I need to go over some things with Svetlana.'

He smiled his sycophantic smile. 'Of course, Professor. Anything to oblige.' He turned to Svetlana. 'Will I see you at Commons later?'

'I'm not sure. My father might want to go out somewhere.'

Sidney's face fell, but he kept the smile pasted on. '*Au revoir*, then.' He sidled out.

When he was out of sight and earshot, Svetlana gave a massive sigh. 'Sidney is really starting to get on my nerves. I used to think it was just Daniel he cared about, but now he won't leave me alone. And my father encourages him. I honestly thought Papa had more sense.'

'I'm afraid your father may see him as a potential suitor,' Emily said gently. 'He is going to be a Jewish lawyer, after all.'

Svetlana made a scoffing sound. 'Bullshit. He's no more Jewish than the pope. And he never mentioned wanting to go to law school before, either. He just can't seem to help trying to ingratiate himself with every person he meets who might be of use to him somehow. It's sickening.' She shuddered. 'And he keeps sympathizing with me about Daniel, but it doesn't feel genuine. One of these days I'm going to lose it and kick him into next week.'

Emily envisioned that kick: with Svetlana's ballet training, it would be graceful, but also highly effective. The picture of a pas de deux between them ending with Sidney flailing through the air to land in an ungainly heap on the opposite side of the stage was a little too appealing.

Svetlana ran her hands over her flawless hair and corrected her posture, as Emily remembered being taught to do in ballet class – *imagine a string attached to the top of your head, pulling you up*. That must be her way of centering herself. 'Anyway, I'm glad you're here,' she said. 'I wanted to ask – have you made any progress? Do you know who killed Curzon?'

'I'm afraid not. We've pursued a lot of leads, but so far none of them looks too promising.' Seeing the girl's crestfallen face, Emily hastened to add, 'But we still have other suspects who haven't been ruled out. Don't give up hope.'

Svetlana's fragile composure deserted her. She put her fists to her temples. 'If only there were something I could *do*! All this waiting and worrying is driving me out of my mind.'

'I'm not sure what you can do in the investigation. But I'm just on my way to visit Daniel and take him some books. I could at least give him a message from you.'

Svetlana grasped Emily's arm. 'My father's not coming to campus till lunchtime. Take me with you. Please? If I could at least see Daniel . . .'

'Of course.' Emily led Svetlana to her car – or tried to, but it was more like leading a cat to its food bowl. The girl kept rushing ahead of her, then turning back as if to hurry her on.

As they drove, Emily gave her an update on how the

investigation was progressing, omitting the fact that she still somewhat suspected Svetlana's father.

'So who do you think did it?' Svetlana asked, as urgently as if Daniel's fate hung on Emily's opinion.

'I really couldn't say at this point,' Emily replied. 'I can't be sure of any one person having all three of the essential elements – motive, method, and opportunity. But we'll get there, don't worry. The truth will out.'

Svetlana sat silent for the rest of the ride, biting her nails and leaning forward as if that would get them there sooner. Emily could not remember a longer few miles of driving.

Colin met them at the front desk of the justice center. He started when he saw Emily's companion. Emily hastened to explain that Svetlana was hoping to visit Daniel as well.

'I'm sorry,' Colin said to Svetlana. 'He can only have one visitor a day, and I've already put down Emily's name. It's too late to change it.' He gestured toward a cubicle furnished with several semi-comfortable chairs. 'You can wait there. Maybe you'd like to write him a note? I could bring you some paper.'

Svetlana's pent-up energy suddenly deserted her. She sagged against Emily, then with an effort righted herself. 'Yes, all right. That would be better than nothing.'

'And could you get her some sweet tea?' Emily said to Colin in a low voice. 'She looks like she needs it.'

Colin nodded and disappeared down the hall. Emily led Svetlana to a chair, determined to make her visit short; the girl seemed about to break. Colin returned with a steaming styrofoam cup and a packet of cheese crackers from a vending machine. Hardly Svetlana's typical healthful fare, but any calories were better than none at this point.

Colin ushered Emily through the security process as before. It took a few extra minutes for the guards to clear the books she'd brought, but soon she was face-to-face with Daniel across a table.

He looked no worse than before – possibly a bit better, as he'd had time to recover from his seizure. But he was still a long way from healthy.

Emily pushed the books across the table to him, and he brightened considerably. 'Thank you so much. You wouldn't believe how bored I've been. I managed to get a pad and pen to scribble some thoughts, but I couldn't do any real work without my books.' He looked over the stack. 'You didn't bring any of the library books, I see. Not sure I'll ever get out to return them?'

'It isn't that. I just didn't know what things were like in here – whether the books might get stolen or damaged.'

'I doubt any of these guys would steal scholarly works on Dostoevsky. They wouldn't even be able to pronounce his name. But I guess you're right about the potential for damage.' He sighed. 'Still, these are a lot better than nothing. Thanks.'

He set the books down and fixed his gaze on her. 'So, have you found any evidence that doesn't point to me?'

'Not evidence, exactly. We've broken a couple of alibis, but unfortunately all that proves is that the men in question didn't want the police to know they'd been in Taylor's office that night. Which is understandable.'

Daniel's face fell. 'I didn't really expect you'd find anything. What could you find? I must have killed her.'

'You still haven't been able to remember anything?'

He shook his head. 'Not a single thing. It's a complete blank.'

Emily huffed. 'If the police were willing to interview everyone on campus, they'd be bound to find someone who saw you somewhere else in that crucial hour. But they won't commit the resources. A bird in the hand and all that.'

He smiled wryly. 'A jailbird in the hand. Can you blame them?'

'If only we could figure out who DR is.'

'You mean besides me?'

'Remember I told you those initials were in Curzon's appointment book for ten-thirty? If it wasn't you, there must be someone else with those initials. Or some other significance to the letters.'

Daniel frowned, then shrugged. 'I'll give it some thought, but my brain's not working very well these days. Not the healthiest environment, you know?'

'I know. I could just go through the college directory and see what I find. That would be a lot less time-consuming than trying to talk to everyone on campus.'

'You know I really appreciate everything you're trying to do for me, Professor Cavanaugh.'

'Emily.'

'Emily. But I don't get why you're doing it. What am I to you besides the guy who snagged all the books you wanted?'

Emily gazed at him, asking herself the same question. 'You're a person in trouble. And I believe you're innocent. That's enough in my book.' Daniel didn't need to know about the personal history that gave this case such emotional resonance for her. 'Don't despair. There must still be some unexplored avenues, and I will definitely explore them, or badger the police until they do. Meanwhile, try to keep your spirits up.'

He gave her a look of utter cynicism.

'I know it's hard. Svetlana came with me today – she wanted to visit you, but they wouldn't let her on the spur of the moment when they already had me signed up. But she's out there in the office writing you a letter.'

Daniel brightened a little at that, and they said their goodbyes. As Colin walked her out, she asked, 'Do you think I could get a look at Curzon's appointment book?'

'I guess so. Why?'

'I'm not sure, I just have a feeling about it. I want to see if I can track down any other DR.'

Colin took her back to the main office and went off to the evidence room, returning in a few minutes with the appointment book in a plastic evidence bag. He handed her a pair of latex gloves to use while handling it. His own hands gloved, he turned the book to the relevant page. 'Right there.'

Emily stared at the initials. They were written together, as capitals with no periods between. 'Could it mean "doctor"?'

Colin looked skeptical. 'Doesn't seem too likely, does it? A doctor's appointment at ten-thirty at night?'

'Not a regular medical appointment, no. But she could have been planning to meet someone who happens to be a doctor, but in some other capacity.'

'But wouldn't she have written the R in lowercase? That's the usual abbreviation for doctor.'

'True, but Taylor was not a usual person.' She skimmed through the entries for the week previous to Taylor's death. 'See, she always writes out a person's name – the first or the last name, at least. There's not a single other entry here that just has two initials.'

Colin leafed through in his turn. 'Huh. You're right. That's kind of funny. But couldn't it be because it was a secret assignation?'

Emily flipped back to the previous autumn and found an entry for Pacifique. 'She was sleeping with this guy, I'm pretty sure, and she wrote his name out. I don't think she'd care about keeping that sort of thing secret. Now, if her mafia guy had the initials DR, that might make sense. But then she probably would have written the initials in Russian. Some Russian letters look like Roman letters, but there's nothing that looks like D or R.'

'Yeah, IB for Ivan Bordetsky doesn't look much like DR either. These letters are pretty clear.'

'Wait a minute.' Emily pulled the book close and examined the letters again, then the other entries around them. 'Aren't they too clear? Her handwriting isn't that great – some of the other entries are kind of hard to make out. But the DR – like you said, it's quite clear.'

'You know, you're right. I never thought of that.'

'I bet it's a forgery. The murderer wrote those initials as just one more way of implicating Daniel.'

'Why not go the whole hog and write out "Daniel Razumov"?'

'Because he didn't trust himself to capture her handwriting. He didn't do that great a job on these two letters. If he'd tried the whole name, you'd have been sure to notice the difference before now.'

'Hot dog. I think we're on to something.' Colin snapped the book shut. 'I'm going to have to run this by the boss and get it over to the handwriting specialist to verify. But I'm sure in my bones you're right. Wharton will have to let me broaden the investigation now.'

Emily glowed. Progress at last, with real physical evidence that Daniel was being framed. She had to tell Svetlana.

But when Colin and Emily entered the cubicle where she was waiting, Svetlana stood. Straight and resolute as a martyr going to the stake, she handed Colin a sheaf of folded papers. 'This is for Daniel,' she said. 'And I want to make a confession.'

TWENTY-THREE

Colin's eyebrows rose toward his hairline. He glanced at Emily, who returned a baffled look. She had certainly not expected this development.

'We'll have to move to an interview room,' Colin said.

Svetlana hesitated. 'May I have Emily with me?'

Colin exchanged glances with Emily again, and she nodded her agreement. 'I guess we could call her your appropriate adult. But you do need to keep quiet unless I ask you something, Emily.'

'Of course.'

He led the way to an interview room – windowless, sterile, devoid of any comfort. Emily felt cold to her core. She could only imagine what Svetlana must be feeling in this oppressive place.

Colin made the necessary introduction for the sake of the recording, then said, 'You said you want to make a confession.'

'Yes.' Svetlana sat rigidly erect, her hands clenched in her lap, her gaze directed straight ahead – not at Colin but at the opposite wall. Her face looked completely drained of blood. 'I killed Taylor Curzon.'

'Right.' Colin cleared his throat. 'Did you plan this ahead of time?'

Svetlana's eyes went wide. 'No! Of course not. I just wanted to reason with her. I went to her office to try to persuade her to let Daniel off the hook. I didn't care what she did to me if she would only leave him alone.'

'You went to her office. I take it you mean on Monday night? What time was this?'

Svetlana swallowed. 'Yes, Monday. I think . . . around eleven?' She cast a telltale glance at Emily as if unsure of the time the police had determined for the murder. A tiny knot of doubt in Emily's mind relaxed at that moment. She was now completely certain Svetlana's confession would be false.

'Did you see anyone else in the building?'

'N–no. Not that I remember.'

'Did you go straight to Curzon's office?'

'Yes.'

'And then what happened?'

'I knocked on her door.'

'Was it shut?'

'Yes.'

'Did she come to the door?'

'No. She called out "Come in", so I went in.'

Colin raised an eyebrow toward Emily. He and she knew that Curzon's office door did not stay fully closed unless it was locked, but Svetlana evidently did not.

'And then?'

'She was sitting at her desk. I went up to the desk and said . . . well, I don't remember my exact words, but I asked her to leave Daniel alone. I said I didn't care what happened to me, but Daniel couldn't work with her pestering him, and he absolutely had to finish his degree this year.'

'And how did she respond?'

'She laughed at me. She . . . called me names. Then she stood up and came around the desk. She got right up in my face and said terrible things about Daniel, too. That his career didn't matter, he'd never amount to anything academically because he was ill. I don't know how she found out about that, but I just saw red.'

Svetlana took in a breath and finished her recital in a rush. 'Daniel's statue was there on the desk, right by my hand – I have no idea how it got there – and I picked it up and swung at her. I didn't mean to kill her. I just wanted to shut her up. Then when I saw what I'd done, I was horrified. I panicked and ran.'

Colin was silent a moment, giving her time to finish. But she said no more.

'I see. You hit her once and then you ran?'

'Yes. She crumpled right away.'

He nodded sagely. 'And you didn't get any blood on your clothes?'

Svetlana blinked rapidly, and Emily could almost hear the

gears of her brain turning over. She knew about the blood on Daniel's jacket; her story would have to account for that somehow.

'I . . . uh . . . I had borrowed Daniel's jacket earlier. I ran into him after dinner and I was cold, so he gave me his jacket. All the blood got on that.'

'And then you took the jacket back to Daniel's room and left it there for us to find. For us to assume he'd been wearing it himself when he killed her.'

Svetlana's eyes went wide. 'No! I never wanted anyone to think that! I . . . I wasn't thinking, I guess. When I saw she was dead, all I knew was I wanted Daniel to comfort me. I ran to his room, and I guess I just took the jacket off while I was there and didn't think about anybody finding the blood.' She buried her face in her hands. 'Why didn't I wash it? Or burn it? Then he'd be free . . .'

Colin spoke gently. 'No, he wouldn't, because we have more on him than just the blood. And I'm afraid this sorry attempt at a confession isn't going to help Daniel either. You seem to know a fair bit about this murder' – he cast a severe glance at Emily, who grimaced an apology – 'but there's one thing you apparently weren't told. Taylor Curzon was not killed by a single blow to the head.'

Svetlana looked up. 'But – I told you—'

'In cases like these, it's what the pathologist tells us that counts. She was struck multiple times. It's possible the first blow was actually fatal, but the killer didn't stop there. He beat her head to a bloody pulp.'

Svetlana turned green and put her hand to her mouth.

'Interview terminated for a comfort break.' Colin stood and opened the door. 'The restroom is right over there.'

Svetlana sped out.

'You'd better go with her,' Colin said to Emily. She needed no urging on that point.

When Svetlana had finished vomiting, Emily helped her clean up and then held her as she sobbed. 'Why didn't you tell me? If I'd had more facts I could have made it convincing. I could have made them take me and let Daniel go.'

Emily rubbed the girl's back. 'I doubt that, Svetlana. Even

if your facts had been convincing, your manner would never have been. You simply don't have the bearing, the attitude, the *anything* of a killer.'

She put her hands on Svetlana's shoulders and held her at arm's length so she could look her in the eye. 'What you did today was very brave, if also incredibly foolish. But the situation is not as desperate as you think. You didn't give me a chance to tell you – we do have a glimmer of hope. Colin let me look at the initials in Curzon's appointment book, and they were almost certainly forged. If that can be proved, it's a strong indication that someone was trying to frame Daniel.'

Hope dawned in Svetlana's eyes for the first time since Daniel had been taken in for questioning. 'Oh, Emily! Thank you! That's the best news I've had in – well, ever. Oh, thank God! Thank God!'

Emily didn't want to prick Svetlana's balloon of confidence, but she knew these grounds for hope were still fairly flimsy. It was one thing to prove evidence suggesting Daniel was framed, but quite another to discover who had done the framing. They still had a long way to go.

Colin called Emily back late that afternoon. 'You were right,' he said. 'The handwriting guy says there's a ninety percent chance those initials were forged. I've never heard him commit himself to that extent before.' He paused. 'Kind of makes me feel stupid for not noticing sooner.'

'You had no particular reason to look closely. The point is, we know now.'

'Yes. And Wharton says we can go back to campus for a more thorough search and door to door first thing Monday morning.'

Emily crossed herself gratefully. 'Thank God for that.'

She allowed herself a true day of rest on Sunday with church, a movie, and cuddle time with the cats. In the evening she called Luke and gave him the news.

'Well, well, well. So you caught Colin out on physical evidence. I'm going to have to rib him about that next holiday gathering.'

'Don't be too hard on him. He feels badly enough about it already.'

'Nah, I'll go easy. He's a good kid. But like all kids, he's got a lot to learn.'

She told Luke about breaking Douglas's and Richard's alibis as well. His reaction was like Colin's on steroids.

'Em, how many times have I told you not to put yourself in a dangerous situation like that? You do not let yourself be alone with a viable murder suspect. You especially don't let him know what you've got on him. Leave that to the police.'

'The police weren't doing anything. Colin would have, left to himself, but Sergeant Wharton dug his fat toes in and wouldn't let him budge. Besides, I wasn't alone with Douglas – Marguerite was there – and I've known Richard for years. Much as I dislike the man, he's too much of a wimp to lash out in cold blood. A crime of passion might be just barely within his scope, but not cold-blooded murder. And in broad daylight, too.'

'I don't care how much you think you've got him figured, you never know what somebody will do under stress. Especially if he's killed before. Promise me you won't do anything that stupid again.'

Emily gave in. Luke might be a little overprotective, but at least it was out of love. 'All right. I promise.'

As for the rest of their conversation, if it had been written in a letter by Anne Shirley to Gilbert Blythe, it would have required a new pen.

TWENTY-FOUR

The weekend's cloudless skies meant Monday morning dawned even colder than the last two weeks had been. Emily resisted the temptation to drive down the hill, but she did take a thermos of coffee with her to the library, knowing she'd need to warm up once she got there.

She knew Colin would be on campus interviewing people again. He was trying to narrow down who might have written the initials DR in Curzon's appointment book as well as confirm who actually was in Vollum during the crucial hour of the murder.

Emily found it difficult to settle to work for wondering how Colin was getting on. But Svetlana was working diligently away on Emily's notes, and she couldn't sit there idly while her assistant labored. So she attempted to read. This was the last week of Paideia; next week she would have to give her desk back to the thesis student who occupied it during term time. She had to make the most of the little time she had left.

At noon Colin called her cell phone. 'Got some stuff to run by you. Want to grab lunch?'

'Sure. Commons?'

'Better off-campus. We don't want to be overheard.'

'Meet me outside the library and we can walk up to Baumgartner's.'

'Mind if we drive? I've been pounding the pavement all morning. My feet are burning and frozen at the same time.'

Emily smiled to herself at the thought that she was more willing to exert herself than this fit young man. But she would humor him. His must be a taxing job, both physically and mentally.

When they had ordered, Colin wrapped his hands around his coffee cup and took a long sip. 'I'm frozen to my core. I guess Bede isn't that big as campuses go, but when you're trudging from end to end in search of folks it feels like the Russian steppes.'

'Interesting you'd choose that simile. It sounds like something I would say.'

He grinned. 'I guess you're rubbing off on me. Or maybe it's all the Russian names and whatnot associated with this case. That plus the weather. But I guess we need a few feet of snow to make it really feel like Russia.'

'That and a further temperature drop of about forty degrees. This is probably like October in Petersburg.'

'Glad we're not there, then.' He shivered.

'So has all your trudging paid off?'

'Maybe. Nothing definite, but some stuff that's suggestive.' He pulled out his notebook, then paused as the waiter delivered their soup and sandwiches. He took a slurp of beef barley soup before continuing.

'First of all, I've confirmed that Richard McClintock was in Vollum until at least eleven o'clock. Once I pinned Douglas Curzon down on his late visit to his wife, he told me he'd seen McClintock in the hallway on his way out.'

Emily's heart gave a little jump, but she reminded herself that she must strive to be impartial. 'So presumably Richard saw him as well?'

Colin nodded. 'Worse luck for us, though – Curzon was definitely on his way out, and he was not covered in blood. McClintock even heard the victim call out something after him, so she must still have been alive at that point. No reason for McClintock to lie to protect Curzon – he'd be more likely to try to implicate him if he could.'

Emily frowned. 'True. So they more or less clear each other?'

'More or less. Though we don't have a witness to McClintock leaving the building. We only have his word he left shortly after that without seeing the victim.'

So Richard could still be guilty. 'How did he justify having lied about his alibi?'

'Blustered a bit, then finally admitted he was afraid of being suspected because of his run-in with the victim earlier that day. He figured Douglas Curzon wouldn't blow his alibi because he wouldn't want to admit he'd been there himself. And McClintock didn't think anyone else had seen him.'

'In which he was correct. Sidney only saw his open door. So, in point of fact, we are no further forward, with those two at least.'

'No.'

'How about Goldstein? Did anybody happen to see him on campus that night?'

Colin held up a finger as he finished chewing and flipped through his notebook. 'Not a definite identification, but your friend Teresa did remember seeing someone with a similar silhouette in the parking lot when she left for the night. She thought it might be the same guy who bumped into her in the library, but he was wrapped up for the weather so she couldn't be sure.'

'Hmm.' Emily mentally ran through the list of everyone she knew who was on campus for Paideia. She couldn't think of anyone whose build resembled Goldstein's, but a slimmer man of similar height might bulk up in layers of winter clothing to resemble his weight. 'So you'll dig further on his alibi?'

Colin nodded. 'And I did have another piece of luck. Potential luck, anyhow.'

'How's that?'

'I found a student who was leaving the library at eleven thirty-five. She saw two men walking together. Crossing that circular drive—'

'Eliot Circle.'

'That's the one. Heading toward Vollum.'

'Did she recognize them at all?'

'No. It was dark and she didn't get close. But she got the impression it might have been a professor and a student. She said the professor one was kind of supporting the other, as if the student was drunk or ill. And she said the one who needed supporting looked taller than the other; he was kind of slumped, but their heads were still about even.'

Emily's stomach went cold. 'That sounds like Daniel. He's tall, and he was in a state to need supporting that night.'

'Yeah. But who was the older man? Douglas Curzon could pass for a professor, especially in the dark, but he's about the same height as Daniel. McClintock's shorter – could have been him – but why?'

'Yes, why?' Emily admitted reluctantly. 'Richard's not the type to go out of his way to help a student, and if he were helping him home to bed they would have been walking the other way.' She drummed her fingers on the tabletop as an inspiration hit her. 'What if . . . I've been saying all along someone was trying to frame Daniel. What if Richard killed Taylor, then found Daniel wandering around disoriented and decided to use him as a patsy? He led Daniel back to Taylor's office, where they "found" the body. He got Daniel to try to revive her – thus getting him covered in blood – while he pretended to call for help. And incidentally wrote Daniel's initials in the appointment book. Then he got Daniel out of there on some pretext – it wouldn't take much given the state Daniel was in – and hightailed it back home, ready to come back in the morning and pretend he knew nothing about it.'

'But then wouldn't McClintock have had blood on his clothes? If not from killing Curzon, then from helping Daniel out of there after he'd touched the body?'

'Probably. But have you examined his clothes?'

Colin stopped with his spoon halfway to his mouth. 'Now that you mention it, no. We never followed up that far on the other suspects once we had Daniel in custody.' He put down his spoon and slapped the table. 'Damn, I could kick myself. Or Wharton. By this time McClintock could have disposed of his whole wardrobe without a trace.'

'Theoretically, yes. But Marguerite always notices people's clothes; if she and I put our heads together, I bet we can remember what he was wearing that day. So at least you'd know what specifically to look for.'

'That would help, for sure.' Colin resumed his interrupted mouthful of soup. 'But look here – we still have to account for the statue as the murder weapon. You keep saying that it was used to frame Daniel, but if McClintock just happened to find him wandering around like you said, he couldn't have planned that.'

'Shoot. You have a point there. But the statue doesn't have to have been part of the frame-up. Taylor could have taken it, as I suggested before, to bait Daniel or bribe him or something. Richard could have seen it and grabbed it on the spot. That would fit with him killing her in a rage rather than a planned attack, as you said the wounds suggested.'

'True.' Colin frowned. 'I don't know, though. It all seems so random. McClintock happens to go into a murderous rage against Curzon that particular night, happens to find a weapon to hand that will implicate someone else, flees the building and happens to run into the very person who will be implicated, who happens very conveniently to be in a fugue state so he can be led around by the nose and covered in blood. What are the odds? Even a planned murder rarely goes right on that many fronts.'

Emily's stomach sank along with her favorite suspect's

likelihood. 'I have to admit you have a point. I always felt the case against Daniel was too neat, too pat, but this one does kind of lean in the opposite direction. Especially since we know of no way Richard could even have known that statue belonged to Daniel.'

She brightened slightly. 'Maybe Richard just happened to catch that tide in the affairs of men which, taken at the flood, leads on to fortune.' At Colin's blank look, she added, 'Shakespeare? *Julius Caesar*? Never mind. But isn't it sometimes the case that real life is more improbable than fiction could ever get away with being?'

'I guess. And I'm not ruling McClintock out, mind you. I'll definitely examine his clothing. And check his handwriting against that DR entry. Goldstein too, while I'm at it. I'm determined to cover all the bases this time around.' His face took on an expression she'd seen on his uncle more than once when they were on the trail of a killer.

They finished their meal and returned to campus, where they tracked down Marguerite in her office.

'Margot,' Emily said, 'do you happen to remember what Richard was wearing last Monday? The day of the murder? When we confronted him?'

'*Bien sûr*. I remember because his sweater was the same color as my dress. A deep bluish red.'

Blood red, Emily thought with a sinking heart. Oh, well, there was always luminol.

'What about a jacket?' Colin asked. 'Or overcoat? Anything like that?'

Marguerite wrinkled her nose. 'Richard has only the one sportscoat, a disreputable brown corduroy that sags and bags in all the wrong places. And in this weather he wears a parka – navy blue with a fur-lined hood.'

Colin gazed at her in admiration. 'What a memory,' he said. 'We should recruit you for the force.'

Marguerite gave him a mischievous smile. 'I will send you the bill for my consultant services.' His eyes widened, and she chucked him under the chin. 'Do not derange yourself, *mon petit*. I am joking.'

Colin reddened and cleared his throat. 'Well, uh, thank you

for your time, Professor Grenier. I'd better be going.' He fled with all decorous speed, leaving the two women to share a chuckle in his absence.

'Go easy on him, Margot,' Emily said with a grin. 'He's going above and beyond for me.'

'Such a young and fresh face, I could not resist. But I will not torment him further. I would not want to bring the wrath of your Luke down upon my head.'

Emily returned to the library, where she encountered Lauren in the lobby.

'Oh, hi, Emily,' Lauren said. 'I was hoping to run into you. I was wondering if you could recommend a book on the psychological profiles of Dostoevsky's characters. After we talked at your house at dinner and again the other night, I've been thinking about that some more, and I'd like to see what's been done in that area.'

'That's more along the lines of Daniel Razumov's research than mine,' Emily replied. 'But I'm sharing his table at the moment, and he obviously can't use his library books while he's in jail. Let's go see what's on his shelf.'

As they passed through the periodicals reading room on the way to the south stacks, Emily said in a low voice, 'This is still pretty hush-hush, but I think Oscar's prospects for a tenure-track job may be improving. Unless I'm very much mistaken, a certain little-loved department head is on his way out.' Richard might or might not be guilty of murder, but he was certainly guilty of plagiarism, and that would get him fired.

Lauren's eyes widened. 'Seriously? How intriguing! I don't suppose you can say any more?'

'Not just yet, no. And don't mention it to anyone else – not even Oscar, for the time being. Nothing is settled yet. But I intend to see it settled by the end of the week, before I go back to Stony Beach.'

Lauren put a conspiratorial finger to her lips, eyes sparkling. Just at that moment they rounded a bookcase and came within sight of Emily and Daniel's table. Emily's eyes were confronted with a scene that her brain took a moment to absorb, it seemed so improbable in that setting. And when she did absorb it, it was all she could do to keep her self-control. Would the past never let her be?

On the far side of the table, Svetlana was backed up against the window, face averted, struggling to free herself from the clutches of a man in a tweed jacket with slicked-back hair. His face was not clearly visible as he strove to mash his lips against Svetlana's while she turned her face aside to avoid him. But that jacket and hair could only belong to one person.

Sidney Sharpe.

The young man who claimed to be Daniel's best friend in the world was making a highly unwelcome pass at Daniel's beloved.

Emily called out, 'Mr Sharpe!' in the sternest tones she could muster while choking back bile. As she spoke, Lauren flew at Sidney's back and jumped up to catch his neck in a chokehold. With her feet dangling six inches above the floor she couldn't maintain the hold for long, but it only took a moment for Sidney to release Svetlana and spring away from her, smoothing his hair as if nothing had happened.

'Svetlana had something in her eye,' he said in his nasal voice, which wavered only slightly. 'I was helping her get it out.'

'Helping her, *my* eye,' Emily retorted. 'You were assaulting her. Lauren, will you please restrain Mr Sharpe while I call the police? I happen to know there's an officer quite close by.' She pulled out her phone and found Colin's number while Lauren twisted Sidney's arm behind his back. That girl must have had some serious martial arts training.

By this time Svetlana had recovered her breath and a modicum of her composure. 'Please, Emily. Don't bother. I'm sure it will never happen again.'

Emily paused with her finger poised to touch the screen. 'Are you sure? This is a serious offense, you know. Even if he doesn't try it again with you, there's no telling who else he might assault.'

'I . . . can't face the police . . . not now. Not after . . .'

'I understand.' Emily slid her phone back into her coat pocket. 'But you should understand this, Mr Sharpe – I will be reporting your conduct to Detective Richards. He won't arrest you unless Svetlana changes her mind and decides to press charges, but he will be keeping a close eye on you from now on. As will Professor Hsu and I.'

Sidney actually managed a shaky smile. 'Always nice to know one is being looked after. Now if you'll excuse me, ladies – things to go, places to see, people to do.' He pushed by Emily and scurried out of the room.

Emily hurried to Svetlana's side and helped her into a chair. The girl looked ready to collapse. Emily knew from experience exactly how she must be feeling, and her gorge rose against Sidney.

'Are you sure you're all right? He didn't hurt you?'

Svetlana shook her head. 'No. He'd only just cornered me when you came in. Thank God for your timing.'

Lauren gave a low whistle. 'That is one curious customer,' she said. 'Caught red-handed and no admission of guilt. Hardly even seemed to realize what he'd done or what kind of bullet he'd dodged with his victim refusing to press charges.' She turned to Svetlana. 'Do you know that guy?'

Svetlana shuddered. 'Oh, yes. He's a . . . a sort of hanger-on. Of my boyfriend, Daniel, primarily, but now I'm starting to think maybe it was partly about me all along.'

Emily pouched her lips in thought. 'I wonder . . . Of course you're very lovely, Svetlana, and any man might be interested in you for no other reason than that. But I wonder if Sidney doesn't see you as part of Daniel's world – his property, as it were – and he's trying to slide into the empty space Daniel has left behind.'

Lauren's eyes brightened with the thrill of discovery. 'Trying to take over Daniel's life. Because he really has none of his own. That's a fascinating thought. Kind of reminds me of Smerdyakov with Ivan. Don't you think, Emily?'

'Good point.' Gears clicked together in her mind. Smerdyakov had constructed a fantastical scenario in his mind and acted according to what he believed Ivan Karamazov was asking of him. 'Of course he's in a different book, and Raskolnikov was really guilty. But I wonder . . .' She realized she was babbling unintelligibly. 'Svetlana, if you're feeling up to walking, I think you'd better take the rest of the afternoon off and lie down.'

Svetlana nodded feebly and stood, pushing herself up with her hands on the desk.

'We'll walk you to your dorm,' Lauren said. 'Just in case.' She and Emily each took one of Svetlana's elbows and helped her out, reserving further comment until they could be alone.

TWENTY-FIVE

E mily and Lauren saw Svetlana safely to her room in the Old Dorm Block, then adjourned to the Paradox across the quad. Coffees in hand, they settled on a couch.

Emily said, 'Lauren, I'd be interested to get your perspective on all the suspects from a psychological point of view. There's so little reliable direct evidence in this case, I feel like we need to approach it more from the human angle.'

'Sure. Who are we talking about? Do I know them all?'

'Most likely not. I doubt you've met Saul Goldstein, Svetlana's father, or Curzon's ex-husband Douglas. I think they've ruled out Douglas anyway. But the one who's probably the frontrunner at this point is someone you do know – Richard McClintock. And it's just beginning to occur to me that Sidney Sharpe might be another – though I have neither evidence nor motive in his case, just a gut feeling there's something very wrong about that young man.'

'I'd certainly agree with that assessment. I think he may even be a psychopath. I'd have to know more to make a real diagnosis, but the complete lack of any feeling of guilt or responsibility for his actions towards Svetlana is a strong indicator.'

'Good point. He lies easily, too – isn't that something psychopaths do?'

'Absolutely. They lie like breathing. And they have no real regard for anyone but themselves, though they can put up a show of being concerned.'

Emily nodded. 'That sounds like Sidney. Though I have to say his show is getting less convincing.'

'And psychopaths don't hesitate to murder when they have something to gain by it.'

'Indeed. But I have no idea what Sidney would have to gain

by this particular crime. Taylor Curzon wasn't out to get him, either sexually or academically, as far as I know; he wasn't even on her radar. At one point I wondered if he might go to some lengths to protect Daniel, but a psychopath wouldn't do that, would he?'

'Not likely, no. Only to protect himself.'

Emily sipped her coffee meditatively. 'What about Richard, then? What's his profile? Because he definitely had both motive and opportunity.'

'Really? What was his motive? He wasn't in love with her, was he?'

'He lusted after her, certainly. But I don't think frustrated lust would have been strong enough to make him kill. I probably shouldn't be too specific at this point, but she had something on him – something quite damaging, potentially career-killing, that he assumed only she knew. He was wrong about that, but that's beside the point.'

Lauren's eyes danced with excitement. 'This is getting better by the minute! Let's see – Richard . . . He doesn't fit the profile for a psychopath, but he is extremely selfish. I'm not aware of anyone he genuinely cares for – are you?'

Emily shook her head. 'Maybe a pet. But even that would surprise me.'

'But he's not a narcissist, either – he doesn't have that inflated ego, that sense of being invulnerable. So in order to take the risk of killing someone, either he'd have to be very sure of being clever enough not to get caught, or he'd have to see the risk he faced in killing as less than the risk of Taylor revealing what she knew.'

Emily grimaced. 'Loss of his career versus life imprisonment. I know which risk I'd choose.'

'Me too, but what else does Richard have besides his career? No family, anyway.'

'And no outside interests that I know of. Certainly no faith. I guess it's possible he'd take the risk.'

'What about the clever planning aspect? He hasn't been arrested yet – someone else has – so presumably it was done fairly cleverly.'

Emily shook her head. 'No, that's the strange thing. It wasn't

clever at all. If Richard did it, Colin and I can't see how it could
even have been premeditated. It seems quite impulsive, and the
opportunity to implicate Daniel completely fortuitous.'

'So we're looking at an impulse killing? That's an altogether
different animal.' Lauren drummed her fingers on her coffee
cup. 'Could Richard be driven to kill on the spur of the moment?
On the one hand I wouldn't think he'd have the guts, but on
the other hand . . . What was the method?'

Emily wasn't sure she was authorized to reveal that detail,
but after all, Lauren was certainly not a suspect herself nor
likely to talk to any suspects. 'This is confidential, mind. But
she was beaten over the head with a bronze statuette. Quite
savagely.'

'Ooh, that does suggest strong, immediate provocation. Hmm.
I think almost anyone could potentially kill that way if sufficiently provoked.'

'And Taylor Curzon was without doubt the most provoking
woman I have ever had the misfortune to meet.'

'Well, there you go, then. I'd say, if the evidence stacks up,
you have yourself a credible suspect.'

Richard McClintock. From nuisance boss and plagiarist to
murderer in seconds flat? Was it possible? Emily could not kid
herself that it would be fair to take vengeance on her ancient
nemesis, the lecherous Professor Jenkins, by helping to convict
a man who merely happened to resemble him. But she could
not deny it would be satisfying.

From the Paradox, Emily and Lauren went their separate ways.
Emily walked toward the library, more out of habit than because
she expected to get any more work done that day; her thoughts
were too full of the present situation to allow her to immerse
herself fully in Dostoevsky's world. Besides, the clouds had
drawn in again, and this time Emily was sure in her aching
bones that snow was on the way. If she were going to be trapped,
she'd prefer to be trapped at home. The library was on the way,
so she could just collect her laptop and head on up the hill.

As she walked, she called Colin. Precisely because she so
badly wanted Richard to be guilty, her sense of justice compelled
her to share with Colin anything that might point toward

someone else as the murderer – even if it was little more than a gut feeling.

'Colin? Emily. Have you found anything on Richard?'

'Not yet. He told me he'd sent that particular shirt and jacket to the cleaners. I'm just about to go in there now.'

'I've had a thought about another line you might pursue.'

'What's that?'

'Sidney Sharpe.'

'Sidney? The student who placed Daniel in Vollum that night?'

'Yes. His evidence wasn't confirmed by anyone else, was it?'

'No. Seems like all the other people in the building were in their offices with their doors closed.'

'My guess is that the encounter never happened. Sidney may have been there, but I'd bet Daniel didn't set foot in the building until later, after that student saw him crossing Eliot Circle.'

'What makes you say that?'

'It's not much more than a gut feeling. But this afternoon I surprised Sidney in the process of trying to force himself on Svetlana. Which makes me think he's not as great a friend to Daniel as he likes to make out.'

'You don't think he actually killed Curzon, do you? What motive would he have?'

'That I don't know. I have a glimmer, but it needs fleshing out.'

'OK, I'll get a swab and see if it matches any of the unidentified DNA we've found. And I'll check out his clothing as well.'

The mention of Sidney's clothing gave Emily another thought. 'That student who saw the two men crossing the circle. Did she say why she thought one of them was a professor?'

'Something about what he was wearing. Just a sec.' She heard the sound of pages flipping. 'He had on a knee-length overcoat and no backpack. She thought that would be odd for a student.'

Emily thought back to when she'd seen Sidney outdoors. 'Sidney wears a knee-length wool overcoat. And he carries a messenger bag rather than a backpack. Plus he's several inches shorter than Daniel.'

'Well, I'll be damned. I never would have thought of that.

But if they're sort of friendly, he might just have found Daniel wandering around disoriented and decided to help him home, right?'

'Possible, but we went over this with regard to Richard – they were going the wrong direction. Daniel lives in the Old Dorm Block, west of Eliot Hall. Vollum is east.'

'Shoot, you're right. OK, I think my priorities have just shifted. Since I'm here I'll check with the cleaners, but then I'm going to head straight back to talk to Sidney Sharpe.'

The conversation had taken Emily as far as the library entrance. Knowing Colin would soon be returning to campus, she settled in at her station in the library instead of going on home. On an impulse, she pulled her copy of *The Brothers Karamazov* off the shelf and began to read near the end – Ivan's conversations with Smerdyakov.

Smerdyakov, Ivan Karamazov's illegitimate half-brother, had at first idolized Ivan and taken his atheistic 'everything is permitted' philosophy much more literally and practically than Ivan had taken it himself. Trying in some way to become Ivan, he had taken it upon himself to commit the dark deeds he was convinced Ivan wanted him to perform – and for which he thus considered Ivan to be wholly responsible.

Immersed in the book, Emily had no concept of how much time had passed when she got a call from Colin. Since the room was apparently empty but for herself, she took the call there.

'Just got through interviewing Sidney Sharpe. He's a slippery character, all right. I couldn't pin him down on anything about his movements that night. Insisted his previous statement was correct, and that after he left the Paradox – where we have witnesses to confirm his presence up till eleven – he went back to his dorm to bed.'

'What dorm does he live in?'

'One of the Woodstocks.' The Woodstock dorms were a group of four largish houses at the far eastern end of campus, beyond the library, which at some point in the college's distant history had provided faculty housing. 'They call it the Russian House, whatever that means.'

'Each of the Woodstock dorms is dedicated to a different language. The students who live there are all studying that language, and supposedly they try to speak it in the house as much as possible. Didn't really work out that way when I lived there back in the day.'

'Oh, that explains it. Couple other students were talking gibberish in the common room. Must have been Russian. At any rate, Sharpe made no objection to my searching his room and confiscating the clothes he was wearing the night of the murder. But he wasn't any too happy about giving me a DNA swab. Claimed an overactive gag reflex and a nasty cold. Only when I suggested doing it down at the station with a doctor present did he finally relent.'

'That's suggestive, at any rate.'

'Yeah. But it isn't hard evidence. We won't have that until the lab gets to work and matches his DNA to something at the scene – preferably some of the unknown DNA found on the victim. I'm taking the swab in now, but it's getting late. Be a while before we have that result.'

Emily glanced out the window and realized the winter day was indeed drawing to a close. She didn't fancy walking home in the dark, especially since she would have to walk past the Russian House.

'Let me know when you find out anything. I'm going to head home and give all this a good think.' She ended the call and gathered her things.

Twilight was closing in as she left the library. The sun, as it dropped from the cloud-whitened sky, drew with it what little warmth the middle of the day had held. Emily shivered, turning the collar of her coat up around her throat and holding it closed with one gloved hand while the other grasped the handle of her briefcase.

As she turned eastward from the library entrance, she caught sight of Sidney walking some way ahead of her, in the direction of his dorm. She thought it odd that he would have left his dorm and be returning to it again in the short time since Colin had left him. Besides, she sensed something furtive in his attitude – he seemed hunched over and kept turning his head to right and left. As he veered off at an angle to pass around the combined physics and biology building, she thought she could see a lumpy shape under his overcoat. What could he be carrying that was too big to fit in his messenger bag?

Sidney paused at the entrance to the educational technology building and looked around more carefully. Emily ducked behind a pillar, wishing she knew more about following people than one could pick up from watching detective shows. After the door closed behind him, she quietly approached and entered the building herself. Sidney was just turning to the left at the end of the hallway. She hurried after him as quietly as the thick soles of her fur-lined boots would allow.

At the end of the second hallway was some sort of opening in the wall. Emily backed behind the turning and peeked around the corner to see Sidney take the bundle out from under his coat and shove it into that opening. Then, with a last furtive glance around him, he scurried toward a secondary exit door at the far end of the hallway.

When he was safely outside, Emily ran to the opening, which was covered by a steel flap engraved with the word 'Laundry'. Underneath that word was a printed sign that read 'Bunny suits only!' Emily put on hold her curiosity as to what place rabbit costumes or Playboy bunny uniforms could have in a college science building and slowly pushed open the flap, praying it would prove to lead only to a bin and not to a chute. She did not feel up to pursuing a chute to its outlet, wherever that might be.

Her prayers were answered. It was a bin, and all it contained was one large white plastic shopping bag with an Eddie Bauer logo on the side, bulging as if it contained something soft. With a stretch that twanged her lower back, she reached in and pulled the bag out.

Sidney's instinct for secrecy must have been contagious. Although the building was empty, Emily shoved the bag under her own coat and looked about for a private place to examine it. Her eye fell on a women's restroom down the hall.

Inside the handicapped stall, still wearing her outdoor gloves, she opened the bag and pulled out a large wad of white Tyvek. She shook it out and saw that it was a sort of coverall. Then she remembered having heard somewhere that these suits, worn in clean rooms or at crime scenes, had the nickname of 'bunny suits'. She supposed they must be used in the computer science department's hardware lab. But there were no lab classes during Paideia, and presumably the suits were meant to stay in the labs. What would Sidney have been doing with one?

She turned the suit around so the front was facing her and looked at it closely. The chest and arms of the coverall looked slightly smeared with a pinkish tinge. And hiding in the shoulder seam she could see a tiny spot of something that looked like blood.

TWENTY-SIX

Emily shoved the suit back into the bag and whipped out her phone to call Colin. He didn't answer, so she left a cryptic message: 'Call me as soon as you can. And don't bother testing Sidney's clothes.'

She wished with all her soul she had her old office back, or some kind of private place on campus where she could keep her discovery safe and be alone with her thoughts. Home it would have to be. She made room in her wheeled briefcase for Sidney's bag, pushing it clear to the bottom where it would be covered by her other things.

She left the restroom and headed first toward the door by which Sidney had left the building. Then she realized that path would lead her directly past the Russian House, where he had presumably been going. She changed course and went back to the main entrance instead. From there she could take a path that led along the far side of the parking lot, skirting the block of dorms altogether.

Darkness was closing in, and with it the clouds that had been lowering all afternoon. The first fat flakes of snow drifted before her as she pushed the door open.

She hurried along the walk, head down to keep the snow out of her eyes. The path was well lit but deserted. Emily would have given much to be surrounded by a bustle of people until she was well clear of Sidney's dorm.

The snow was escalating rapidly, forming a soft carpet that muffled her footsteps as she walked. That meant it would also muffle the steps of anyone who might be approaching. She raised her head and looked around, but the snow was already so dense she could not see beyond the halo of the streetlight under which she was passing. She wondered if her project of walking home was really so wise after all. Maybe she should have begged shelter in Marguerite's office instead.

She passed out of the light's halo into darkness. Now she had to focus on the path, which she could barely discern as a smooth gray space between two swaths of more textured gray on either side. As she approached the next streetlight she raised her head again, and looming out of the darkness beyond its halo she saw a shadowy form.

Emily slowed, her heart in her throat. Should she turn and run? Pass on as if all were normal? Or take her stand under the light and confront this shadow, which she was sure must be Sidney?

She took a deep breath and reminded herself that Sidney did not know she had found the bunny suit. He had no reason to think she even suspected him of the murder, let alone that she had what was probably proof of his guilt. She could simply act normally and nothing untoward would happen.

God willing.

The shadow moved into the light. Between the layers of coat, scarf, and hat she could barely discern a pair of round, wire-rimmed, cold-fogged lenses. Sidney.

As if on cue, they both put on bright smiles. Emily hoped hers didn't look as fake as Sidney's did.

'Professor Cavanaugh,' he hailed her. His voice held an edge of something – hostility? fear? – beneath its surface cheer. 'What brings you out on a night like this?'

'Just trying to get home,' Emily replied. 'Although I must say that looks a lot more difficult now than it did when I left the library. I can't believe how quickly this snow came on.'

'Let me escort you. I can't claim to have snow-melting superpowers, but at least I can catch you if you slip.'

Emily thought fast, not allowing her smile to waver. The last thing she wanted was to be alone with this young man, either on the street or, God forbid, in her own home. But it was probably a good idea to keep him close until she could get in touch with Colin.

'You know, on second thought, I'd rather wait out the storm on campus. I think I'll go back to Paradox Lost and have some hot chocolate. If you'd like to join me? I'm buying.'

'How can I resist such a charming proposal?' He offered her his elbow. As she was hesitating – trying to overcome her aversion to touching him, even through layers of cloth, so as not to arouse his suspicions – another shadow loomed up behind him.

Colin's voice spoke out of the whirling snow. Emily's relief was palpable.

'Emily? I got—'

Before he could say more, she interposed loudly, 'Detective Richards! Mr Sharpe and I were just on our way to Paradox Lost for some hot chocolate. Care to join us?'

Colin's mouth snapped shut as Sidney turned back to face him. That had been close. If Colin had said anything to betray that Emily was on to Sidney – well, she didn't want to think about what might have happened.

'That would just about hit the spot. I'm frozen to my core.' Colin stepped between Sidney and Emily and offered Emily his arm. Thank God he'd inherited his uncle's chivalry. 'Where is this Paradox Lost? You're not talking about the regular Paradox, I hope? That's clear across campus.'

'No, this is an outpost right here in the science building. Just around the corner.' They headed back the way Emily had come.

Colin kept up a breezy chatter as they walked, but Emily could feel the tautness of his arm through the layers of gloves and coats. He was on the alert lest Sidney make any move to escape, or worse.

But apparently Sidney was still at the stage of caution where he felt, as did Emily, that acting normally was the best defense. They reached the café without incident.

Emily stepped toward the counter, but Colin moved ahead of her. 'Allow me. Three hot chocolates, please,' he said to the barista. Then he ushered the other two toward a table. All his actions sent the message that although he'd been late to the party, he was in charge of this encounter.

That was fine with Emily – in fact, she was grateful – except that Colin still didn't have all the facts. She racked her brain for a way to communicate with him without Sidney hearing, or at least suspecting something.

She positioned her briefcase on the floor between her chair and Colin's and unzipped it, pretending to look for something. With a lightning glance at Colin that she hoped was full of urgency, she held the compartment open for a moment and pushed her books out of the way so the plastic bag was visible. There was no way to communicate what it contained or how she'd come by it, but at least Colin seemed to get the message that the bag was in some way significant, and that this significance should not be betrayed to Sidney.

They talked about the weather – which at this point was worth talking about – until their drinks were ready. After a few sips, Sidney excused himself, looking quite uncomfortable, and headed toward the restroom. Emily supposed his bowels had absorbed the fear he was trying so hard to conceal.

When he was out of earshot, Colin whispered to her, 'There's no other way out of here, is there?'

'Not that I know of. Not even a window in the restroom.'

'Good. Now what's in that bag?'

Keeping an eye on the restroom door, she related to him in an undertone her experiment in covert surveillance and what she had discovered. 'The coverall's been wiped off, but it still has pinkish smears on the front and one tiny spot in the seam that looks like blood.'

Colin gave a low whistle. 'Sounds like we've got him.'

Emily hushed him with a look. 'He's coming.'

Colin whipped out his phone and sent a text. *Backup*, he mouthed to her. He just managed to slide his phone back into his pocket before Sidney reached the table.

Emily divined the need to keep Sidney in place and unsuspecting until the backup arrived – which, given the weather, could take a while. Time for a spate of gripping small talk. Not, unfortunately, her strong point.

'Paideia's drawing to a close, I'm afraid,' she said to Sidney. 'Have you managed to accomplish whatever it was you set out to do in this time?'

His smile seemed sinister, but perhaps it was just her imagination. 'I believe so,' he said. 'At least, the really important things.' He volunteered no information about what those were. Surely he couldn't have come to campus this month with the express goal of killing Taylor Curzon and framing Daniel for it. 'What about you, Professor? How is your research coming along?'

'Pretty well, all things considered.' This was an exaggeration, but perhaps after tonight she'd be less distracted. She ventured on another tactical fib. 'I've decided to narrow my focus somewhat. I'm concentrating on Dostoevsky's treatment of repentance and restitution. The redemption of the fallen man.'

Sidney bared stained and crooked teeth in a derisive grin. 'Redemption? An outmoded idea, surely. People don't change – at least, not for the better.'

'Oh, but I believe they can and do, with the help of God. Dostoevsky certainly believed that. Look at Raskolnikov. Or Dmitri Karamazov.'

'Spending their lives in exile? You call that improvement?'

'I'm talking about internal change. They were both determined to live better lives, to overcome the demons within them. And they'd made a start on that by the ends of their respective stories.'

'But what about Ivan Karamazov? Or Rogozhin from *The Idiot*? You can't say they were redeemed.'

'They lacked faith. Descent into despair or madness is often the lot of those who lack faith, if they're faced with a crisis.'

He snorted. 'And what about Prince Myshkin? He had faith, and look where it got him. A gibbering idiot with no hope of recovery.'

'Myshkin was a martyr. His mind was defeated by its own illness and by the actions of the people around him. That doesn't mean his soul was damned. I'm sure that even through the wreck of his physical brain, his soul was held tenderly in the hands of God.'

At this point Emily realized that both her companions were staring at her uncomprehendingly – Sidney because he had no understanding of spiritual matters, Colin presumably because he was not familiar with Dostoevsky. And perhaps he had no understanding of spiritual matters either. One could be a good cop without believing in redemption, she supposed.

'I see Dostoevsky as focusing on retribution,' Sidney said. 'People get what's coming to them in his stories. Exile, imprisonment, madness, murder.' His eyes darkened and a shadow passed over his face. 'Suicide.'

A shiver passed through Emily as she remembered Smerdyakov's untimely end. It occurred to her that perhaps being arrested would prove to be Sidney's salvation – from himself.

Sidney stood suddenly, jostling the table and sloshing hot chocolate out of all their cups. 'If you'll excuse me—'

Colin leapt to his feet a split second after Sidney and grabbed him by the elbow. 'I don't think so, Mr Sharpe. You're coming to the station with me for further questioning.'

Sidney spluttered, attempting vainly to wrench his arm free. 'You have no right—'

'I have every right. Because of something Mrs Cavanaugh has right there in her bag.'

Emily pulled out the white plastic bag with its distinctive Eddie Bauer logo and held it well out of Sidney's reach.

He lunged for the bag, toppling the flimsy table and spilling hot chocolate everywhere. Emily retreated out of reach, shoving the bag under her now-sopping coat. Colin grabbed for Sidney's coat collar, but Sidney twisted away and made for the door.

The door opened from the outside. Two uniformed policemen stood in the doorway.

'Grab him!' Colin shouted. And they did.

To her astonishment, Colin invited Emily to ride along with him to the station while the uniforms took Sidney in their black-and-white. 'I'll need to get a formal statement from you about finding that bag. May as well do it now.'

Emily would have preferred to wait until they could drive in snow-free daylight, but she supposed time was of the essence. 'Of course.'

'I'm hoping Wharton will be gone for the day and the captain will let me question Sharpe on my own. You can watch through the two-way mirror if you want.'

Emily's natural curiosity warred against her compassion – or was it merely squeamishness that made her reluctant to witness Sidney's further degradation?

'We'll detain him for now while we get the bunny suit tested. Unless we get a confession – then we can arrest him right away. Otherwise, once the suit tests positive for Curzon's blood and Sharpe's DNA, we'll arrest him and let Daniel go.' He blew out a long breath as he inched the car through the swirling whiteness. 'And then I'll find some excuse to hightail it out of town, because Wharton is going to be out for my blood.'

'Why? If you've found the real murderer?'

'Because I'll have done it all on my own – with your help, of course, but behind Wharton's back. I will have exonerated his pet suspect and grabbed all the glory for the real catch. Not the way to win friends and influence people at this station.'

Emily had no response. Of course, she knew cops were people too, as fallible as anyone else; but it saddened her that they would let personal jealousies and resentments take precedence over the conscientious execution of their duties.

'At least I'll have to put up the best case I possibly can so the captain will back me up. You worked out how Sharpe did it?'

'I think so. In fact, Sidney as the killer makes better sense of the Bronze Horseman statuette than any other theory we've looked at. He knew where Daniel kept the statue and what it meant to him. He was always hanging around the library; he could have taken it at any time.'

'OK, I see that. But that makes the killing totally premeditated. And why frame Daniel? I thought he worshiped him.'

'Worship can so easily go sour, especially if the idol proves to have feet of clay. Daniel's only human. I don't know what specifically he may have done to turn Sidney against him, but I imagine it wouldn't have taken much to tip the balance.' She thought back over the scenes she had read that afternoon between Smerdyakov and Ivan. 'Or, conceivably, he could have set Daniel up in order to provide himself with a safety net – not planning on Daniel being arrested, but ready to drop him in it if Sidney were arrested himself.'

'Hmph. Well, setting that aside – walk me through how you see it playing out that night.'

'This is pure speculation, of course, and I haven't had time to iron out the wrinkles yet. But let's suppose Sidney planned ahead *how* to do the murder, but not *when*. He stole the statuette and the bunny suit in preparation, maybe even carried them with him in his bag. Then Monday night he ran into Daniel wandering around in a fugue state and he thought, here's my chance. He must already have known Taylor was still in her office – in fact, he was most likely telling the truth about having been in the building at ten-fifteen.'

'Yeah, no reason to think otherwise. Maybe that bit about seeing Daniel there was on the level too.'

'Possibly. But he wouldn't have wanted Daniel around while he was actually doing the murder – in case Daniel remembered it later on. Maybe Sidney took him along to the Paradox to establish his alibi and parked him there, hoping he'd stay put. Then Sidney went back to Vollum, put on the bunny suit – possibly in the restroom, though he'd have risked being seen – then went to Taylor's office and killed her. He stashed the bunny suit somewhere, planning to dispose of it later. Maybe he even had the gall and the incredible luck to wash it off in the Vollum restroom without being observed.

'After that, he went to get Daniel, who may or may not have stayed in the Paradox all that time, but anyway, Sidney found him. He took Daniel back to Taylor's office, where they "discovered" her body. Somehow Sidney got Daniel to touch the body – probably encouraged him to check for signs of life, maybe try to revive her – so Daniel got her blood on his clothes. Oh, and at some point in this whole process, Sidney wrote Daniel's initials in the appointment book.'

Colin shook his head. 'This "plan" has so many variables, it blows my mind that it almost succeeded. I guess even for killers there's some equivalent of beginner's luck.'

'I know. Fortune favors the bold, I suppose. Anyway, after that he probably escorted Daniel back to his dorm and put him to bed, making sure he didn't change out of his bloody clothes.

'As for what Sidney did with the bunny suit – where he stashed it, why he didn't put it in the dedicated laundry bin right then – I have no idea. Maybe he had a hiding place he thought was secure, but after your last interview with him he got the wind up and decided the bin would be more anonymous, less likely to be traced to him.'

'But surely he would have known his DNA could be on the suit? He may be crazy, but he isn't stupid.'

Emily shrugged. 'Either he forgot about that, or he trusted the suit wouldn't be found and linked to the crime. Or he thought he himself would never be suspected and tested. If he is indeed mentally ill – and I think he is – that kind of arrogant assumption wouldn't be out of character.'

By this time they'd reached the Hawthorne Bridge, where the colder pavement over the water risked turning the growing carpet of snow into ice. Colin slowed to a crawl, although he had taken the time back on campus to put chains on his tires. 'Once we get over the bridge we're almost there,' he said through gritted teeth. 'God, I hate snow.'

Emily had always loved snow in the past, but tonight it did seem sinister. With the swirling whiteness obscuring all the modern buildings and freeways around her, she could almost believe herself to be crossing the Neva, heading toward the majestic Baroque streets and squares of St Petersburg. She could be inside one of Dostoevsky's novels – where anything might happen.

TWENTY-SEVEN

At the station, Colin led Emily to the observation area next to the interview room. He went to the lab to drop off the bag with the bunny suit, then returned to check in with her before going in to question Sidney. Behind Colin was a tall gray-haired man whom he introduced as Captain Ramirez. Emily stood to shake the captain's hand.

'I understand we have you to thank for our suspect here,' he said. 'Ordinarily we don't like members of the public to get this involved in a case, but Richards tells me you come highly recommended. I served with his uncle Luke many years ago, back in our army days. Good man. And I think I even remember him showing around a picture of a beautiful redhead. Could that possibly have been you?'

Emily gave a shy smile. 'I certainly hope it was. Luke and I fell in love all those years ago, but then life got in the way and we didn't get back together until last summer. He seems to have connections everywhere.'

'Indeed he does. Quite the people person. Young Richards here has inherited his uncle's persuasive powers – he's talked me into letting him lead this interview. I'm going to sit in for form's sake, but this one's all yours.' He clapped Colin on the shoulder. 'If all this goes well, you could be heading for a promotion, son.'

Colin's Adam's apple bobbed and his mouth twitched, as if he were trying not to smile. 'Yessir. Thank you, sir.' He cleared his throat. 'You OK, Emily? Can I get you some coffee, glass of water?'

'Too late for coffee – I'd never sleep – but I'd love a cup of tea. I haven't quite warmed up yet.'

'Coming right up.' Colin sprinted down the corridor and returned in a few moments with a steaming styrofoam cup, Lipton tag hanging off its rim. Emily suppressed a grimace. She'd been spoiled by Katie's imported loose-leaf tea, brewed and served in fine china. But at least this was hot.

She cradled the cup in her hands and nodded to the two men as they left for the interview room. Behind their backs, she made the sign of the cross in the air. They were going to need all the blessing they could get.

She'd been watching Sidney through the two-way mirror as she waited for Colin to return from the lab. He'd sat nearly motionless, arms crossed over his chest, staring inscrutably at the door. The glare of the bright ceiling light off his round lenses concealed his eyes and made it impossible to discern his expression. It was as if he had simply shut down, waiting for something to happen. A robot needing human contact to bring him to life.

When the door opened to admit Colin and Captain Ramirez, Sidney leaned forward, uncrossing his arms. The light no longer hit his lenses, and she could see his eyes. They focused on Colin with an intensity that made Emily devoutly thankful she was not in the room with them. Sidney Sharpe was not a physically powerful young man, but the psychic energy he radiated in that moment could have felled a giant.

The fact that Colin did not flinch raised him a notch in her estimation. She'd liked him all along, but now he was showing a mettle to match his uncle's. Luke would be proud.

Colin switched on the recorder and went through the spiel – date, time, names of those present.

'Mr Sharpe, you were observed earlier this afternoon entering the educational technology building on the Bede campus, where you dropped a white plastic bag containing a clean-room coverall into the designated laundry bin. That coverall was retrieved and found to be stained with blood. Would you like to tell us about that?'

Sidney gave a smile that reminded Emily of a serpent. 'What's there to tell? You seem to know all about it.'

'First of all, what were you doing with that coverall? There are no classes involving the clean room during Paideia.'

'Oh, I borrowed it for a project of my own. I'm building a computer from scratch in my spare time.'

Colin made a note, presumably to have the clean room searched for evidence of such a project. 'Why didn't you put the coverall into the laundry as soon as you'd finished with it?'

'I'd nicked myself with one of the tools and bled on it. I wanted to clean the blood off right away, before it had a chance to set.'

'Very public-spirited of you. Still, you could have done that right in the building and then put the coverall into the bin. Why take it away?'

Sidney blinked twice. 'I was in a hurry. I had to be somewhere.'

'Which would mean the blood would have time to dry anyway. So there really was no point in taking it away.'

Sidney's mouth opened and shut. He gave a self-deprecating smile. 'Silly me. I just didn't think of that at the time.'

Colin raised one eyebrow. 'So when was this? That you used the coverall and took it away?'

'This morning. Right before lunch. I had arranged to meet Mr Goldstein for lunch.'

'So he can verify that?'

'Well, I'm not sure. He didn't show up, so it's possible he'd forgotten all about it.'

That Sidney certainly was a slippery character. But he was clearly making this up on the fly; it was impossible that it would all hold up under scrutiny.

'So why did you wait until late afternoon to return the coverall?'

'I got busy. One thing and another. Including being interviewed by you, Detective.' He shrugged. 'I figured since the blood had set, there was no hurry. I waited until I happened to be passing that way.'

Colin flipped back through his notebook. 'I interviewed you in your dorm room, finishing at four oh five p.m. The dorm is southeast of the ed tech building. But you were seen approaching the building from the west at four-fifteen. Not much time to have done some other errand and be passing back that way.'

Sidney swallowed visibly and shot out a pointed tongue to wet his lips. 'I, uh – I went over to Vollum to see my advisor. But he wasn't in, so I headed back to the dorm. I had the coverall in my bag, so I stopped by the ed tech building and dropped it off.'

Colin's stare bored into Sidney until he dropped his eyes. 'We'll be checking on all that, of course.' He gave that a moment to sink in, then went on. 'Let's leave the coverall for the moment and go back to your movements on the night of the murder.'

Sidney blinked and adjusted his glasses. 'Remind me, Detective, which night was that?'

Emily watched Colin's nostrils flare as he absorbed this obvious delaying tactic with no verbal reaction. 'Monday the fourteenth. A week ago today. As you remember perfectly well.'

'Of course. Silly me. So much going on right now. I'm afraid I got a little muddled.' Another smile. This one might have looked convincingly innocent on someone else.

Colin absorbed this without comment. 'Let's start with your previous statement. You said you saw Daniel Razumov in Vollum Center at ten-fifteen that evening.'

'That's correct.'

'What were you doing in Vollum at that time?'

Sidney licked his lips again. 'Another attempt to see my advisor.'

'At that hour?'

'He, uh . . . he tends to keep late hours. But he wasn't in that night.'

'Who is your advisor?'

'Professor Banerjee.'

'And where exactly is his office?'

Sidney swallowed with a grimace. His voice came out raspy. 'Could I have a glass of water?'

Colin nodded to the uniformed officer standing by the door. He went out, then came back in with a small paper cup, which he set before Sidney.

Sidney downed the water in one gulp. 'His office is on the main floor. Room two-thirteen.'

'So what were you doing on the third floor?'

'Did I say I was on the third floor? I think I said I saw Daniel coming down the stairs from the third floor.'

Colin flipped through the folder of statements next to him on the table, then back through his notebook. He took his time with this, and Emily could see the sweat starting to bead on Sidney's brow.

'Your original statement was vague as to your own where-abouts. But you told Professor Cavanaugh later that you had seen Professor McClintock's door open at that time. That puts you on the third floor.'

'Does it?' Sidney gave a nervous giggle. 'How odd. Oh, I remember now – I went up to use the restroom.'

'Isn't there a restroom on the main floor?'

'Yes, but it was . . . closed for cleaning. Yes, that's right.' He gave a triumphant smile.

At some point Sidney was bound to talk himself into a corner he couldn't talk himself out of, but he was creative – it could take a while. Emily admired the patience of the two policemen – especially the captain, who had sat motionless all this time, leaning back in his chair with his arms crossed, narrowly observing his suspect.

Colin gave Sidney a stare that would have wilted Emily, but Sidney kept smiling, although his hands, clasped on the table, grew white-knuckled with his effort to keep them still.

'Leaving that for now, you said you went from Vollum to the Paradox Café. Did you see where Daniel went?'

'Oh, ah . . . he came with me. Didn't I mention that?'

'You did not. We have witnesses to confirm you were at the Paradox from ten-thirty to eleven. Was Daniel with you the whole time?'

'Yes. In fact, I . . . I left him there.'

Emily was certain Sidney was only admitting this because he knew it could be confirmed. But it did fit in with her theory.

'And where did you go then?'

'I went to my dorm and to bed. I'm not one of these night owls who can stay up to all hours. I need my beauty sleep.' He made an attempt at a jocular grin.

'Can anyone confirm that?'

Once again Sidney licked his lips. 'I'm afraid not. I went straight to my room and didn't run into anyone else.'

Emily fidgeted, knowing that from here on Colin would be flying without a net. They had no witnesses to confirm that Sidney had been anywhere other than his dorm from eleven o'clock on – except the one student who had seen the two men crossing Eliot Circle over half an hour later, but she would not be able to swear to Sidney's identity. And the lab work to confirm that the blood on the coverall belonged to Taylor Curzon would take some time.

If only Emily and Colin had had more time to talk about Sidney's psychology, his motivation for the crime. She might have been able to give Colin clues about how to approach this next bit, how to hit Sidney where he was most vulnerable to shake him off his guard. She doubted whether Colin had sufficient experience to guide him in the right direction. He would have to trust to his instincts.

And perhaps to a bit of subterfuge. 'The thing is, we have a witness who saw you out and about later on. At' – again, Colin consulted his notes – 'eleven thirty-five, as near as she could place it. Crossing Eliot Circle toward Vollum. With Daniel.'

Sidney's mouth fell open. With painful slowness he closed it and swallowed. 'More water?' he croaked.

'Maybe later. Would you like to explain what you were really doing in those missing thirty-five minutes?'

Sidney's eyes darted around the room, as if he were searching for answers in the texture of the paint on the walls. 'I . . . oh, I remember, when I left Daniel I decided to go looking for Svetlana. Daniel seemed to be in pretty bad shape, but he wouldn't let me take him to his room. I thought Svetlana might be able to persuade him.'

'And did you find her?'

'No. She was out. Maybe went somewhere with her dad.'

'Mr Goldstein told us he had an early night that night. And the hotel staff where he's staying confirmed it. No mention of Svetlana being with him.'

'Well, I don't know where she was, do I? The library, maybe.' For the first time a hint of annoyance crept into Sidney's tone. Perhaps this was the initial sign of a crack in his façade.

'Anybody confirm this version of your story? Run into anyone at Svetlana's dorm?'

'No. Her roommate was out too, or at least didn't answer the door. I suppose all the other good little girls were asleep.'

'Right. So you didn't find Svetlana. Then what did you do?'

'I went back to the Paradox. I thought maybe if I couldn't get Daniel to go to his own room, I could persuade him to come back to mine, where I could keep an eye on him. He didn't look as if he should be left alone.'

'I see. And he agreed to this?'

'Well, I told him a tiny fib. I said we were going to the library to look for Svetlana.'

'You left the Paradox at eleven and presumably came back for Daniel at eleven-thirty, or thereabouts. Svetlana's room is in the Old Dorm Block, right across the quad from the Paradox. It took you half an hour to go there and back?'

Another swallow. 'No, of course not. But it took me a while to persuade Daniel to come with me. And then we had to move pretty slowly – he was leaning on me with most of his weight. And I'm not all that strong – I lift books, not barbells.' A deprecatory smile with a hint of pride behind it. Like Cecil in

A Room with a View, Sidney no doubt gloried in being 'a chap who is no good for anything but books.'

Colin did not look convinced. 'So Daniel spent the night in your room?'

'Ah – no. After we passed the library entrance, he sort of woke up and demanded to know where we were going. I admitted I was taking him to my dorm, but he shook me off and headed in the opposite direction. I guess he went home to bed.' A feral grin. 'Or back to Vollum to commit a murder.'

All this would be impossible to disprove, and Emily had to admit it was just as plausible as her own theory about how Sidney had committed the crime – in other words, only barely. But she was sure in her bones that Sidney was lying about everything except what he knew others had witnessed – and about the reasons even for that.

Time for the psychological approach. Emily crossed herself with a prayer for wisdom for Colin – the wisdom of the serpent, to match Sidney's own.

Colin leaned back in his chair, as if to suggest the serious part of the interview was over – they were just chatting now. Sidney's posture relaxed fractionally in response.

'You seem to have been awfully concerned about Daniel's welfare.'

A bright smile. 'Of course. He's my best friend.'

Colin raised one eyebrow. 'Really? That's not what he says. I believe he referred to you as' – Colin pretended to consult his notes – 'a nuisance. And a creepy nuisance, at that.' He flipped a page. 'Ah yes, here it is. He said you were a leech.'

Sidney's nostrils flared. 'I don't believe you. Daniel would never say that.'

Colin shrugged. 'Believe what you want. But he said it. Pretty emphatically, as I recall.'

Sidney's mouth worked, as if words were fighting each other inside it. His eyes stared past the two policemen at some scene playing out in his own mind. 'That Judas. After all I've done for him. How could he?'

'Just what have you done for him?'

Sidney's breath came labored. 'Stood up for him with Curzon. Even tried to get her to focus on me instead of him. And when that didn't work . . .' A smile of genuine self-satisfaction spread across Sidney's face. 'I solved his problem for him. Made it completely go away.'

'What problem?'

'Curzon. I made Curzon go away.' He sat back in his chair and snapped his fingers. 'Just like that.'

TWENTY-EIGHT

Sidney clammed up after that; Colin couldn't get another word out of him. He simply sat there, his eerie smile fixed on his face like a rigor mortis grin.

'Never mind,' Colin said to Emily after the uniformed officer had taken Sidney away to a cell. He went docilely, not seeming to notice what was happening to him. 'That last admission was near enough to a confession to be going on with. We'll get the full story out of him sooner or later. Meanwhile, I'd love to release Daniel right away, but I'm afraid it will have to wait for morning for all the paperwork. Be tough to get him home tonight, anyway.'

Emily nodded. 'Speaking of getting home . . .'

Colin clapped his hand to his forehead. 'Shoot, that's right! You came with me. Well, I guess we'll have to brave it. I don't want you to have to spend the night in a holding cell. I've done it once or twice in a pinch – believe me, comfortable they're not.'

'You know what, I don't want to make that drive any more than you do. I'll just get a room in a downtown hotel. Then you'll only have to drive me a few blocks.'

Colin's face brightened. 'Do you mind? That would be terrific. Only I'm not sure I can get the department to pay for it – you are here sort of unofficially, after all.'

'Don't worry about that. I can afford it.' She smiled. 'I think I'll go to the Benson, if they have a room open. I've always wanted to stay there but never had an excuse before.'

'Perfect. Then I can let Goldstein and Douglas Curzon know they're free to leave town. As soon as the weather clears, at least.'

She called ahead, not wanting to risk Colin having to drive to another hotel if the Benson was full. The desk clerk demurred at first, but Colin got on the line and lent his authority to the request and the clerk finally admitted that they could find Emily a room. 'All we have is a suite on the tenth floor,' he said. 'I'm afraid it's rather pricey.' He named a figure, and Emily flinched. Her old average-income sensibilities were still with her.

But she reminded herself that she was wealthy now. 'That will be fine,' she said. 'Is it possible to purchase necessities in the hotel? I got trapped downtown unexpectedly – I don't have any luggage.'

'Of course. The room is stocked with basic toiletries, bathrobes, and a hair dryer, and the hotel shop has anything else you might need.'

Colin got her to the hotel safely and escorted her to her room, since Douglas's and Goldstein's rooms were on the same floor. She was still admiring all the suite's amenities – including what would have been an impressive view of downtown had she been able to see past the snow – when she heard a soft tap at the door. Assuming it was Colin with a last check-in, she opened the door with a smile, then was startled to see Douglas Curzon standing before her.

He gave a sheepish smile. 'Now that you know I'm not a murderer, could I possibly persuade you to have dinner with me? I promise to behave like a perfect gentleman.'

Emily hesitated, but in truth she had no wish to spend the entire evening alone. The specter of Sidney's madly fixed smile still haunted her. And now that she thought about it, she was starving – it was well past her normal dinner hour. 'Will you promise to moderate your wine consumption as well?'

'Certainly. That won't be difficult now that the stress of being a suspect is past. In fact, callous as it may seem, now that the immediate shock of Taylor's death is past also, I feel a bit like celebrating. I'm a free man at last.'

Emily grabbed her purse, and as she closed the door behind her, Douglas added, 'Oh, and did I tell you? I got my painting back! The police found it for me, of all things. You'll never guess where.'

Emily had a sudden inspiration. 'On the back of the icon in her office?'

His face fell. 'How did you know? That's exactly right. The witch had cut the painting out of its frame and stapled it to the back of her contraband icon. Nothing was sacred to that woman.'

'I'm so glad you got it back. But I'm even more glad that once the police have finished with it, the icon will be returned to where it belongs – in a church somewhere in Russia.' At least, she hoped that would be its ultimate fate.

Once they were settled in the restaurant and had placed their orders, Douglas said, 'Can you tell me anything about this person they've arrested?'

Colin hadn't said anything about confidentiality. She supposed at this point it couldn't hurt. 'He's another of Taylor's students. Sidney Sharpe.'

Light dawned in Douglas's eyes. 'Odd-looking sort of chap, dresses more like a stereotypical professor than a student?'

'That's the one. Did you meet him?'

'Not to say *meet*, but I did see him exiting Taylor's office as I was about to enter it. The Friday before the murder.' He colored deeply. 'She taunted me with him, in fact. Said I stood no higher in her estimation than he did, in . . . one particular respect.'

Emily graciously avoided probing him on that issue. 'Did you get the impression Sidney had just been . . . shall we say, proposing himself as a replacement for Daniel?'

'I did indeed. And she had laughed him out of the room.'

'Did you mention this to the police?'

'No. It didn't seem relevant, since it happened several days before the murder.'

'It does contribute to establishing his motive, though. Colin may want you to add that to your statement before you leave town.'

Douglas gave a resigned sigh. 'No rest for the wicked. Oh well, it looks like I may be trapped here for at least another day, anyway, with all this snow.' He looked meditatively out the window, then asked, 'Do you suppose that was young Sharpe's entire motive? That she had rejected him?'

'Not really. I think it was a great deal more complicated than that. Are you familiar with *The Brothers Karamazov*?'

'I've read it. Some years ago at this point.'

'I think Sidney was a sort of Smerdyakov to Daniel's Ivan.'

Douglas's eyebrows rose. 'Indeed? So you believe he killed Taylor because he thought Daniel wanted him to?'

'Something like that. Only he also tried to frame Daniel for the murder, so clearly his motivation was more convoluted. This afternoon I caught him making a pass at Daniel's girlfriend. I think on some level he was trying to take over Daniel's life.'

Douglas blinked. 'That sounds . . . rather mad.'

'I think he is mad. And I'm quite relieved that he is now in custody, where he can't hurt anyone else.'

'Thanks largely to you, it seems.' He raised his wine glass toward her. 'To the smartest and most beautiful lady detective I know.'

Emily acknowledged both compliments with downcast eyes. 'And I propose that for the rest of this meal we forgo all further talk of murder.' She gave him a stern glance. 'And all personal compliments.'

He grinned. 'Agreed.'

Emily spent the night in luxury that surpassed even that of Windy Corner – soaking in a hot Jacuzzi with a glass of champagne and a box of fine chocolates at her side, dressing in the filmy negligée she'd chosen from the hotel gift shop (which after this she intended to save for her honeymoon), and sinking into a bed that seemed entirely composed of down.

Before surrendering to sleep, she called Luke. Not only did she want him to know everything that had happened and how much cause he had to be proud of his nephew, but she needed to process the whole course of events by talking it through with someone who had not been directly involved.

When she finished her recital, he said, 'You know, I'm actually glad it turned out not to be McClintock. I couldn't help but feel you were beating a dead horse on that one. I mean, if you'd had a chance to put away the guy who really assaulted you all those years ago, that would have been one thing. But to take it out on somebody who just reminds you of him – you're better than that, Em. That would have haunted you for a long time.'

Emily bridled. 'I would never have tried to pin a murder on an innocent man.'

'I'm not saying you would, and I doubt Colin would have gone along with it anyway. I'm just saying you might have felt that way – you would have blamed yourself for letting your feelings cloud your judgment. And for gloating over your enemy's downfall. This way, all that doesn't arise.'

Luke knew her so well. 'Yes, it is better this way as far as I'm concerned. It looks like I will have a chance to gloat over Richard's downfall, though. But for something he really did. Taylor's accusation of plagiarism was for real. Marguerite and I got the evidence from the student involved, and she's taking it to the review board. Richard will be out on his ear.'

'Win-win, then. You'll never have to see him again. You and I can bury those old memories together.'

'Amen to that.'

Emily awoke late, refreshed and lightened by the knowledge that an innocent young man had been vindicated, largely by her efforts, and would soon be restored to his home and the woman he loved. The fact that a guilty young man would soon meet his well-deserved fate gave her no joy at all.

She was still wearing the cushy-soft hotel bathrobe and breakfasting on strawberries and a fresh croissant – along with a bit more champagne – when Colin called. 'Daniel's being processed out right now, and I'm going to drive him home. I thought you might want to come along, if you're ready.'

Emily looked around the beautiful room with a sigh. Her house on Woodstock would seem like Raskolnikov's garret compared with this. It would be so nice to linger until checkout time. She could always get a cab home.

But Daniel would be shattered after his time in jail. He would need a friendly face and ear – not those of the policeman who'd arrested him, however much said policeman regretted the mistake – until she could deliver him into Svetlana's waiting arms. 'Can you give me half an hour? I'm not decent yet.'

'Sure. It'll take us that long anyway.'

Emily dressed and bagged up her new belongings, then went down to the lobby to check out. At the desk she encountered Saul Goldstein on the same errand.

'Mr Goldstein,' she said. 'I trust you've heard the good news. Daniel is innocent.'

Goldstein turned a scowling face toward her. 'Doesn't change anything in my view. He may not be a murderer, but he's still a sickly egghead who'll never amount to anything. Nowhere near good enough for my Svetlana.'

She regarded him narrowly. 'And you are clearly such an excellent judge of character – since you thought the real murderer was worthy of your daughter's hand.'

He hmphed and spluttered. 'Different thing altogether. Villain can pass himself off as plausible, but you don't get a man out of a scarecrow.'

'If I were you, I would be wary of judging any book by its cover. I think you'll find that once Daniel gets regular treatment for his epilepsy – which I personally plan to guarantee – he will show all the strength of mind and character even you could wish for. He'll never be a lawyer, of course, but I believe he has a brilliant academic future ahead of him.'

Goldstein continued to scowl, refusing to meet her eyes.

'And I also believe – no, I know with absolute certainty – that Svetlana will never be happy if you force her to give him up.'

He turned toward her, face red. 'Why don't you mind your own damn business, lady?' Then he picked up his bags and stomped out of the lobby. But something in his walk told Emily he was not quite as resolute as he appeared.

She had just finished checking out when the doorman summoned her to Colin's car, idling at the curb. The snowfall had ceased in the night, and the temperature was already rising; the streets and sidewalks were covered in slush. But Emily hoped the lawns and trees of the Bede campus would still bear their pristine blanket of white. The storm had been nightmarish, but its aftermath was a lovely dream.

Emily climbed into the back of the car next to Daniel. He raised a ravaged face to give her a shaky smile. She squeezed his hand.

'Thank you, Emily,' he said in a voice that sounded as if it hadn't been used in a month. 'I understand I owe this to you.'

'You owe it to your own innocence,' she replied. 'The truth was bound to come out in the end.'

'I don't feel like an innocent man,' he said with a sigh. 'I still don't remember what happened that night. It's like a horrible black hole in my mind, populated with imagined horrors that won't go away. I accept that Sidney was the one who actually killed her, but the fact remains that I wanted her dead. And I'm pretty sure Sidney thought he was doing me a favor by getting rid of her. That makes me morally responsible.'

'It does nothing of the kind. Other people who care about you knew her death would be a boon to you – Svetlana, I myself – but we didn't take it upon ourselves to kill her. And you never asked for Sidney's hero-worship; in fact, you did all you could to discourage it. Sidney is a sick young man, Daniel. The sickness of his soul is much worse than that of your brain, and I'm afraid much less treatable. Oh, and speaking of your brain, I have some good news for you. Dr Zimmerman told me the college insurance has changed – they'll be able to cover the medication you need from now on.'

Daniel's face brightened at that. 'That is good news. I thought I could tough it out, but after this whole ordeal – well, let's just say I never want to go through anything like that again.'

Colin's phone rang, and he answered it via the car's Bluetooth. Emily and Daniel heard a voice on the other end say, 'Better get back here, Richards. Sharpe's hanged himself in his cell.'

TWENTY-NINE

'I'm so sorry,' Colin said to Emily and Daniel as he turned the car to head back over the Hawthorne Bridge to the station. 'I'll try to be as quick as I can.'

He left them in the informal waiting room Emily had occupied on a previous visit and disappeared down a hallway. Daniel sat with his head in his hands, unreachable and oblivious to the world around him as he wrestled with his private demons. Emily retreated into prayer, examining her own conscience with regard to Sidney and the case as a whole, and interceding for Sidney's soul. In the eyes of the Orthodox church, suicide was an even more serious crime than murder, since it left the perpetrator no opportunity to repent; but she knew mental illness was regarded as some mitigation. Ultimately, the church did not pronounce on anyone's salvation or lack thereof, but left all to the mercy of God. And Emily knew that mercy to be unfathomable.

She would need some of that mercy herself. Although, looking back, she could not see how at any point she could in good conscience have acted otherwise than she had, she questioned her own motivation. Had her determination to exonerate Daniel been entirely altruistic, or had there been a measure of pride involved – a wish to justify her own assessment of his character? And as for Sidney, she had never liked him, never made any real effort to understand or help him. Had she not felt some measure of triumph when she discovered she was right about him and about Daniel? And then there was Taylor. Had Emily ever entertained a single charitable thought about her?

And as for Richard – she had never once given him the benefit of the doubt, and all because of an accidental resemblance. It was true that emotions she could hardly control, arising as they did from buried trauma, had played a big part in her attitude toward Richard; but even so, she could have made more of an effort to think and behave charitably toward him. Now that everything was over – now that she knew Richard was not a murderer, Taylor would never harass a student again, and Daniel and Svetlana would be able to recover from her persecution and get on with their lives – Emily was surprised to realize the only emotion she still felt toward Richard was pity. Pity for the deep sense of inadequacy that must have informed all his behavior, from sneering at Emily's good fortune to stealing a student's paper in an attempt to enhance his own reputation.

The wheels had been set in motion for Richard's prosecution for plagiarism, but Emily would feel no pleasure in it now. Rather, she felt she could even pray for him. And someday, perhaps, she'd be able to pray for Professor Jenkins as well – though she felt certain he was already receiving his just deserts in eternity.

Emily made a mental note to set up an appointment with Father Paul for confession before she left town. That would be the best way to cleanse her soul from the evil that had surrounded her and, to some extent, seeped into her over the last few weeks.

She looked over at Daniel, whose face was invisible but whose posture suggested he had a long way to go before he would feel himself cleansed and at peace. And he had no active faith to help him along that path. She added a prayer for him and for Svetlana, who would bear the brunt of supporting his recovery.

Colin returned and collapsed into a chair. 'I've done all I need to for now,' he said. 'We can get going. But I thought you might want to read this first.' He handed her a rumpled sheaf of lined notebook paper with the indentations of a heavy scrawl showing through the back. 'His suicide note.'

Emily wasn't at all sure she really wanted to read that, but in some obscure way she felt she owed it to Sidney. She took the papers cautiously, as if they might burst into flames in her hand.

The note began with no address or preamble.

You've all figured out that I did it. I killed Taylor Curzon. So there's no point in denying it anymore. I have no intention of standing trial or going to prison, so this will be my only opportunity to explain myself. And it really was such a clever plan, it would be a shame to leave it unexplained. Even though your pedestrian minds will undoubtedly never fully understand. Daniel might, and that's all I care about.

I'll go back to the beginning – to meeting Daniel. I knew right away he was my destiny – another extraordinary mind, untrammeled by convention, clearly intended for higher things. I made it my mission to emulate and serve him. I knew quite well people didn't like me, couldn't fathom the mysteries of my superior mind. But they did seem to like Daniel, though he never stooped so low as to cultivate their liking, so I thought I could learn that secret from him. Not that I cared if all you peons liked me, but it helps in the early stages when one is trying to attain one's rightful place in the world. Once I'd achieved power, I'd be able to dispense with mere popularity.

For some time, I believed that Daniel returned my regard. We needed none of the tawdry outward signs of mutual esteem that ordinary people depend on – the hand-shakes, the clappings on the back, the invitations to 'hang out' together – all so vulgar. There was simply an under-standing that existed between us without ever being overtly expressed. I would have done anything for him, and I believed he was similarly attached to me.

When Daniel's difficulties with Professor Curzon began, I set myself to the question of how I might solve his little problem for him. Knowing Curzon's rapacious tendencies, I assumed reasoning with her would be point-less. But I thought I might be able to divert her attentions from Daniel to myself. I had been studying his ways with the beautiful Svetlana and welcomed this opportunity to practice them.

But my plan backfired. Apparently playing the dark Byronic hero only works if you have the looks for it. Curzon laughed in my face. Not only that, but she told me that she and Daniel had laughed at me together behind my back. What I had thought of as our wordless understanding was apparently only one-way after all.

It was then I decided they would both have to go. Curzon would undoubtedly strive to hinder me after that encounter, and Daniel would only stand in my way, occupying the place in the world that was rightfully mine. I would eliminate them both and slide into the hole Daniel had left behind. I must say, I did contemplate the prospect of sliding into Svetlana's good graces with some considerable relish.

But I couldn't bring myself to harm Daniel directly. He still meant too much to me. So I conceived my brilliant plan: Curzon would die, and Daniel would be convicted of her murder.

Everything fell together so easily once I'd made my deci-sion; it was obvious the universe was on my side. That statuette of Daniel's – so easy to abscond with, so clearly linked to him, so potentially lethal. The bunny suit was easily accessible and (as I thought) easily disposed of, with no link to me. And then Daniel's blackout on Monday night. What could have been more propitious? Once I'd seen him wandering the campus like a sleepwalker, the entire plan unfolded before me in all its glorious detail. Use Daniel to establish an alibi, bash the bitch's head in, then bring Daniel back and make sure he got nicely covered in her blood – and he would never remember a thing about it. You have to admit it was awfully neat.

And it would have worked, if it hadn't been for the damned bunny suit. After I put Daniel to bed, I stashed the suit in the laundry room in the basement of his building, the Old Dorm Block, where if it was found it would be taken as one more proof of Daniel's guilt. But then after that policeman and that über-bitch Cavanaugh started snooping around, I realized Daniel had no connection with the computer science department and therefore could not be supposed to know about the bunny suits stored in the clean room. So I thought it would be safer simply to put it where used bunny suits normally go. And it would have been – if I hadn't been seen. It must have been Cavanaugh who saw me; no one else would have thought anything of it. If only she had never come back to campus, I'd be a free man now, with Daniel out of the way and a clear path to greatness before me.

I don't suppose I'll have any opportunity for direct vengeance now. But she's such a sniveling do-gooder, I know my death will weigh on her tender conscience, and that will have to suffice for my revenge. Yes, I did say my death: by the time you find this, I will have gone to my eternal reward. Except that, of course, there is no such thing. There is only darkness.

But I don't mind. Darkness and I have always been good friends. And if I can't stand in the spotlight, darkness is where I prefer to be. Out, out, brief candle. Life is a tale told by an idiot, full of sound and fury, signifying nothing. The rest is darkness.

Emily handed the sheaf of papers to Colin and fell back in her chair. She felt cold to her very core. A sorrow too deep for tears welled up in her – not so much because Sidney had committed physical suicide as because his soul had been dead already. He had chosen darkness, and the darkness had overcome him.

Colin offered the note to Daniel to read. He hesitated, and Emily shook her head. 'I wouldn't if I were you, Daniel. Don't let his venom poison you. I think you already understand why he did it.'

Daniel nodded and dropped his outstretched hand. 'I think I do. I think I've always known. I just didn't want to believe it.'

Emily stood and wrapped her coat around her in a vain attempt to dispel her inner chill. 'Let's get him home,' she said to Colin. 'He needs Svetlana now.'

THIRTY

Emily had Colin let her out on campus along with Daniel so she could seek out Marguerite. She didn't feel like being alone right now.

Marguerite made coffee in her French press, and they sat in her office for privacy while Emily told her all the parts of the story she didn't yet know. '*Le pauvre* Daniel,' Marguerite said when she had finished. 'But now all will be well, yes? His demons will have been purged by his suffering, and he and Svetlana will make a life together.'

'I hope so, yes. Provided Sidney doesn't haunt them forever.'

The practical Marguerite dismissed this possibility with a wave of her hand. 'Much good will come of this evil, you will see. We are free of Taylor Curzon, for one – we and a whole generation of her potential victims.'

'True, though even she didn't deserve to go that way.'

'And we have sniffed out the transgressions of Richard. I have reported him to the committee, and I am confident he will be out by the end of the year. Also, a little bird has hinted to me that I am next in line to take his place as division head.' She gave Emily a significant smile. 'And you know what that means.'

Emily brightened for the first time. 'A real job for Oscar?'

Marguerite nodded. 'An assistant professorship on the tenure track. I have it all mapped out in my mind.'

Emily gave her friend an impulsive hug. 'Bless you, Margot. He won't let you down, I'm sure of it.'

'I am certain of it as well – otherwise I would not recommend him for promotion. I would do much for you, *ma chérie*, but sabotage my own division I would not. Oscar will do very well.'

'And then he'll be able to get his own apartment and marry Lauren. Maybe they'll even have children; she's young enough. My own nieces and nephews at Windy Corner! Oh, that would be bliss!'

Emily started off into a happy dream, but Marguerite recalled her to the present. 'Do not count your chickens too soon, *chérie*. Lauren strikes me as a woman with a mind of her own.'

'She is that. But I think she really loves Oscar, and her biological clock is sure to start chiming before long. I'm going to be optimistic until I have reason to be otherwise.'

That afternoon, after running home for lunch and a change of clothes, Emily forced herself to go back to the library and address her research. She had only three days left in Paideia after today, and the student who normally used her desk could reappear at any time. She needed to wrap things up.

Svetlana had been amazingly efficient, considering how many distractions she faced, and had managed to enter and organize all the work Emily had done so far on to her laptop, so Emily was able to review it quickly and see where she still had gaps to fill. Armed with that knowledge, she brushed off her dormant typing skills and succeeded in collecting all the information she still needed by Friday morning. Of course, it would take months to synthesize all this raw data into her own treatise; but she could do that in the comfort of Windy Corner. Perhaps if she didn't invite any more retreat guests until she was finished, she would be able to maintain some peace and quiet there – although she was beginning to feel as if she were destined to carry murder and mayhem with her wherever she went.

Over the weekend Emily would be packing up her belongings from the Woodstock Boulevard house and returning to Stony Beach. But before she did that, she wanted to say a proper goodbye to the people here who meant most to her – Oscar, Lauren, Marguerite, Daniel, and Svetlana. She decided to throw another dinner party. With Daniel's permission, she invited Colin as well – he was, after all, part of her family now. She wanted to invite Luke but told herself he would be busy, and anyway, she would see him the next day at home.

This time Emily asked Marguerite to help her cook, and they produced a sumptuous repast worthy of a celebration. Everyone was gathered and they were bringing the steaming dishes to the table when the doorbell rang.

'Who on earth can that be?' Emily muttered, wiping her hands on her apron as she rushed to the door. 'Whoever it is, their timing stinks.'

She opened the door to a grinning Luke, champagne bottle in hand. 'Room for one more?' he said.

She threw her arms around him right there in the doorway with the freezing air pouring in. 'There's always room for you. But how did you know?'

'I have my sources.' He winked over her head, and she turned to see Colin blush.

'I didn't think you'd mind,' Colin said. 'I haven't seen Uncle Luke in ages, and I wanted to talk the case over with him.'

'Just don't do that in front of Daniel and Svetlana, OK? Save it for after dinner.' She gave Luke another squeeze. 'I'm so glad you're here. Now my party is complete.'

Oscar scrounged up a chair, and Marguerite laid another place between Emily's and Colin's. As they all gathered around the table, Marguerite poured champagne and Emily raised her glass. 'To Daniel's freedom,' she said and, after everyone had sipped, 'and to Oscar's improved prospects.'

'Which we both owe to you,' Daniel said. 'To Emily!'

She blushed as everyone cheered.

'And I have another one,' Daniel went on. 'Svetlana's father has – not exactly given his consent, but withdrawn his opposition to Svetlana deciding for herself what she wants to do with her life. So after graduation, she's going back to ballet – and she has agreed to become my wife.'

Emily's heart made a leap worthy of Svetlana's balletic talents. Having herself missed the opportunity to spend her whole life with the love of her youth, she, more than most, appreciated what a great gift that was.

'To Daniel and Svetlana! Many happy years!' Glasses clinked again as the young couple kissed, starry-eyed.

Oscar whispered something to Lauren, and she nodded with an impish grin. 'Not to steal your thunder, you two, but we have an announcement of our own.' Oscar cleared his throat and drew himself up. 'I'll be competing with Daniel for the honor of luckiest man in the world. Beyond my wildest dreams, this amazing lady has said yes, and we hope to be married within the year. As soon as we can afford a decent place to live.'

'How about here?' Emily said impulsively. 'This house is promised to Peter and Lillian through May, but after that it's mine to dispose of. Since I've definitely decided to retire, I won't be needing it anymore. The mortgage is paid off, so you're perfectly welcome to live here rent-free – as long as you let me stay for a night or two whenever I come to Portland.'

Oscar and Lauren gaped at each other in astonished delight. 'That means we can get married this summer!'

Oscar turned to Emily. 'We accept! And that wedding at Windy Corner at New Year's was so lovely. Could we possibly do that too? We may have a few more guests than they had, a little more hoopla all around. Do you think Katie could handle it?'

'Katie can handle anything. We're going to have her own and Jamie's wedding there in a few months, and after that Luke's and my reception, so she'll get plenty of practice. Windy Corner may become a regular wedding chapel. Friends and family only, though,' she hastened to add. 'We are definitely not going public.'

She raised her glass one more time. 'To Oscar and Lauren!'

They kissed enthusiastically, and everyone sat down. The two couples were each completely absorbed in their partners. Colin and Luke took the opportunity to violate Emily's ban on talk of the case, but they kept their voices low, so she left them to it. Emily and Marguerite were left to chat on their own.

'That was impulsive, *chérie*, offering your home to your brother,' Marguerite said. 'Generous, but impulsive. Are you certain you will not regret it?'

Emily let her gaze drift around the house she'd inhabited for twenty-five years. From her seat she could see most of the ground floor. It was a cozy house, a friendly house, and until recently she'd expected it to be her home for the rest of her life. But now it seemed like a mere way-station on her journey. She felt not a single pang at giving it up.

'If there's one thing these last few weeks have proven to me, it's that this house . . . Bede . . . Portland . . . isn't my home anymore.' A vision of the library fireside at Windy Corner came over her, complete with the three cats dozing on the hearth, Luke playing with Lizzie on the rug, and Katie serving tea. Her heart swelled with longing.

'I'll miss you and Oscar when I go back tomorrow, but honestly, I can't wait to get home.'

AUTHOR'S NOTE

Attentive readers of the previous books in this series may notice that Emily's college has changed its name. This is not a reflection of any event in the real world but simply an authorial convenience. Setting an entire novel on campus necessitated improvising on a number of aspects of the college that were either unknown to me or had changed since I was a student there in the seventies. In addition, I would not wish the nefarious persons and events depicted in this novel to be in any way associated with my actual alma mater.